MW01268590

BOIL AND BUBBLE

The Amazon Women of Kansas

By

James D. Yoder

Cover Credits: Mural on the wall of The Pittsburg, Kansas Public Library Reading Room, "Solidarity, March of the Amazon Army," by Kansas Artist, Wayne Wildcat. Permission granted. www.waynewildcat.com.

ISBN 0-7414-6717-8

Printed in the United States of America

Published August 2011

INFINITY PUBLISHING
1094 New DeHaven Street, Suite 100
West Conshohocken, PA 19428-2713
Toll-free (877) BUY BOOK
Local Phone (610) 941-9999
Fax (610) 941-9959
Info@buybooksontheweb.com
www.buybooksontheweb.com

*Dedicated to all the miners of
Southeastern Kansas who lost their lives
in the coal mines.*

A NOTE FROM THE AUTHOR

When I was perusing Lora Jost's and Dave Lowenstein's fine book, *Kansas Murals - A Traveler's Guide* (University Press of Kansas, 2006), and began reading the descriptive text about "The 1921 March of the Amazon Women," I was captivated. It was a "must" for me to look further into this historical event.

I owe a debt to many authors, librarians, and to Kansas artist,Wayne Wildcat, who painted the mural, "Solidarity: March of the Amazon Women." This mural is on the west wall of the Pittsburg Public Library reading room.

In addition, Wayne's wife, Dr. Tolly Wildcat, published an overview of the march and history of the painting, entitled: "Mining History for Art: The Story of Wayne Wildcat's Solidarity," *Journal of the West*, Winter, 2004, V. 41, No.1. This article stimulated me to look further into the tragic events of the Kansas coal miners and the abhorrent conditions that brought on the labor conflicts, strikes, and the womens' famous march.

For those readers who want to know more about the sad story of coal miners in Kansa's "The Little Balkans," I heartily recommend, in addition to reading this novel, a field trip to the Pittsburg, Kansas area and visit the many little coal mining towns and historic sites, including Pittsburg and Franklin. I give readers more information regarding these sites in the "Acknowledgment" section at the end of my novel.

James D. Yoder, Hesston, Kansas

CHARACTERS

PROTAGONISTS:

Milan, Danika, Neda, and Toma Cratnick, principal characters.

Mary Skubitz, considered "the leader" of the Amazon Women's March.

Alec Howat, President of District 14 Miners Union.

ANTAGONISTS:

John L. Lewis, President of the United Mine Workers of America.

Henry J. Allen, Governor of Kansas, 1919-1923.

Harvey Otis, a sleazy mine operator.

Myrtice Hester, a two-faced widow.

IN ADDITION:

An assortment of male and female characters, both fictional and actual.

CHAPTER ONE

Chicago, 1916

"No doubt about it. The scoundrel's guilty." John P. White, president of The United Mine Workers of America, leaned back in his swivel chair, while biting down on his Torano cigar. "We've had enough of Alexander Howat's impudence over there in southeastern Kansas, diddling with all those foreigners."

White cut his icy blue eyes toward secretary Percy, lips drawn grimly across his shoe-box face. His eyes caught on Percy's stare at the mention of Howat's name.

White continued. "Well, it's a bitter memory, Percy. We don't want war breaking out down there like it did in Trinidad, Colorado."

"Oh, no! A frightful memory. Terrible." Percy dug for his handkerchief to wipe a sweat bead from his brow. "You're referring to those unfortunate miners who were mowed down with machine guns by the National Guard. Ordered by Governor Ammons, too."

White lifted a starch-cuffed wrist and ran his fingers through his wavy hair. His legs shifted underneath his massive desk.

"Well, I've found out that Alec Howat is a documented troublemaker. "They don't call him 'Bull of the Woods' down there without some real reasons."

"Yes, Mr. White, but wasn't Howat expelled from District 14 after the fracas he caused? The last one?"

Pettygrew cleared his throat. "You don't expect him to cause Trinidad, Colorado kind of trouble, do you?"

"Well, I demanded that he step down as president of the district, until his lawsuit against the operators' association is settled. I've changed my mind. I think Alexander Howat is guilty."

"That certainly puts a different perspective on it, doesn't it?" Percy added.

"Well, that dark-skinned little mucker has grown defiant, Percy. He's ignored my directions one time too many. What would you do with a feisty cock like Howat? They say the Scottish have skin thicker than a black oak plank."

John White stood, his long legs sheathed in narrow-cuffed striped pants. His Sacque-suit coat of expensive wool flannel flared open showing a heavy gold watch chain.

"But since you asked him to step down, isn't he off the map, so to speak?" Percy smiled as if he had rubbed Cloverine Salve on John White's ruffled disposition.

"Off the map?" White bellowed. "I've just received a copy of an affidavit accusing that mischief-maker of receiving $25,000 in a bribe. A dirty bribe! And the money sneaked from our Southwestern Union, too." He glanced at Percy, wondering if his fancy little secretary could see that his blood pressure was close to blowing the petcock.

"Well, a bribe is something, indeed, with which to be concerned." Percy's words bounced. His mouth drew into a pucker. He shifted a shiny two-toned spectator shoe.

"Not only the *bribe*, Percy, but he has allowed himself to be put back into the leadership in District 14 in spite of my orders."

Percy's eyes bugged. He clutched his note pad and pen, waiting for his boss to search for solutions as White stared out the office window, untangling his thoughts.

I knew Alec Howat's sneaky, but he's done himself in this time. Let him rot over in Pittsburg, Kansas if he hasn't already choked on the coal dust and grime.

Flooding our National offices with scurrilous letters, some unsigned, denigrating the national leaders. Ignores the National directives to stop the strikes.

"Percy," he snapped, lean cheeks flushed. "We're going to file a lawsuit. Suit against Smart Alec Howat and the operators there for defrauding the Union. Call the garage and have my Pierce-Arrow ready. You and I are going to visit Federal Judge Grosscup."

"Yes, President White. Yes, indeed." Percy scurried to his desk, his celluloid collar nearly choking him.

"We're going to demand that insulting little upstart's resignation as a District Officer. Fire him. Percy, we're going to fire Alexander Howat! Good riddance of that dung beetle rolling his ball of manure across that corner of Kansas. We've got him this time." He yanked at his watch chain.

****

Alec Howat, a deep-chested man of Scottish lineage and coal miner since the age of ten, eased into a club chair in the living room of his modest bungalow on West Park Street in Pittsburg, Kansas. The house nestled on a quiet street very near Playter's Lake, once an old strip mine.

His wife, Agnes, sat in a Victorian upholstered chair opposite him in the burgundy wallpapered room.

"Alec, dear. Do we have to fight this again? The election is over for the Union President. John White's in command now. Can't you let go?" Her fingers locked beneath her bosom.

"They've brought a lawsuit against me, Agnes. A federal lawsuit. Alec decided that this was the time for the full disclosure.

Agnes leaned forward, her fingers, tightening around her handkerchief, lifted to her chin.

"*Lawsuit*? What on earth for this time, Alec?"

"Some dirty skunk has dumped garbage on the desks of the International Union Officers claiming that I've accepted bribes to pay for stoking ballot boxes in the last election and paid mine operators here to ignore the strike injunction."

Agnes raised herself from her chair and stepped to his side. The soft pleated A line skirt of gray crepe swirled as she walked. She rested a small hand on his shoulder, an opal ring catching the light cast by the Faville-glass Tiffany lamp.

"Alexander, my dear husband. You've been loyal and faithful to the miners here. Always concerned with their welfare. You've proven your trustworthiness. Nobody could even count the times you've put yourself in jeopardy for them." Her hand slid across his broad shoulders.

He rested his brown-haired head against her bosom, sighing as her hand shifted to his cheek.

Fatigue and weariness. How long do I have to fight for our rights? How long, this time? Facing prison bars? For what? Bribery? God help us all.

Agnes knelt beside his chair on the worsted rug with the intertwining roses border and reached for his hand. His hand, coarse-palmed and scarred from years of near slave labor in the pitch darkness of the mines, contrasted with her soft, white palm.

She held his hand in silence, allowing her tears to stream down her plump cheeks.

Their silence was interrupted by the rustling of a burr oak in a stiff wind outside, its leaves silvered by the moonlight.

But where was the moonlight in their souls?

Howat found his voice. "They demand that I resign as a Union Officer until this is settled in court, Agnes."

Alec could see the fear slide across her face.

"What will you do? Surely you won't do such a thing."

"Agnes, you know what I'll do. I'll find my old pick and shovel and go back to the coal mines and dig coal until I'm proven innocent. Yes. Back to the mines."

CHAPTER TWO

Attorney Walsh's Office, Pittsburg, Kansas

Alec Howat could do little about the scurrilous letters, telegrams, and publications John P. White and his cohorts circulated, denouncing him as a traitor. Every local official had received the incriminating letters and telegrams full of distortions and lies.

"Well, if my skin is as thick as everyone says, then I'll challenge that turncoat, White, to a debate in every one of our districts." His heart pumped with furor, his resolve strong as steel posts in a coal tipple.

Alec turned to attorney, Frank Walsh, whom he'd hired to represent him. "We'll take the case all the way to the Federal Court in Kansas City, if necessary."

"I don't know, Mr. Howat. You're dealing with people who've flooded the country with letters denouncing you as a traitor. We couldn't possibly gather all the material together. If President White agrees to come to Pittsburg for a debate about these charges, then challenge him to come on down. If anyone can expose scoundrels, it's you, Alec."

Attorney Walsh waited for Alec's decision.

"He agreed. Mr. White, agreed to come to Frontenac, to Arma, to Scammon, but the only debate he confirms as settled is the one scheduled in the Opera House here in Pittsburg."

"Then I'll help you prepare, Alec. We'll fortify ourselves with copies of those slanderous letters. We'll certainly counter sue, if necessary."

Alec's dark blue eyes conveyed a perpetual sadness begotten by his own slave-like labor in the mines with their cave-ins, blowouts, poisonous gases, and the ever-present face of Death.

Attorney Walsh continued, "If the suit is directed toward District 14, then we can surely rake up the funds, even if the Southwestern Coal Operators' Association has taken over our books. The Illinois District has already sent a thousand dollars for your support, and I'm certain more will be coming from the West Virginia miners."

Howat lifted his head, hair carefully parted, a far-off look upon his face. He raised his square chin and turned to the attorney. "I'm truly grateful, Frank."

"You're known here and as far away as Indianapolis, Indiana as an orator, Alec, one who can speak the truth. What do they call you? 'Bull of the Woods?' Even The New York Times correspondents are writing about these disputes. Someone from the Times will be there and your own simple language and leadership skills won't let you down." Walsh grinned. "I can hardly wait to hear you let loose, Alec. Yep, let loose."

A trace of a smile crept across Alec's hard-hewn face. "I can tackle John White in a debate, Frank, but you know the Opera House can't possibly hold all of the miners and their families who'll show up."

"It'll be a rowdy crowd. The streets outside will be overflowing." Walsh leaned back in his desk chair, a hand smoothing the gray flannel pant-leg of his tailored suit.

"Let's go get em, Alec!" Walsh said as he closed his notebook and stood. "I'll tell my clerks to give this the highest priority. We won't let you down."

****

For twenty-one months, Alec Howat's muscles hardened as he abandoned his desk job, grabbed his pick and shovel, his carbide lamp, and the ever-necessary two-gallon lunch pail and descended into the mine shafts of southeastern Kansas. He lived and dreamed coal mining. He so identified with his fellow miners that they considered him the Angel of Good Fortune among them.

If anyone knew mining, it was Alexander Howat.

Along with the hardening of his muscles and the growing calluses upon his knees from kneeling in the shallow, narrow tunnels, he vowed to fill the required number of coal cars on his shift, and even more. Though the walls of the shafts darkened around him, the light in his spirit flamed brighter.

Skilled at almost every mining task, he took his turn; filled in when a miner fell or disaster struck. When it rained six inches on the surface above, the creek overflowed its banks in a ferocious torrent, the shaft ceiling collapsed and the mine began to flood. Alec, disregarding his own safety, waded in to rescue three miners in imminent danger of being swept away in the roaring waters.

When needed, he held the breast auger, driving the drill into the coal seam with his breastbone and the weight of his body.

When a cager missed his shift, he took over, heaving the coal onto the cars, aligning them at the bottom of the mine and replacing them upon the track above when emptied. He was called upon to be shift boss under the caustic frowns of the mine supervisor. He'd bent his back at the picking table, a sorting table where he hand-picked the shale from the coal.

He rode the trip, a number of coal cars headed for the tipple, riding on the black chunks to attend to the attachments and signals.

He had gotten into a fist fight with a burley check-weighman at the top of the cage when he discovered the crooked weighman had been shortchanging the poundage of their cars, pocketing the money. He had left him cold on the tipple floor, awaiting the long arm of the mine operator.

An overworked and slightly-built miner fumbled, leaving the charge hole too wide and angled. The miner inserted the blasting cap, lit the fuse. They made ready, flattening themselves against a wall. There had been a violent blowout, due to the incorrect cartridge placement. Gases and coal particles from the windy shot plastered men to the walls and pillars, blasting them with dust, sharp-edged chunks of rock and coal, knocking them down, three with their legs buried underneath the avalanche of coal.

Alec, freeing himself, grabbed a pick and began digging with his powerful arms to release the half-buried miners.

At night his dreams ushered him back into the pitch-dark caverns. In one alarming dream he suddenly realized that their carbide lamps had ignited a seam of methane gas. The flames leaped toward him as he waited, waited, and waited, choking, gasping as time stood still for the deadly flash.

Agnes, when awakened by his struggles, shook him until he emerged from the horrors of the nightmare.

And worst of all was the disaster dream where all the men of his shift were silently overcome by the afterdamp, a gas composed of carbon monoxide and carbon dioxide that most usually followed a blast gone awry. In this dream he saw himself floating above his body, stretched upon the mine floor among a dozen silent, prostrate comrades.

CHAPTER THREE

Pittsburg Opera House

The sun had sunk beneath a hazy sky due to the mixture of coal dust, smoke arising from the many steam-powered locomotives on tracks from 2nd street to 11th street. Among the lines: the Kansas City, Fort Scott, and Memphis Railway, the Frisco, the Santa Fe, the Kansas City Pittsburg and Gulf Railroad, and the Missouri Pacific.

Noxious air drifted from a dozen smelters on South Broadway. Nevertheless, a golden afterglow lingered over Pittsburg on the balmy September evening.

By 1916, Pittsburg, Kansas, named after the industrial city of Pittsburgh, Pennsylvania, roared into the twentieth century, stretching its boundaries. Contractors erected prestigious buildings, designed by leading American architects imported from New York, Chicago, and San Fransisco. One goal was foremost: Pittsburg, Kansas would be destined to become a leading industrial city in the heart of the country.

Alec, Agnes beside him in their Chevrolet Classic Six, chugged along from their home on a maple-tree-lined street in Pittsburg's eastern residential area.

He turned the car onto a street leading past an array of offices, stores, tobacco shops, saloons, and bordellos. Agnes couldn't help but glance over to the opulent three-story brick house with huge front windows, draped in rich velvet. Glass globes reflected red lights. Tinkling piano music flowed from the open windows, drifting to her ears:

"Love, oh, love, oh, careless love...."

Agnes, whose eyes were beginning to water from the air drifting in the westerly breeze from the zinc works and the brickyards, dug in her purse for a handkerchief.

Alec realized that it was impossible to approach the building from the front entrance. He steered the car into the parking lot behind the imposing three-story Opera House with its corner silo-like cone-roofed tower.

It seemed as if an all-nations assembly had filled the streets and sidewalks, pushing up to the doors of the elegant building at an intersection on Broadway Avenue, across from The National Bank. Among the wing-whirl from a flock of pigeons, the murmurs and gush of flowing tongues gave evidence to the lively expectations of the waiting people.

Miners, returning from their shifts, arms encircling their ever-sacred lunch pails, lifted soot-smudged faces as if already they could hear the voice of their cherished leader.

Blue-uniformed police guarded the entrance to the heavy opera house doors. The Howats were aware that every seat would already be filled: scores standing at the back and along the sides, where allowed.

The officers growled their commands, "Get back! Stop pushing or we'll have to make arrests!" The intermingling voices in Italian, English, German, Slavic, and mix of broken dialects overshadowed their words. It was common knowledge that upon any Saturday night, fifty different languages could be heard on the sidewalks of this new Pittsburg.

****

A mine operator named Angelo Degaspri, his waxed mustache above his broad grin, ushered Agnes to an elevator taking her to the upper level where she had a reserved seat in front of the stage, sporting two lecterns.

Giving evidence of his pleasure at seating the wife of the famous Howat, Degaspri held his hand across his waist and bowed to Mrs. Howat, who was wearing a loose fitting belted two-piece dress with tight cuffed sleeves, trimmed in buttons and braid.

Agnes's skirt hung eight inches from the floor. Her matching hat sported a wide brim and a derby crown. Her shoes -- a smart pair of two-toned boots.

Alec, wore a blue serge suit in line with the sack style of the times, shortened coat and tapered, cuffed pants. His feet were shod in a pair of black oxfords with tool-worked caps. He was quickly led up the stage stairway and would soon be seated behind one of the lecterns.

Agnes glanced to the right and noticed two women whom she recognized from her visit to the Franklin Union Hall, where she had addressed the small gathering on her recent European travels.

The one on the right she remembered as a Mrs. Danika Cratnick, a big, broad-shouldered woman, hair almost completely covered by a simple hat, pulled low. Agnes observed her obviously home-made dress. The woman sat alongside her miner husband, a ruddy-cheeked man, giving the appearance of having made every attempt to scrub off lingering coal smudges. A young boy and a teenage girl sat alongside the parents, patiently waiting.

Agnes recognized a young woman with bobbed hair and bright eyes, Annie Stovich. Next to her sat a stocky woman, leaning forward as if she was impatient for the debate to begin. Agnes believed her name was Mary Skubitz. A strong woman, as she recalled, and a member of the Socialist party, from Ringo.

Upon the stage, a deep red velvet valance hung under the proscenium with matching side curtains drawn open into soft folds. She saw two straight-backed chairs, slightly to the side of each of the two lecterns, where the debaters would be seated. Between the oak lecterns rested a small table and chair, upon which sat the debate moderator, Samuel Wilder.

****

White stood, bowed augustly, his dark serge suit tailored to fit his long frame. His brownish hair shone beneath the lights.

A modest applause arose but faded in a few seconds. However, in the back of the opera house, at least fifty or more persons, mostly men, let forth loud-mouthed hoots as they clapped robustly. Shrill whistles erupted, showing their approval of their National President. Wilder waited for the racket and applause to die down, then gave further instructions.

"I need to remind the audience that we have gathered here for a debate, not an argument. The rules for this evening require full respect shown to both gentlemen. We cannot allow shouting or hooting."

The listeners murmured, then fell silent.

Agnes wondered if worry showed openly on her face as she straightened her shoulders, waiting. She did note, however, a drift of alcoholic breath from her left. Bourbon, perhaps?

"I now introduce to you a man who in these mining counties needs no introduction. A friend to many here, a coal miner himself who knows mining from the inside out." Wilder lifted his chin above his round-edged collar, surveying the audience.

Rumbles of approval and nods.

"Your Local mine leader, Alexander Howat who...."

At the mention of the Howat name wild calls erupted from throats. At least a half of the audience rose from their seats, whistling, cheering. One yelled out, "Flatten him, Alec, he don't know nuthin bout mining!"

Moderator Wilder banged his gavel. "Silence. You were warned. Respect! We need full respect for both of our debaters. I will not allow such a commotion."

He frowned and banged the gavel three more times.

Wilder continued: "Our Local President Alec Howat of Pittsburg, has called for this debate and The Honorable John P. White has responded affirmatively. Their topic tonight concerns a matter of how the bookkeeping is done at the local, state, and national levels as well as specific charges the National Office has leveled against District 14 President, Alexander Howat.

"And now may I present the first debater, The distinguished John P. White."

A weak and scattered applause echoed as John White's long legs led him to his lectern. He surveyed the crowd, reaching with his fingers to feel his silk cravat.

"Ladies and gentlemen." He smiled handsomely, leaning forward, arms resting on his lectern, gold cuff links visible.

"I have been invited to this debate by your own Mr. Alexander Howat" He gave a spare nod toward Alec.

"I want to unfold before you the rocky road we have traveled with this District 14, here in Pittsburg, Kansas. Mr. Howat has frequently challenged us at the national level by calling for a considerable number of strikes."

Giggles rippled across the audience.

"Nearly three hundred strikes, according to our records." He paused as if the grins before him were a bit more than unsettling.

Agnes's shoulders twitched as she heard a voice, obviously a miner's behind her speak audibly, "Well, ain't that sumpin?"

Though the crowd may have reflected a touch of unfriendliness at first, it seemed that President White was confident that, with his looks, his long pedigree, his language skills (who could understand the guttural grunts of these aliens?), and his experience before audiences much larger than this, he didn't have to doubt himself. Not at all.

He unfolded his points. His long finger wagged toward imaginary listings in the air to the right. His voice ascended in pitch.

Members of the audience settled in. Some of the miners gave their tobacco chaw an extra chew, folded their arms before their chests and stared.

White outlined his points: First: Their district president had dared to sneak funds from the National Office to the tune of twenty-five thousand dollars.

At the mention of this amazing amount of money, giggles again rippled across the room and a huge miner's wife near the back called out, "Wish he would a taken fifty."

Supportive clapping ricocheted approval.

Moderator Wilder, now a definite look of worry about the possibility of losing control, stood and tapped his gavel on the lectern to the left of President White. "Folks, folks, I have to admonish you. Quiet, or I'll have to call on security!"

He turned toward White, his nervousness obvious on his face. "Please continue, sir." He nodded toward White, his face flushed.

White cleared his throat and grabbed both sides of his lectern as if to keep it from flying away.

"Now where was I?

"Yes, point two. This man you call Alec is not only careless about the money matters, but belligerent. We subpoenaed him to come all the way to Indianapolis to clear up the matter. We had a whole sheaf of incriminating documents disclosing his guilt. Guilt!"

He scanned the audience to check their understanding.

He saw mostly blank cow-like stares and turned-down mouths.

Next, White rambled on about the insulting letters Alec and his devious cohorts had "dumped" upon them at all levels - district, state, and national offices.

"The absurdity of it! The unprofessionalism of it. The sneaky, childlike modes of operation."

By now Agnes's chin was up, her eyes beaming her own horror toward White's face.

"And thirdly: The outright lies concerning such a felony, a felony serious enough to put a man in prison for years.

Think of it."

White, still anchoring his lectern, dared take a quick glance to see how their Alec was taking these disclosures.

His eyebrows lifted in amazement as he fixed his eyes upon their wonderful Howat, slumped upon his chair, legs crossed, one foot shaking back and forth as he pared his fingernails with his pocketknife.

White's Adam's apple bobbed. as he looked upon a man demonstrating openly as if this was the most ho-hum experience he'd ever been asked to endure.

White's neck twisted back toward the audience as he made attempts to reconnect.

"Now my opponent has one thesis..."

Agnes realized John P. White had made a mistake by uttering that word, her belief supported by waves of giggles. A man at the end of her row openly placed his left thumb in his ear and wagged his hand at White. " A tousled-headed older miner called out in a raspy voice: "We're all trying to learn English, here, Mr. White."

White fumbled for his place on his notes. "His one, uh, uh, argument will be that he is not a manager of funds and that he is innocent. He is a man in a responsible position and it is his fiduciary responsibility to...."

Agnes couldn't believe he had actually spoken the word "fiduciary." She leaned back, drawing her handkerchief to her lips to cover her own giggles.

Eight minutes of the scurrilous listings and rantings by White against their beloved leader by now had solidified the mining crowd firmly together, their mouths puckering as if they'd been forced to taste bitter alum.

The moderator intervened. "Time up, President White. I must call time."

White, stuffing tattered notes into his pocket, seemed confused by the quick passage of time. He nodded with a less than enthusiastic smile toward Wilder.

"Yes, Moderator Wilder. Yes, indeed. It is time to hear from my opponent. He bent over awkwardly to snatch a note page that had slipped his grasp.

****

23

Alec's turn.

There was nothing "ho-hum" about Alec's appearance before his lectern. He raised his shoulders to their full height. He turned his chiseled face from side to side, focusing his ever sad eyes, sporting grayish circles.

He surveyed the assembled miners and their families, along with the city dignitaries scattered throughout the crowd. He clasped large, work-worn hands before him.

"My honorable opponent," he turned, flashing a gracious smile toward White.

"I do not have a thesis to unfold." He noted a sea of faces spread with grins, as if he had uttered a nasty word.

"No, not a thesis, but the truth. Just the simple truth. He turned, remembering that regardless of the subject, smile at your opponent.

"Now our own esteemed President White has traveled a long distance and taken considerable time, already, to inform you that I am a sneak and a scoundrel."

At those words half of the miners stood, voices shouting in various dialects: "He wants the truth. Give him the truth, Alec. Tell him what it's like to work in hell!"

Supporting cries echoed as moderator Wilder scurried to the lectern to again pound his gavel.

Alec waited for Wilder's fit to be over. He drew in a huge breath and released it, a trace of a smile across his weathered face. "I was, to use the legal term, *subpoenaed*, to travel all the way to Indianapolis by the officers of the International Miners Union of America. Yes. All the way to Indianapolis."

At the mention of the term *subpoenaed*, looks of astonishment spread, as if he had emptied a shovelful from last year's back house upon the stage.

Alec paused, noting Agnes's grin beamed toward him.

"When I got their scores of mine operators, union officers, and corrupt lawyers piled layers of telegrams, scurrilous letters, and accounting ledgers before the judge. Exhibit number one, exhibit *number two.* "

He paused for the words "number two" to settle as eyebrows raised.

"Oh, yes. The auditors, those paid to inspect the accounting books, tried to prove my misuse of Union funds. I don't need to declare, tonight, my friends, about my innocence. I spent Union money. Yes. I spent it for timbers to shore up the mines. I requisitioned money to insure that we had proper venting fans so that we miners would not gag and suffocate in the cold and darkness, where we prayed for air."

Groans could be heard. Whispers: "God bless im."

"I requisitioned - even sent the checks to pay for helmets for our heads. Something proper for a miner to protect himself instead of rag caps or felt hats."

Wilder had to step lively to the lectern and fumble for his gavel again as the yells arose:

"Tell em, Alec. Tell 'm. Tell em we still need them helmets to perteck our noggins!"

"Of course," Alec continued, my request was denied. *Denied.* And, dear friends," he paused. "They kept the money anyway."

His long pause was calculated. He waited for the words to sink into the thirsty soil of their souls.

"Our own District 14 monies paid in by you. You the steady, hard-suffering miners who have to accept company script and be forced to spend it at company stores. Forced to buy your own shovels, picks, and carbide lamps at inflated prices."

A prolonged booing swept from the back all the way to the stage.

"Of course, our reputable debater here, President White," Alec turned to nod toward him, remembering to smile, "performed his faithful duty by asking me to resign my position. Well, you can see that I honored his request. And I think you all know that I don't have to defend myself against false charges that I paid people to vote for me rather than our Honorable White."

Someone called out, "That'd be OK, Alec. OK with me!"

Wilder dropped his watch upon the floor, picked it up and stepped lively to the lectern.

"Not only did I have to listen to those degrading accusations, but under our prestigious debater here, Mr. White, I was thrown in jail."

Boos bounced upon the ceiling.

"Far from my home, my friends, my wife, Agnes, lonely. Forsaken by the International Officers and their henchmen. I held onto those jail bars as I watched the constable shake his head in his own confusion. I ..."

"If we had been there, Alec, we'd have skinned them," a tough-looking man with handlebar mustache yelled.

"I'll tell you who your friends are, you mining folks. Dozens of financiers, stock and bond buyers and sellers contributed to a fund called 'The Yellow Dog Fund.' You know what that sorry deal was, don't you? They were buying yellow legislators and all of them had a yellow streak in them."

"Let's get paint and give em a stripe, Alec, We'll do it," a grinning, almost toothless old codger hollered.

"So sorry, Mr. Howat. Sorry, but your time has expired." Wilder stood, wild-eyed as if he'd just seen a ghost.

Alec turned from the podium, slid his hands leisurely into his side pockets and sauntered back like Charlie Chaplin to his empty chair, while the august President White shifted his feet back and forth.

Moderator Wilder, shaky and bug-eyed, led his esteemed debaters and the agitated, noisy crowd through the remaining steps of the debate: cross-examinations of speakers, negative rebuttal, positive rebuttal, and on to the conclusions, relief apparent upon his face when it ended.

****

The end of the story hadn't yet been fully told. The notable John P. White agreed to appear for several debates, to Arma, to Frankfort, and other coal towns nearby, however, he never appeared.

The second debate was scheduled for the very next evening in Frankfort. President White was a "no show," even though a crowd of several thousand had gathered to wait.

Months passed as Alec Howat's attorney, Frank Walsh, kept pushing, studying, laboring over the case. Auditors reexamined the ledgers. Suddenly one of the accountants explained, "I've checked the bank checks and vouchers and I've discovered that the mysterious $25,000 dollars Mr. Howat was accused of stealing was misplaced by an incorrect ledger entry."

"Alexander Howat is, indeed, innocent of all those charges."

Agnes's dear Alec was awarded a check for $7,000 in damages.

The story of coal is always the same. It is a dark story.
For a seconds' more sunlight, men must fight like tigers
for the privilege of seeing their children's eyes by
the light of the sun. Mother Jones

CHAPTER FOUR

Franklin, Kansas

Milan Cratnick's worn overalls whipped in the wind as he tromped along with his fourteen-year-old son, Toma. The boy carried the salt and baking powder, Milan, the sack of flour as they ambled toward their small plank house in the coal miners' town of Franklin, Kansas.

Milan, a medium-sized, broad-chested man with wiry hair, and skin that bore the residue from his labors in the mines, lowered his eyes to focus upon his scarred shoes, wondering how much longer they would last.

Coal tipples loomed and slag heaps humped against the gray sky and across the sullied countryside. His bent shoulders and dragging feet betrayed the near hopelessness in his heart.

His eyes, black as the coal he dug, cut upward toward a sapling along the gritty roadside when he heard the song of a mockingbird. He was mindful of the contrast between the beauty of the long-tailed bird's song and the dismal blight around him. He, however, was only partially aware of the fact that he had neither the skills nor the words to express such contrast. He had resolved, though, not to allow the dread in his soul and the poverty of the hours to usher his family into deeper despair.

Other than the the bird's trilling, there was only the sigh of the southeasterly wind. The puffing, coughing, and bellows from the squat steam engines, which supplied power to the mines, were quiet, due to the strike.

His thoughts were occupied by how little the boy, Toma, knew of his parents' Slovenian background; their births and early years across the ocean in a distant land. He resolved, some day, when the sun again spread light across the countryside of his soul, to tell Toma and his sister, Neda, more fully why they had left their homeland.

Of course, everyone labeled folks in these whereabouts who had emigrated from Europe to find work, aliens: Germans, Irish, Welsh, Slovenians, Polish, and many more, including the whole town of Frontenac, where all those "noisy Italians' lived. Surely the people here were from fifty or more differing countries.

What did Governor Henry Allen in Topeka call this part of the country? The Little Balkans, wasn't it?

Milan's wife, Danika, however, had shared bits and pieces about the old country with its cities and castles, forts and villages, farmlands and vineyards, skipping over the accounts of poverty, the serf-like conditions of the masses, the wars, and their near-starvation.

Sure, the folks around Pittsburg Kansas, rejoiced that the Great War had ended and President Wilson had signed the peace treaty.

He could hear Danika's words. "Toma, you ought to get down and kiss the Kansas dirt for our freedom and the opportunities we have in this good land."

Well, if the opportunities are so wonderful, why do we have nothing to eat but roots and vegetables from that little patch behind the house? When can I again provide a beef roast for the family table? Even a soup bone would be welcomed.

Besides the leanness of their table, Milan worried about the coal strike.

When could the miners return to their work? And how many strikes had there been? Almost three hundred?

He turned toward Toma, sharing his thoughts.

"You know the new International Union President, John Lewis, threw our leader, Alec Howat, into jail and ordered all the miners back to work. Course, most of us refused since Lewis put that Van Bittner in Alec's place. To make matters worse, Bittner turned around and hired scabs to take our jobs."

"Pa, just what are scabs?"

"Part-time workers. No loyalty to the Union. Know little or nothing about mining coal. Just interested in getting a fast buck." He spat into the dust as if emptying his bitterness. "They sneer at us for going on strike, while they pocket our money. Real money, not Company script."

He was aware that Toma knew the family was more than in a bad way. The boy knew also that Alexander Howat was nearly worshiped by almost everyone in the mining camps.

"Alec's jailed over in Girard this time." Milan spat a second time. He vowed to find the reasons why the International leader, John L. Lewis, jailed all their District 14 leaders.

Lewis's actions weighed on him like a chunk of the bituminous coal they mined.

In a sentence or two, he told Toma about how John L. Lewis, with his bull dog looks, had thrown Alec Howat in prison back in Indiana, a few years ago.

Their feet crunched on a mixture of dirt, sand, and coal particles as they approached the company mining camp. He was glad Toma and Neda were aware that not all of Kansas was blighted by the soot. Railroads everywhere, trolleys and coal trains. Hoots and whistles. Black smoke, steam, gray fog, gray mist, gray sky, and, he thought, sometimes the people themselves even looked grayish, including himself.

He'd been beyond the nearly three hundred coal mines around Pittsburg once on a visit over west of Scammon. There the sun had cast dazzling shafts upon the waving leaves of corn and cane. Wheat fields rolled in the wind like a sea of velvet. The rivers rippled and flowed, abounding with fish. He had been amazed at the Kansas green beyond the coalfields.

Sure, in eastern Kansas they had abundant rains, the plants and grasses grew tall, the soil in the river bottoms was black and fertile. There was even a river not far away called *The Verdigris*. Didn't that mean "green?"

As they approached their shack-of-a-house squatting among the stark rows of a hundred or so company houses, he sighed, thinking of his daughter, Neda, scrambling to find some kind of job down in Pittsburg to help put food on the table and clothes on their backs.

They stepped to the back porch of the crude house, entering through the patched screen door. He began to unpack the staples on the kitchen table.

Danika, flour scattered on her apron bib, turned to greet the menfolk. Her smile spread across her face, darkened by her toil under the hot sun. Her hand, large as a man's, reached for the salt and flour, stashing them in a pine cupboard leaning against the wall.

She turned to Toma, who stood waiting, eyes upon a pot of potatoes on the cast iron range, evidence of his hunger showing in his eyes as he leaned forward, hands buried in his back overall pockets. Steam rose from a skillet of simmering dandelion greens and a strip of salt pork.

Milan saw the worry in her eyes as she turned to speak.

"Why, Toma, I was just thinking. Maybe after we eat our dinner, you and your pa can dig out those fishing poles under the porch and see if you can get to a creek and yank out a good old catfish or two this afternoon."

Toma smiled, his face reflecting that he thought it a superb idea. His eyes drifted back to the top of the tiny black stove with the iron hearth.

Milan's grin, too, confirmed the soundness of Danika's suggestion. Maybe as he and Toma waited for the fish to bite under a cooling willow, they both could talk about those questions.

Is a strike the best way for the miners to settle their problems?

Is striking for a cause or better wages a part of aiming at that justice Father Pompeney talked about over at St. Philip Neri Church?

CHAPTER FIVE

Girard, Kansas

Toma's shoulders rocked with the sway of the trolley as he and his mother, Danika, rolled along in the crowded car toward Girard, Kansas. His heart thumped at the possibility of seeing the famous Alexander Howat, nicknamed "Alec" by the District 14 Mine Workers. Lean forward on tiptoes in the pressing crowds and cheer, if as promised, the jail warden allowed their beloved chief to speak to them.

Would President Alec really wobble out in chains onto the jail porch and address the cheering hordes -- the prisoner whom most of the folks in Franklin hailed as the one who could rescue them?

Sure, Pa wanted to be here, and wouldn't he bellow with his lifted fist in devotion to Alec and his faithful miners? Cheer lustily and loudly? But Pa, who was recovering from near pneumonia, sat on the back porch in Franklin trying to absorb the warmth of the sun.

Though he needed to heal and rest, Pa also sacrificed the trip to Girard in order to be at home when Toma's sister, Neda, arrived back from Pittsburg on the evening trolley.

They had all rejoiced when the seventeen-year-old brunette landed a clerking job in the small gifts department at the Five and Dime. Course, she'd had to spend her entire first week's salary to buy some new duds, which had been on a marked-down sale, so she could look nice like the other girls.

A lightning streak of pain shot down Toma's back all the way to his buttocks as he thought of his father's burns when his carbide lamp ignited a vein of methane gas, burning his shirt right off his back. Pa'd lain on his belly, writhing in the sweat of his bed, pleading to God that his son would never have to descend three hundred feet into the bowels of the earth and grovel on bended knees for a twelve-hour shift for less than three dollars a day. Not even to mention being out of work three months a year.

He remembered that Pa had been working in the mines since he was twelve years old. And, Ma didn't want it mentioned that she had worked in the coal mines in Illinois when she was a teenage girl, after her pa died. Toma knew that was rare. Yes, rare indeed for a woman.

Toma leaned over to help his mother struggling to open the grimy window. He surely thought it a blessing to see the coal tipples (the tall frameworks where the coal was dumped into the rail cars below) slide behind them. He was eager to rock through the countryside, away from the smoke and grime, the streaked black-and-weathered grayness of the landscape and shabby buildings.

Within the car the stink of sweating bodies circled in the September heat. His eyes scanned over the heads of the seated folks. The trolley was overcrowded with striking miners and their wives; children in faded overalls and patched pinafores, packed five to a bench. Desperate people, aliens from almost every country in Eastern Europe clacking onward toward Girard.

The Little Balkans, that's what Governor Allen called their corner of Kansas. And the governor expected this part of his state to blow up, even starting a war like that big World War the U.S.A. had helped to win back in 1918.

What else had the governor called them? Folks from Pittsburg, Frontenac, Franklin, Mulberry Grove, and the other coal camps scattered all the way westward toward Chicopee, Cherokee, Weir, and Scammon? Aliens, Communists, and Socialists. Big words, bloated with meanings beyond Toma's full grasp. But, according to Governor Allen, those words surely described people he didn't trust.

Governor Allen seemed certain that what he called "these stiff-necked" coal miners and their families were "ready to overthrow the government." Called them Bolsheviks, whatever that meant. He knew it had something to do with Russia and the Communists there.

Toma began to relax as the wobbling trolley carried them farther away from the smoldering slag heaps and tailing piles of the mines: Central Number 51, North Edison, Frogtown, Washer, and Ringo.

At least the tiny porch with the leaning rails attached to the back of the trolley, packed with an assortment of ragtag folks, hadn't fallen off, pitching a disgruntled miner into the water-filled ditch alongside the track. That'd happened in The Toonerville Folks comics last week. When the platform plopped off, old man Wortel was pitched onto the track, then rolled into the ditch.

Yes, the car was overcrowded, but so far no one had tumbled off this one or been trampled upon. Hopefully they had a better "Skipper" than did the Toonerville Trolley.

The trolley leaned and the wheels screeched on the rails as it maneuvered a curve. Toma scanned the rise and fall of the farmland with its patches of timber and wide willow-lined creeks. A touch of envy spread in his heart as he focused his eyes upon white houses and painted barns and outbuildings. He sucked in the air from the open window, absorbing the freshness from new grass shooting up as a result of the recent rains.

Suddenly his ears ached at the clanging of the bell as the car approached a country road crossing. The conductor pulled his levers, bringing the trolley to a halt, allowing a hat-rack-of-a cow to saunter on across, her bag swinging, bellowing her disdain at the interruption.

He glanced over at his ma and pity gripped him as he thought of her toiling from four o'clock in the morning until she dropped upon a canvas-and-corn-husk mattress at night. How could he even begin to list her endless efforts: baking, cooking, cleaning, scrubbing, sewing, nursing them when they were sick? Racing to the back-lot garden to chop and drag the hoe with callused palms and blistered fingers. Not to mention wringing a young Leghorn's neck, scalding it, plucking it, and preparing it for a Sunday dinner.

He knew that those chickens would last only so long and now, with the strike, just what would Ma do? He was glad that Pa'd insisted that she come to hear their imprisoned leader make efforts to spark encouragement in the hearts of the despairing miners. And Pa'd said, "Toma, you must go with your ma," in spite of the trip costing them nearly thirty cents.

But Ma was surely silent so far. He hoped that her weary bones would get some rest as they rocked along. He glanced at her broad olive-skinned forehead, and surveyed her bulky body overflowing her half of the bench. When she turned and momentarily stroked the back of his hand, a trace of a smile graced her lips. He recognized that her eyes, the color of a rusted iron pot, radiated a deep love and warmth.

Worry showed there, too, in the lines on her forehead and the way her chapped hand crept up across her mouth when she stared forward as if she was viewing the coat tail of one of the three horsemen in the book of Revelation that Father Pompeney brought to their attention.

Yeah, he thought, maybe Ma can do something to lift the burdens from the backs of the ten thousand coal miners around Pittsburg, Kansas. Help release them from near slavery and, at times such as this all-out strike, rescue them from gnawing stomaches and the ugly face of starvation.

Sure enough. Ahead in the car he recognized the reddish cap of his buddy, Cecil Otis.

What would Cecil be doing on this car? Both eighth-graders, they'd been pals for seven years, even though Cecil was the son of the mine operator of the Jackson-Walker Mine Number 17. Toma had been inside the Otis's monstrous three-story house, with its velvet curtains and oriental rugs, which surely could be called a mansion. Right on the block in Franklin that butted up against the paved street with electric light poles.

Cecil's mother, Ophelia, had a Irish maid, and a gardener who kept their grounds trimmed and drove Operator Harvey Otis to the mines and union meetings in that long midnight blue Packard.

A wide gulf existed between Operator Otis and most of the struggling coal miners. Harvey Otis favored Governor Allen's Industrial Court Law, passed in the legislature last year that, according to Pa, would keep the miners on their knees if they yielded to it.

The new law prevented the miners from striking at twelve-hour shifts and starvation wages, not even to mention the horrific working conditions.

Toma had overheard Ma and Pa, when he was supposed to be on his cot sleeping, talking in hushed voices about the the mine disasters last year. Over a thousand accidents and fourteen miners dying from cave-ins, firedamp, and blowouts from faulty mining caps. Not even to mention his friend, Carl Mishmash, whose father was killed in the Dean and Reliance strip mine five or six years ago.

Young Carl, barely fifteen, had stepped forward, grabbed a pick and his Pa's hat and carbide lamp and descended into the hellish darkness to keep his family from going hungry.

Not even settled yet, Carl not getting his full wages and the whole family eating boiled turnips and whatever game Carl could shoot.

Toma knew that situation was part of the reason for the present strike, and for their beloved Alec being thrown into jail for defying the hated Slave Law, as his pa called it.

Since that law was passed, all their miners' disputes had to be brought before Governor Allen's Industrial Court in Topeka for settlement before a board of three judges, selected by the governor himself.

What did they know about what coal miners faced?

Pa said, we've got to be just like Andy Gump in the funny papers, loaned to him by Cecil, who stomped and railed against the hard-shelled blowhards.

Pa'd named them, too, the blowhards. First was John L. Lewis, President of the International United Mine Worker's Union, who had those forest-like eyebrows. Then Henry Allen, their governor. Lastly that weak-kneed Van Bittner, put in as president of their local 14 after they'd dragged Alec Howat off to jail and thrown out the District's Vice President Dorchy.

Well, hadn't Cecil Otis, who kept up on the latest slang, said it right? "Half the world are squirrels and the other half are nuts."

"Why, it violates all sense of decency and the miner's freedom," Pa'd said. "Don't call Governor Allen's law anything else but a slave law!

Toma looked up and saw his ma adjusting the self-knitted hat as the trolley crept around a bend, approached an intersection and rolled on toward downtown Girard. He could tell by the bending trees alongside the tracks that a wind had come up.

Maybe Ma should have worn something heavier than her old hand-knitted gray sweater.

In front of them, three other yellow and red trolleys were unloading. He could see folks shoving and leaning forward, running toward the county jail beyond the imposing courthouse.

Toma and his ma struggled to wedge toward the front of the jail as the cheers of the shoving crowds rose about them. He turned, looking backward up the main street, and saw the street was packed from curb-to-curb with marchers headed their way.

Why, the line must be at least two miles long.

Toma focused his eyes upon a few placards and signs on sticks with the words "The future lies with the Socialists" in bold letters on them.

Well, Toma had to admit that he didn't quite know what all that the word Socialist meant. But he knew that Girard was called a "Socialist" town and that some really well-meaning but loud-mouthed women had been here several times.

His ma liked them both, Mary Heaton Vorse, and the old, old one with her spectacles shoved down to the end of her nose, called Mother Jones. She could outyell a Pentecostal preacher.

As far as Toma knew a Socialist was someone who worked in behalf of all of the people and that the industries that paid them were controlled by the working people.

Pa'd said that both coal mining towns of Arma and Dunkirk had men on the school board and such, and that they were Socialists. Governor Allen, he was sure, though, was certain that it was leading them straight to Communism like in Russia and that a revolution lay just around the corner.

Toma and his ma settled into the crowd, made up of French, Italians, Germans, Slovenians, Irish, and a host of other immigrant miners and family members. A chorus of voices rose into the air: "Give us Howat! Give us Howat!

Would this be the day their relief began?

CHAPTER SIX

Jailbird Howat

Danika and Toma pushed through the multitude of people wherever they could find openings. They finally stood at the edge of the sidewalk, outlined by dandelions and new tickle grass. Opposite them, the two-storied stone jail rose, imposing, threatening, with its gloomy windows at the foundation, signifying who-knew-what? lying below.

The Italians from Frontenac began to roar the loudest. Their staccato-and-broken-rhythmed voices bounced above the mongrel mixture of tongues. Here and there were the harsh Gs and the JAs of the Germans. Danika drew her dingy sweater closer to her shoulders, betraying the fact that she should have worn a heavier wrap. Her feed-sack dress whipped around her cotton-stockinged legs.

They both recognized some folks from Franklin, catching glimpses of them through the spaces between shoulders and heads.

Well, what is Myrtice Hester doing here?

Widow Myrtice, whose husband had been an overseer at the H&J mines of the Mackie Fuel Company, received a steady monthly pension. Her station in life was considerably above that of these ordinary miners shoving up around them. Didn't have to rely on company script like the rest of them.

Wouldn't Myrtice Hester stand with the John. L. Lewis supporters instead of Mr. Howat?

A part of Danika hoped she didn't bump against the nosy woman.

God only knew where Myrtice stood, spreading her gossip from house to house all the way over to Frontenac.

Danika shoved these thoughts to the corner of her mind, since she didn't want to miss out on the most important thing, the two uniformed guards up on the jail porch waiting for the warden to bring out their King of Miners, Alec Howat.

"Ma, will he really be in chains?"

"I can't say for sure, son, but the way Mr. Howat keeps standing up against the governor and his henchmen, they're not gonna give him any extra leniency." The din of voices around her almost deafened her.

To the right, wearing a tightfitting wine-colored felt hat stood Mary Skubitz, standing alongside a slender teenager, Clemence DeGruson, who already had one of those new hair bobs. Danika breathed a sigh of relief when she recognized that most of the crowd were supporters of the miners' cause.

The question was, though, who was embedded in the horde who stood with Governor Allen and Bull Dog John L. Lewis? Danika swallowed, straining to focus her eyes to see more clearly. She was glad that the sun had sunken behind some clouds in the southwestern sky, enabling her to get a clearer view.

Suddenly the guards opened the heavy double doors. At first all she saw was the darkness.

A hush swept across the vast crowd, mostly from Cherokee and Crawford counties.

Only the caw of a crow on a telephone pole disturbed the silence. As Howat stepped awkwardly forward, she could then see their beloved President Alec. He was no taller than her husband, Milan. She stared, her hand raising to her mouth, as the medium-sized, wide-chested man swaggered from side to side in his approach to the porch rails.

Sure enough. His legs were manacled with heavy clanging chains. Worse yet, he was decked out in black-and-white prisoner's clothes that bagged like old underwear. Yes, she thought, you could tell just by looking at him, Alexander Howat was one of them.

He was a coal miner. He had that haunted look.

The prisoner's heavy trousers bunched at his high-topped shoes. His brown hair, graying at the temples at only age forty-four, lifted, whipping in the sudden wind.

No doubt about it, one could see "miner" in his stature and his bearing. Hadn't he gone into the mines when he was only ten?

Suddenly the silence was broken by a wave of cheers rolling toward Alec, yelling his name in dialects familiar to them. Work-worn hands with crooked fingers stretched into the air. "Alec, Alec! Give it to em, Alec!"

Danika hoped there would be no foul words spoken with Toma standing right beside her, but she did sympathize with the passionate, their necks raised from wrinkled collars, stubbly mouths opened widely, showing bad teeth.

They screamed their love for their deposed president. She knew that most of the cheering laborers wished that John Lewis and Governor Allen were both banished to the fartherest end of yonder, not even to mention that Van Bittner, put in by the governor to take Alexander Howat's place.

How could one lone man standing on that porch address such a crowd?

Danika and Toma stared as the warden, who was suited up in a black double-breasted suit, a smart homburg hat cocked on his wide head. He grabbed a megaphone from one of the guards, cleared his throat and raised his arms.

The crowd grew silent. Straining.

"Citizens! Citizens!" he called through the megaphone, voice like the bellowing of a frog. "We're going to allow this prisoner to speak to you but only by the generous order of Governor Allen.

Again, wild cheers broke loose.

Now holding the megaphone, Alexander Howat, in and out of coal mines for thirty years of his life, lifted it to his mouth with a muscled hand.

He turned his head slowly, eastward, southward, looking across the vast expanse of citizens, described by Governor Allen as "aliens and dangerous radicals."

"I thank Warden Simmons for this opportunity to speak to my fellow miners and their family members who've made the sacrifice to be here." The megaphone lowered.

Danika and Toma strained to hear his words.

"Friends, this time I've received a three-year sentence. Your fellow officers of District 14, five of them, have been sentenced to a year in jail. I've even lost count of the times I've been imprisoned. But today, that's not important. What is important is the message I'm sending along with you and to the powers that want to keep us in poverty."

Gnarled hands thrust into the air, accompanied by a chorus of cheers.

"I am imprisoned because of that Slave Law which prevents us from striking when our backs are burdened with loads too heavy to bear. Wages are lower than they have been in years. We've endured a three-year strike called by that rat in Indianapolis, John L. Lewis."

An explosion of booing rose at the mention of the name considered infamous by the majority in Cherokee and Crawford counties.

Howat's sentence made Danika twitch. She noted that a man wearing a faded fedora in front of her did not raise his hands and cheer. She was aware that the Lewis supporters here were waiting, watching, listening for ways to further divide them from their District 14 leaders, withholding salaries over trifles, and with this recent strike, sending in scabs (non-union members) to fill their places.

She glanced quickly to the side and noticed uniformed police at street corners, holsters tightly buckled at their waists. Their tense bodies and stares gave evidence of their fear of a possible riot.

Girard was, after all, a Socialist Town, some people even dubbing it the Eugene Deb's town. The town where they printed that newspaper, The Appeal to Reason. In less intense moments than these, however, she thought both of those words, "appeal" and "reason," sounded non-threatening and reasonable. She'd have to talk more with Milan about them.

Howat continued.

"You all know about young Carl Mishmash. His father, broken down by the strip mine operators, died on the job. Several years ago."

Moaning voices lifted in the wind.

"Carl, a teenager, picked up his father's shovel and pick and went to work to keep his family from starvation."

Again groans of identification with the situation could be heard.

"Three years the family waits for their compensation. But, no, a problem which could easily have been settled, as the mine constitutions and ordinances declare, has been neglected by the very mine operators themselves and that skunk, Governor Henry Allen, up in Topeka."

Booing swept upward with the whirring wings of a flock of pigeons. "Give it to em, Alec. We're standing with you. You call a strike, we strike!"

The folks screamed acclamations of support.

"Now I do thank Judge Andrew Curran who sentenced me to jail. I read in the newspaper where he called me a 'Sturdy American.'"

Danika remembered the short article and had been confused by it.

"They talk," Howat continued, "about Sturdy Americans who send men to jail who have committed no crime. The men and women of this part of Kansas are going to attend to these Sturdy Americans when they get the opportunity."

A thundering roar beginning at the fartherest edge of the crowd rippled toward the jail porch, and Howat's baggy-kneed jailbird trousers billowed in the wind.

Danika could see a smile creep across Alec's Scottish face. Her fingers interlocked tightly below her heavy bosom.

"The miners of District 14 are engaged in one of the most remarkable fights in the history of the nation." Howat leaned, coughed, then again put his mouth to the Megaphone. "Striking against a law that itself, that very law, causes strikes.

"We, the people of Kansas are demonstrating right now. Demonstrating to the people of America that we stand for our constitutional rights. The day has past, my friends, when a few conniving politicians, International Union Presidents like Lewis, and a few unscrupulous lawyers can chain workers to their jobs like slaves."

"Tell em, Alec. Tell em! We're with you, Alec. Tell us more!" The roars were deafening.

A struggle broke out to Danika's left. A woman, no doubt overcome with emotion or going too long without any decent food, had fainted. Howat waited to allow the collapsed woman to be carried to a less crowded area by a lamp post.

"You need to know, my fellow citizens, that the bankers, the business owners in our cities, and most of the professionals stand with the governor and Attorney General Hopkins. We won't step down. Vice President Dorchy and I will stay in jail until they take us out in boxes!"

By now Toma had to wipe his own tears with the back of his hand. He could hear the sounds of women weeping.

In the Sunday School, hadn't he learned that the Lord was on the side of the poor?

Didn't those who governed over them know that what the Lord requires is justice, and it showered down like rivers of righteousness?

He resolved to ask Pa what some of that really meant. Maybe this. This opportunity for justice. Right here in Crawford County, Kansas.

CHAPTER SEVEN

Neda

Neda Cratnick dug in her little beaded handbag for her lipstick, the very cheapest one that the Five and Dime put out on discount. Not that Ma'd scold her for sure, but she hadn't wanted to take any chances.

Bobbing her hair like the other girls in the store had done was pushing far enough, wasn't it?

At least she hadn't dyed her hair henna.

She was thankful for the Interurban rocking into Pittsburg. She considered herself lucky to be close to a town, city actually, of 22,000 people. In a mining district, too.

Of course she knew from when she was in the eighth grade and studied Kansas history and geography that Kansas was the third largest coal producing state in the nation. Wasn't so bad at all, living in Franklin once one rode on through the rotten coal smelling air and the ramshackle look of things.

She surely would, though, appreciate an extra room or two built on their company house. Ma threatened to take in a coal miner boarder. But where on the green earth would he sleep? Neda didn't need to be told that the family could use the extra money. That fact was evident.

Well, wasn't she helping, doing her very own part?

Of course they'd been set back with pa's broken bones and burns. Don't even mention the coal strikes.

"God bless, Alec Howat" she breathed to herself. And wouldn't I have loved to have ridden with Ma and Toma over to Girard to hear the Miner's King?

As far as Neda knew, the International Miners' Union hadn't given Alec and the local 14 officers a fighting chance. When the Carl Mishmash case dragged on and the mine operators refused to pay the full salary to Carl, Alec had called a strike. Sure, the miners called out in unison, "Alec, we're with you," laying down their picks and shovels.

Well, Neda knew she came from Slovenian background and she didn't rightly know much about that old European and immigrant family history. Weren't they far too burdened down keeping food on the table and Toma in school to spend much time looking backward? Hope lay in the future, that's the American way!

What did the Statue of Liberty say?

"Give me your tired, your poor, your huddled masses yearning to be free...."

Lots of old grannies and their husbands told tales of crowding the rails of immigrant ships and how they pointed, lifted babies, genuflected, and prayed when they cast their travel-weary eyes upon The Lady, lifting her lamp beside the golden door.

The Interurban pulled in at the Pittsburg station. The working girls descended, along with businessmen in wide-lapeled suits, heads topped with homburgs, derbies, and fedoras. Neda wondered if the rest of the girls who clerked in the variety of stores up and down the streets were as anxious about their looks as she was.

Yes, her Mary Jane shoes with the strap were shiny and black. She'd tried to ignore how the narrow toe pinched. Her beige stockings were rolled properly, just below her knees.

Oh, Poppa, how things changed when the soldiers came home from France and Germany only three years ago. And the songs: "I'm here for you girl, whatever you need...."

Why, the women, first thing, pitched out those heavy hats weighing at least a pound. Yanked off those black woolen stockings and, would you believe it, let their dress hems creep all the way up to mid-calf. Good thing, too. Who wanted a long skirt dragging through all that horse manure when you crossed the street? She had to admit, though, that some of the Flapper gals' hems had crept up too far even to talk about.

Well, she felt reasonably secure that her light-green dress with the drop waist and skirt filled the bill for these times. Every girl wanted to "fit in." Of course, the big busted ones struggled to flatten their bosoms so they could wear these new fashions, but, so far, Neda had no cause to worry. Besides, she had read that the doctors were saying that if young women flattened their breasts, they would give birth to babies that had rickets.

She liked it that her hemline "dithered," sarong-like. The air had a chill in it, and a wind had sprung up this morning. "I could use a little scarf or a throw over my shoulder," she thought, stepping briskly.

She was satisfied with her beige cloche hat which fit smartly on her head. The girls saved those head bands for evening wear, feather stuck up in back as they crossed their legs and dangled a shoe. Not to mention a cigarette in a holder, poked fashionably into the air. Something she definitely hadn't tried.

Neda noticed that the lights were on in the Five and Dime. She reached for the handle of the big brass doors. She was expected by nine-thirty at her counter where there was a display of an assortment of affordable china, teapots, clocks, little clay Indian pots from way out west, and other special gift items. She'd made it in plenty of time.

Not gonna catch Neda Cratnick being late if I can help it.

She'd already remembered to spit out her gum.

The little bell tinkled as she stepped through the door, always welcomed by the cheeriness and glitter of the spacious store. A sense of well-being and actual delight moved through her. She felt herself smiling at proprietress

Lena Lotlie. She guessed that Lena's husband, whom everyone called "Hank," must be working on the books in the back room.

Lena finished dusting the shelves of picture frames and carnival glass with a whisk of her feather duster. She greeted her recently-employed clerk with a syrupy "Good morning, dear."

Neda glanced at Mrs. Lotlie's mid-calf blue chiffon pleated dress. She knew that it had been written that blue was the best all-around color for a steady woman. Avoid black, unless your are over sixty. White only when in a coffin. Lotlie's long black onyx beads were conservative and appropriate, Neda thought.

Neda knew, since she'd had the job only two months, that she was still on trial but with her self-confidence this morning, and the expectations of meeting new customers, she felt like she could have just whistled her greetings.

Instead she spoke her "Good morning, Mrs. Lotlie."

"Hon," Mrs. Lotlie said, "I want my girls here to be especially careful with that new green-and-rosebud painted china that came in last week. A salesman is coming in sometime this morning to bring some extra pieces."

Well, Neda already knew that some of the "higher up" ladies of the town had been eying that china and were waiting for the shipment of the special pieces.

"Why, that's just dandy, Mrs. Lotlie. "I'll be expecting the gentleman."

They usually were men, weren't they? And those men liked to lean across the counters at the young women clerks, and finger their mustaches, forgetting parts of their sales pitches. Some even dared a wink.

One had to watch, that's for sure.

Six other girls had taken their stations. One could hear the tinkle of their cash registers as each checked her money drawer. Neda loved the smell of the dime store, the newness and sparkle of it. The smell of waxed wood. The little tubes rising from the counters to the ceilings. Vacuum tubes, they called the little pipes. Shooting the customer's money and the salesclerk's ticket all the way up to the mezzanine where the cashier counted the cash and shot the change, if any, back down to the waiting clerk and customer. Nobody around here needed to mention Kansas City for being up-to-date. Nope, not with cutting-edged equipment like that.

And that place up there called the mezzanine impressed her so much she'd have to be careful saying that word around the folks in Franklin and coal mining camps. They'd snicker and think she was stuck-up.

Mrs. Lotlie stepped over to Neda's counter. She cleared her throat and lifted a hand, topaz-ringed finger outstretched. "I think it is just a terrible thing. Lord knows that the miners' families need cash. But they're robbing themselves. Going on strike like that."

Neda felt as if her Mary Jane shoes were suddenly glued to the floor.

What had the girls talked about yesterday during their morning break while sipping cherry phosphates?

Why, they'd whispered about the fact that the bankers and businessmen and most of the professionals were on the side of the state and the hated slave law.

She knew the extreme caution among the merchants regarding their salesclerks joining a union. Neda knew that some of the girls at the Five and Dime were union members.

"You know, Neda," Lena leaned in toward Neda to make her point, sharp chin lifted. "They're cutting off their noses to spite their faces. Mr. Dorchy and the Governor have offered good pay for these times. You know with such a widespread strike, the merchants here in town are going to suffer."

Neda felt her calf twitch. A vein in her throat began to throb. She hoped her cheeks didn't turn red.

What if the old biddy had to go without butter, let alone bread?

Neda cleared her throat and added, "The miners do have to take a stand. You know that Mr. John L. Lewis of the

UMW of America has lowered all the coal miners' wages since the War." She refrained from mentioning that heavy-eyebrowed Lewis had called a nationwide coal strike which had lasted three years.

Should I have mentioned this bare fact?

Lena's eyes suddenly looked cooler, her crepe eyelids hooded. She drew her hand back, clasping it with the other one behind her back. "And, I might as well inform you right up front, Miss Cratnick, that I really don't want to hear about any more of my newly hired girls joining that Clerks' Union. Mr. Lotlie and I pay good wages here, and so far, our girls have no complaint." Lena, making her point turned as she marched to the front door to turn the sign to "Open."

****

By eleven o'clock Neda had already had the good fortune to sell one of the china clocks with the French figurines to a banker's wife who wanted it for a birthday gift for her granddaughter.

Next, she'd sacked up three small matching picture frames, wrapping them in tissue paper first. Every time her vacuum tube returned with the change and the bill, she not only felt relief, but success. So far she hadn't made any mistakes. Not even belched from the frothy sarsaparilla they'd had at break time like Dorrie Reed had done over at the next counter, right in Clara Crutchman's face, the town plumber's wife.

No, the day was good. Sales rolling along. She felt certain that old lady Shuston, who had rifled and fingered at least a dozen assorted items from counter to counter, messing up the handkerchiefs on Twila Tilson's front shelf would return to her counter and buy one of those little glass dresser sets. She'd almost clinched the sale on the pink three-pieced set. She'd actually noticed proprietress Lotlie had glanced her way several times and had flashed a quick smile of approval.

She didn't know why, but when she saw Lena's long chin, the words from that Shakespeare play Mr. Woodman had them read and study in Senior English, suddenly flitted through her mind.

> *Double, double, toil and trouble;*
> *Fire burn and cauldron bubble.*

She guessed it was the tall man in the brown suit with a matching fedora cocked on his head that made her open her eyes a little wider. He carried a merchant's case, which pulled his shoulder to the right.

He put down the case and extended his greetings to Mrs. Lotlie over at the notions counter. Neda couldn't help but notice how Lena bowed and scraped.

Well, he certainly was a looker, wasn't he?

She'd admit that to herself. She liked curly hair and he had blond curls dangling from underneath the front of his hat, which he quickly removed.

Looked like Lena'd clinched a deal, then she ushered the thin, but well-built man right over to her counter.

"Miss Cratnick," Lena spoke in a honeyed voice. "This is Mr. Colburn Teer, up from Joplin. I'm purchasing the three tea sets. You know, the green-and-rosebud china I mentioned when you came in?"

Yes, Neda remembered. She felt her cheeks flush as the man, surely not more than thirty years old, set his case down, holding his hat.

"Why, howdy, Miss --, Miss--"

"Cratnick," Neda was certain she was blushing. "Neda Cratnick."

Why do I suddenly feel so hot?

"Well, pleased to make your acquaintance." His voice had a husky mellowness, deeper than Lena's honeyed tone. "Neda, well, well, one doesn't hear that name too often." His grin widened.

Neda threw back her shoulders, making certain that her posture was correct. "Pleased to meet you." She waited, trace of a smile on her lips.

Should I have extended my hand?

"May I rest my hat here on the counter? he asked.

"Oh, certainly, certainly, Mr. Teer."

Am I too eager to please?

Colburn began to lift out the three tea sets, his handsome fingers unwrapping the tissue paper enveloping them. Neda half-turned toward her back display shelf where she had just the right place for them.

Neda noticed that Mrs. Lotlie hung close by, one hand smoothing her skirt. Other hand fiddling with her beads, eyeing her.

Salesman Colburn placed one entire set in front of Neda on the glass counter. A pang of desire gnawed through Neda. How she'd love to purchase that tea set for Ma for Christmas. Never had Ma had so pretty a present. But now, she knew that such a purchase would have to be deferred. Delayed for a long time during these strike days.

Neda noticed three town women sauntering over toward her counter, new-looking hats fitted well on their heads. Their conversation drifted: "You know that trial over in Girard is over, and the warden there is going to allow that Alexander Howat to speak to a crowd." The one with the brown cloche puckered her lips and frowned.

"You mean that mine president who's been deposed? I thought they put all those jerks causing the lay-offs in jail to stay," the heavy-set one added.

Neda couldn't believe what she was hearing. Then she remembered that her father had warned her, "Don't trust all the town people. Especially the merchants and business owners. Most of them are John Lewis people. They want to keep the miners under their feet."

Then, salesman Teer, after he'd lifted out the third set and placed it upon the counter, made the decision to add to the conversation he'd overheard. No doubt, he thought it was appropriate in this environment. He seemed to be getting ready to lean on the counter and pass the time of day with Neda.

Neda wouldn't have minded at all having a little chat with this exciting summer-tanned man. She glanced up and saw the twinkle lines at the edges of his snappy eyes. An electric current tingled at the base of her stomach; but the ugly womens' words, circling around her like the screech of starlings, began to sour her stomach.

Grinning, Colburn, elbow resting now on her counter, hands clasped before him, stared in her face with his delft-blue eyes. The mistake he made was in his selection of words.

"Well, that's right, don't you think, Miss Cratnick? Miners causing so much trouble. Stopping sales and shutting down businesses. Why I think it'd be a good thing for that Girard crowd to take that Alexander Howat out and hang him on the nearest tree."

He had hardly finished the word "tree" when a shattering crash resounded all the way to the back of the room. Broken china clanged and clunked to the floor.

Neda Cratnick, unable to control her hands and arms, had grasped the gorgeous tea pot with the painted roses and crashed it over Mr. Colburn Teer's handsome head.

Neda Cratnick, newly employed salesclerk, right there in the Five and Dime in Pittsburg, having landed a real-for-sure job and good wages, now caught in this disaster?

CHAPTER EIGHT

Take Me to the Loony Hospital

Quicker than Neda could mouth any words at all, she felt her arm gripped by Lena Lotlie's clawing fingers, her face a boiled-beet red. She hissed as she sucked in air. Neda stumbled and banged her hip on the sharp-edged counter as feline Lena dragged her towards the back office.

"You stupid heifer! Hank warned me about hiring trashy coal mining camp girls like you!"

Hank, green celluloid visor shading his eyes as he worked on the books, looked up as he heard the commotion.

"I--uh--," Neda's tongue tangled. Her bruised hip throbbed in pain. She felt herself being shoved down onto a hard chair.

"Don't say a word. Hank, make out a check. Figure it up, it can't be more than four dollars." Lena gasped in another gulp of air. "This ignorant girl just cost me over twenty-five dollars with her stupid escapade. Can you imagine! Crashing that beautiful tea pot over Mr. Teer's head?"

Hank turned to survey the thin girl in the flapper shift, leer on his slick lips. Neda's eyes, wide like a doe's, caught in a Model T's headlights.

"Well, he said with a snicker, "I could a taught her a thing or two."

Lena's eyes bugged back at him, her face now toad-like. "You're an idiot too. Give me that check." She snatched it, lips turned down.

"Here." She shoved it at Neda. "Don't you ever step into my store again! Ever!

Christian businesswoman like me trying to do my duty by giving you a chance. Other merchants warned me. My father always said: 'You can't make a silk purse out of a sow's ear.'"

Neda stood, knees trembling, not knowing whether or not she could even take a step. She found her tongue: "I'm so sorr--"

"Don't say a word. You're lucky I didn't slap you right out there at the counter among those real ladies. Lucky, too, that I didn't call the sheriff. Yes, lucky, I'd say. Now get going, and good riddance!" She gripped the back door handle and jerked it open.

****

Neda found herself stumbling out onto the narrow back alley. Limping from her bruised hip, her steps faltered. She wasn't even sure how she ended up on the sidewalk along Broadway. Shattered, she jumped and leaned to the side of a building when the driver of a Tin Lizzie squeezed the bulb of his horn at a horse-drawn ice wagon.

Looking up, the frazzled girl noticed that she was leaning against the wall of one of the many Pittsburg saloons, doors wide open, in spite of the prohibition laws. She gathered her feet under her and shuffled on.

Head hanging low, feet stumbling indeterminably, she didn't even glance up once to notice the grandeur of the graceful dental building in the morning light. The edifice, designed by the great Lewis Comfort Tiffany himself, and the famous architect, Harvey M. Grandel, was a marvel of southeastern Kansas.

What'll I do? I can't go home. Oh, Papa, Oh, Mama, how can I face them.

Tears scalded her cheeks. She realized that she had to brace herself, couldn't be seen crying out on the street, three women stepping briskly toward her. What'd they think?

Her feet dragged the rest of her down the sidewalk past a prestigious church, and there were many in the city. Her eyes fixed upon the train station across the street. Ignoring the traffic (another blare of a horn from some kind of an expensive car driven by a man with a homburg hat), she hurried her steps, wondering if she could lift her feet when she came to the curb.

The fat driver in the homburg rolled down his window, whistled at her and called out, "Hey, babe, wanna go for a ride?"

Her head hung lower with the shame of such an invitation, mortifying her.

Finding herself in the expansive station, the thoughts tumbled in her brain.

Now what? I can't go home. How will I spend the day?

Then she realized she'd left her cloche hat on the peg in the back of the store.

No, a team of Clydesdales couldn't drag me back there and face that old witch.

Double, double, Kansas trouble:
Fire burn, and cauldron bubble.

Neda hunched in the fartherest hard-backed bench of the waiting room like a child ordered to the schoolroom corner by a scornful teacher. She was aware the Stationmaster was eying her but right now her brain was shutting down.

What'll our family do now? I so wanted to help out. Oh, dear, dear, Lord Jesus, help me.

She was certain that Mary Magdalene, tears streaming and on her knees before the blessed Jesus, begging forgiveness for her sins, wasn't as low down a sinner as was she.

Where was St. Barbara, the patron saint of miners? Could girls like her call out for her mercy?

It seemed as though all her past sins weighed down on her: the time she read Angela Degaspre's note from her boyfriend, Adolph Smith, and wasn't supposed to. The time she'd let Tom Bellezza sneak her a kiss at the side of the schoolhouse, when she promised Ma she'd never do such a thing.

On and on she numbered her sins, not to mention the time she reached for the biggest bowl of ice cream last summer before Toma could get to it. Oh! Surely the blessed Jesus was too pure to ever again look her way.

Now she knew that she would never be able to face Father Pompeney with such a sin weighing upon her heart.

My soul is like that poisoned toad under a cold stone.

She heard a rustle and looked up. There stood the Stationmaster, a kindly-looking man, white hair below his visored cap. "Young lady, are you wanting a ticket for the eleven-fifteen to Joplin?"

Neda looked into his spectacled eyes, kindly eyes.

But surely no mercy for a sweltered-venomed girl like me.

She lifted her head up from her slumped body. Why, why -- no sir, I--I'm just--just waiting here."

Now wasn't that crazy? For what? A lump of clay and knobby knees. Surely I'm losing my mind. A loony hospital. Yes, not far from here in Nevada, Missouri. Take me to the loony hospital.

"Well, the Stationmaster said, his voice, warm and deep. "I take it then that you are waiting for someone coming down from Kansas City on the 10:50?"

She finally gathered herself together, tottering toward the door. "Thank you, Sir, I, I -- uh--I was just needing a rest. Yes, a rest. Thank you. Thank you very much."

****

After walking a few blocks eastward, eyes focused upon her feet lest she'd have to greet another person "out for the air" stepping her way. She turned in at a very pretty park with tall, sweeping trees and a wide spread of green grass. Beyond, just over a little rise, lay a lake.

What was it? Why, the sign pointed toward "Playter's Lake."

She headed into the peaceful-looking park, noticing the contrast in the lawn cast by the shade from the trees. A few more steps and she was at the edge of the water. *Clear water.*

Wonder if this was an old pit mine?

Seemed like she'd once heard something about this park, but her family didn't have either the time nor the money to travel here and picnic.

The water. Yes, the rippling water.

Three ducks circled, about twenty feet from shore. They quacked when they saw her approach. Park attendants had placed large rounded stones suitable for a person to sit upon right at the edge of the lake. Fatigue hit her. She slumped upon the middle gray stone, feeling the coolness below her hips. She sat in silence. The only sounds were the sighing of the wind through the tall oaks and willows with the interspersed quacking of the ducks.

The water. Wonder how deep it is?

Her mind, slowly awakening.

Why, those old mines are filled with cold, cold, water. Could be forty feet deep. And if it had been an old strip mine there would be no shelf or shallows. Go straight down.

Yes, deep enough. Maybe even a few water moccasins hiding in it.

"That's it," she said to herself, dragging a leg out from under her, not noticing how the rough stone had ruined her stockings. "That's it."

The waves sloshed in the brisk wind that had arisen. The three ducks had already waddled ashore, now grazing in the grass.

Neda tossed a quick look over her shoulder.

Nobody coming. Nobody here.

She allowed her body to slide on the downward lake side of the stone.

Gravity itself a blessed thing, wasn't it?

Her heart pumped. Seemed like it was knocking her ribs right out of the side of her body.

Judas took a rope, didn't he, but he had a tree on a cliff....

The water whispered.

Suddenly her ears registered human words. A child's voice.

"Mama, a lady, a pretty lady."

"Yes, darling, a young lady. "Why don't we just step over by that beautiful tree and make her acquaintance?"

Neda realized she'd waited too long.

CHAPTER NINE

Around the Cratnick Table

The Cratnicks sat around a pine table which Milan had nailed together soon after he and Danika were married. Their homes had always been company houses like theirs that could be easily knocked down, loaded on boxcars and hauled off to a new mining camp when the mine gave out.

Milan had taken care that he'd washed his hairy arms and hard-callused hands as carefully as one could in the little granite wash basin on the back porch bench. He found it difficult to scrub off the grime, and Danika's small bar of lye soap was tough on his skin.

He'd raked through his thick graying hair with the family comb, which had a few missing teeth, still, some strands shot upwards in the back. He'd shaved his heavy beard this morning, guiding his straight razor by glancing at the fragment-of-a-mirror nailed to the unpainted wall. His razor strap hung, swinging in the wind. He was aware, though, that he always wore what people called "a five o'clock shadow."

He appreciated the fact that Danika tried to keep things tidied up as they say. But in this company house their furnishings were spare, worn, and plain. She'd worked hard saving enough of the slick parts of newspapers and old magazines, passed on to her by Myrtice Hester, to paper the kitchen, using flour-and-water paste. The pattern on the patch of linoleum covering the cracks between the floor boards had long since worn off. Milan knew Danika longed for a new piece.

He was aware also that Danika relished the idea of someday adding on a new room. A wish which was about as soon to be fulfilled as seeing an elephant lift a cage full of miners up out of a mine with its trunk.

Two choices when it came to occupying a company shack. Either rent one that looked like a boxcar on a side rail or this sixteen-by-sixteen-foot square one, which Ma'd preferred. How do you divide up a house with only 256 square feet of living space?

Milan glanced out the east window to the row of forlorn shacks. About a hundred of them, each occupied by an average of five people.

He and Danika had the only tiny bedroom, which was furnished with their second-hand iron bed with the corn husk mattress. The dresser was so small one had to stoop to look into the mirror to put on the finishing touches before going to church.

Danika had saved all the old rags and worn out overalls. After she'd boiled them to get the coal grit and grime out of them and cut them into strips, she braided a right pretty oval rug to put one's feet on when sliding out of bed, mornings.

Toma slept on the wobbly imitation leather dufold in the front room which doubled as a couch in the daytime. Ma'd tacked heavy reddish billing paper onto the studding, which kept some of the bitter winter wind from shooting through the cracks.

Neda slept in that curtained-off place at the west end of the kitchen, furnished with a sagging cot, a tiny table made of an orange crate smacked in the corner, and a pine cupboard, which Pa'd nailed together, a place for her to hang her sparse "wardrobe."

The house sported a center tin-lined hole in the roof from which spouted their blackened stovepipe.

As he glanced out the east window, Milan shook his head in negation at the wasteland-look of the shacks, screaming poverty and disillusionment.

From November until May, endure the mud, endless black, sticky gumbo mud. Drop into the mine shaft in winter-morning blackness. Drag out of the onyx-black hole, weary and bent and slosh homeward, boots buried in the mud.

Son Toma had memorized a poem.

What was the verse?

> *"Nothing but blackness above*
> *And nothing that moves but the cars....*
> *God if you wish for our love,*
> *Fling us a handful of stars!"*

Milan's mind returned to his family around the table and evening supper. He shook his head to clear his thoughts.

Milan appreciated it that his wife had put a flowered, opened feed sack on the table, even though it was thrown on kitty-cornered, leaving bare spots at the four corners. They'd drawn up their chairs, two of them Civil War era bentwood chairs, which he and Danika sat on. Toma, at his right, perched on a wobbly green chair which he'd rescued from a pile of junk from behind the Company Store. Neda, sitting in her plain shift-of-a dress, sat in a decent-looking chair he'd made himself out of a few pieces of walnut he'd salvaged.

Milan tried not to mumble as he and his family members crossed themselves and began praying the words: "Bless us, O Lord, and these Thy gifts which we are about to receive from Thy bounty, through Jesus Christ our Lord, Amen."

He realized that for a more abundant bounty, he'd have to wait until the strike was over.

Right now" the bounty" was a bowl of potato soup served in chipped and cracked bowls and a tin plate of hot soda biscuits.

Now, what to do about everyones' long jaws since Neda'd gotten fired down in Pittsburg?

Faces hung as the faces of the three walkers on the way back to Emmaus in St. Luke's account. Their leader, Jesus, having died cruelly on a cross and leaving them alone.

What did those men mumble to themselves? "We had hoped?"

Sure, they'd all hoped. More than hoped, almost panted for joy. And frisky young Neda, swinging her beads, kicking up her heels like she'd just won the summer singing contest down at the Roof Garden by the Franklin Hotel when she'd landed her job. And she'd promised herself, already, to learn to dance that Charleston, swinging her beads and knocking her knees.

No, they hadn't railed at her when she returned home at dusk from her mishap, face swollen, still wiping her tears with the back of her hands. If anybody knew about "being out of work," it was men like Milan Cratnick and Alec Howat.

Neda'd raced to her bedroom, yanked the curtain shut. They all knew she lay face down on her mattress trying to stifle her sobs.

Milan and Danika were certain they knew the reason for Neda's tears.

Disappointment was a frequent visitor in the coal camps where the atmosphere was steeped in agony. Churchgoing folks knew for certain what it meant to be like Jesus, "acquainted with grief." The ones who were severed or taking vacations from the church knew it, too, each in his or her own way. Poverty and a lean plate was no respecter of persons in the mining camps.

Anyway, a person can only stay in one's bedroom so long before nature itself forces one out. After Neda'd been to the privy, Milan caught glimpses of her at the wash bench. She'd changed back into her work shift of yellow muslin. She'd rolled off her stockings and shoved her feet into her old garden shoes, etched with dried mud. Next, she'd splashed some cold water on her face from the basin on the back bench. Not once had she glanced into the mirror.

Pride glowed in Milan's chest, as he glanced at Neda across from Toma. She had more than a little grit. She'd survive. Like the rest of them, she would learn that opportunities come at unexpected times and that the day wasn't over. All wasn't lost.

He and Danika had talked about it at night. The firing.

"Don't blame her, Milan," cautioned Danika. "I tried to warn her about holding her tongue down there in Pittsburg. But I forgot to mention the rest of her body."

"Well, Neda's got a little fire in her, and I admire it," Milan added.

****

At the supper table, Neda laid down her spoon, slow grin sliding across her face.

"Well, Pa, you taught us to stand up for what was right. It was definitely not right for those women and for that salesman to say such terrible things."

"Yeah, it'd about make a preacher cuss, bucking up against what we have to in these parts, Neda. Criticism blasting the air and attacks leveled toward striking miners. Most of what Governor Allen and John L. Lewis, up in Indianapolis, spout out have been lies or half-truths. We have to remember that at least ten to fifteen percent of folks in these coal towns are John Lewis supporters."

"Well, why does he keep fighting with Mr. Howat, Pa?"

"Well," Milan added, "I think it's personal. Our Alec ran against him to be president of the United Mine Workers Union. Nearly won, too. Don't think Lewis ever forgave him. Sometimes I think he's a bitter man."

"You have to remember, though, a number of miners and their families are grateful. You hear them say, "Lewis saved the miners by his tough negotiations and fighting for their rights." Danika leaned back in her chair.

"Have to agree with your mother, Toma, we're under a lot of distress. Lewis asked the new Miners' Union leader,

Van Bittner, to order our men back to work. To make matters worse, when not enough returned to get the mines operating fully, they combed the streets for scabs."

"Yes and they brought in some negroes from Arkansas." Danika took a sip of water from her shell-and-pearl glass tumbler.

"And that's what's caused some of the bitterness. A few miners returned to their jobs. Can't blame them in some ways, but we are all needing more food on our tables. Besides, we've always had a settlement of black miners in some of our towns around here. Course, they keep pretty much to themselves. Elijah Benning is a black miner in our mine at Central, along with Amos Whipple, over south end of town."

"Then Governor Allen gets nervous, knowing that there really are some Socialists among us. I think Mary Skubitz is a Socialist. No wonder Henry Allen thinks about sending in the troops." Milan dragged a leg back under his chair.

"Well," Milan continued, facing his rosy-cheeked wife opposite him, forehead beaded with sweat. "The governor out in Colorado sent in the troops with guns when those miners struck, two years back."

Milan remembered the ghastly scene, called "The Ludlo Massacre," where at least thirty miners and family members were gunned down by machine guns, ordered by a "strike buster's" detective agency, hired by the mine operators.

Governor Elias Ammons called in the Colorado National Guard when the miners' wives decided to go on a protest march.

"With the crooked operators, the detective warriors, and the National Guard, the situation worsened. Soldiers with rifles formed a line. They shot unarmed women, killing several as well as three children." Milan fingered the side of his cheek as the tragic history weighed at his heart.

Poverty-stricken miners in tent cities found their camps on fire, burning to the ground. Dead bodies of striking miners had lain for an entire day on train rails leading into

Ludlo. Finally, a passenger train stopped; conductors and passengers removing the bodies.

And, thought Milan, all the miners wanted was a ten percent wage increase, getting rid of crooked weighmen shortchanging them, and an eight-hour working day.

"Yes," Danika said, "those miners and their families are bitter until this very day.

We all have to hold our tongues. At least count to ten as my Ma used to say. Maybe to a hundred. But there is a time to speak out at injustice."

Neda hung her head, then raised it. "Well, I didn't remember to count to ten and I let my anger leap out."

Milan decided he'd better do his best to draw his family together. He believed it important not to give in to despair. Help each other put salve on wounded spirits. There had been several suicides of miners, as everyone knew, with the ever-present strikes.

Don't need anyone with a prolonged depression in the household.

Maybe there were solutions to labor disputes other than strikes? It sure wasn't Governor Allen's Industrial Court Law.

"I'd like to know what you thought of Alec Howat?" Milan's question directed to Toma about his recent ride on the Pittsburg and Joplin Interurban over to Girard with his mother.

Toma swallowed a spoonful of potato soup, his slurp belying his relishing the mixture of diced potatoes, onions, and milk from Clementine, grazing in the back lot.

At least the conversation turned from Neda's disaster.

"Why, Pa, I thought seeing Mr. Howat and listening to his words was, well, what do you say? Inspiring? Yeah, Inspiring. You ought to have heard them yelling and cheering. Ma and me, too. Course there were people in the crowd thinking he was giving em the bum's rush but I thought it was a real whoop-de-do."

James D. Yoder

"Sorry I couldn't go, son, but now you know what he and the miners are up against."

Milan reached for another soda biscuit on the cracked plate.

CHAPTER TEN

John L. Lewis, Indianapolis

1920

Back in Indianapolis John L. Lewis, President of the United Mine Workers of America now for a year, raked his heavy fingers through the thick hair on his leonine head. He sat in his walnut-paneled office, leaning back in his leather-upholstered chair behind the mahogany desk.

He called to his executive secretary, his voice a low, coarse vibration, akin to a growl.

Secretary Edrea, a tall thin woman dressed in a somber dropped-waisted dress with long sleeves, stepped into his office. Her hair, pinned high on her head, marked her reluctance to change to the worldly bobbed hair her boss detested. She stood just inside the threshold of his office, pen in hand over her stenographer's pad. Her mouth, a tight line, betrayed her chronic nervousness.

"Yes, Mr. Lewis." She waited, pen raised.

"Get me Henry Allen out there in Topeka, Kansas on the phone." His black Welsh eyes riveted upon her face. His thumb locked in his vest pocket just above a heavy gold watch chain.

"Of course, Mr. Lewis. Governor Allen, Yes, of course." Her thin voice piped. She turned to her desk, heels of her black Sure Shine pumps buried in the thick carpet, giving no sound.

Lewis chuckled to himself.

Give old Henry out there in the hick country something to make him have the jitters. Funny Papers coming out now with a little rascal named "Henry." Both of em bald as a billiard ball. Yeah, that's a good word. Give him the jitters.

His snicker, nearly lascivious.

"You may pick up your receiver, Mr. Lewis." Edrea's voice now obviously strengthened by her successes with the various "Centrals," each with her whiny "Number please," she'd contended with.

His massive fingers, grown broad from his own labors in the Iowa coal mines, gripped the receiver, lifting it to his dark-skinned, low-slung ear. He did appreciate that Edrea had maneuvered the lines successfully.

The voice of the governor of Kansas now echoed in his ear.

"That you, John? Well, surely pleased you called. We got us a powder-keg out here in southeastern Kansas."

Governor Allen's voice appeared well-modulated to Lewis but he knew before the conversation was over, the chances were good that the governor's voice would have more than a wobble in it.

Well, wasn't he a kind of sissified dude with all that pushing-a-pencil correspondence background? Na, didn't shoulder a gun in The War - out there with the Red Cross and stuff. Pictures of him looking pious down his long nose like he was a Presbyterian preacher or something.

"What's the latest, Henry?"

Oh, I'd love to drag out the vowels on that word but better hold back now.

"Well," Henry Allen said, "We got Alec Howat and Dorchy salted away in the jail over there in Girard. They'll soon be moved to Columbus. You don't have to bother with them for awhile."

"Oh, you got em, Henry, you got em." He noted that Allen's voice had a hint of a "give in" tone. "Your Socialist woman, the big one, what's her name, Skubitz? Mary Skubitz? Then you got those *communists* who'll be waving red flags and marching, if they haven't already, at these arrests and street mobs. Gathering like that only because we're standing by the law!"

Of course he meant the Kansas Industrial Court Law, which, Lewis hoped, would soon be the law of the land for strikers. Have to stave off an appeal to the Supreme Court.

"Well, I don't know, John. Lot of good hard-working people down there around Pittsburg and Girard. Good people, but you know since that strike you and President Wilson called back in '19, people haven't gotten their sled runners back under them."

Lewis chuckled. "Well, I hear they call your part of the country The Little Balkans. Isn't a compliment, Henry. You got ammunition piles out there?"

It pleased Lewis to hear of the turmoil. Easy to squash. Miners of District 14 trying to tell him the strike wasn't just over that pitiful little Mishmash case.

"Well, Governor Allen," he emphasized the word Governor.

Let the paunchy little outlander wiggle a little.

"We would've held out back in '19, held our guns for higher wages. You know, Henry, they don't call me 'the benevolent dictator' for nothing."

There was a pause on the telephone. He heard Allen clearing his throat.

"Well," Governor Allen said, after the embarrassing silence, "uh - uh -uh, we can always call in the troops if the situation gets any worse."

Just what I want to hear. Lewis licked his thick red lips.

Little Allen's getting scared. Topeka's not far enough away from Pittsburg, Kansas. Bet he's beginning to wish he was back in Germany with the Red Cross.

"What's that I'm reading in the papers out there getting way back east into the New York Times?"

"Yes," Governor Allen said, "there's a lot of publicity. Too much, in fact. And you, out in Indiana, don't have to contend with the Socialists in Girard. We've got that half-baked Eugene Debs still writing columns for *The Appeal to Reason.*"

"Oh, I get that paper, Henry. Don't you think I know it all?"

Well, shouldn't have said that, he'll think I'm pompous, which I might be, but it'd give him ammunition.

"Listen, Henry, I don't cotton to those miners of our Union sending in thousands of dollars to Howat's rag-tag people. We've got better uses for that money. I'm going to personally turn off the spigot."

John Lewis waited during a pause. The line crackled. He heard Allen clear his throat again.

Was that squeaking sound from his swivel chair?

"You have a lot of respect from the miners, John. This is a test case in Kansas. You and I both have won a victory if the Industrial Court Law becomes the law of the land, like I said." Henry waited.

Lewis guessed that by now Henry Allen was digging for his handkerchief to mop his bald globe. He heard a growling sound in his own throat.

"Well, John," he boomed, "If I got a lot of RESPECT, then why on God's green acre did that infamous paper out there write this paragraph?"

The coup de grace.

Silence, only the rustling static on the line. Lewis knew he had him.

Let him stew.

He slipped his glasses over his stub-of-a nose and bellowed loudly over the phone.

"Lewis's actions, since Howat has gone to jail, cannot be justly characterized as anything else but the foulest treachery, not only to the Kansas miners, but to the labor movement of the United States and Canada and of the cause of humanity."

Lewis chuckled to himself.

Yep. Bet little Jack Horner out in Kansas is going to pull something besides a plum out of his pie if he doesn't watch out. Gotta be nice to him to his face at conventions and when I come to Kansas.

Course I don't plan on taking the train out there if they don't keep out that old lady Mother Jones, always stirring things up.

Finally Lewis heard a wobbling squawk as Allen attempted to speak. His supplicating words slid along the line connecting them.

"Why, uh, President Lewis, I'm real sorry about that, those words. Maybe I'll have to have my driver take me down to Pittsburg again. Maybe even set up my governance in one of the hotels. That is, if things get worse."

That's it, Lewis thought. I can hear him wilt. Got him where I want him. Running scared. What a laugh. Setting up governing in Pittsburg, Kansas. Make a donkey hee-haw.

CHAPTER ELEVEN

Mary Heaton Vorse

Danika Cratnick's feet shifted on the hard floor as she hurried to poke the rest of the green beans into her Bell jars, cold pack them and stow them away before she tidied herself up. She was anxious about missing the trolley headed up to Arma, north of Franklin.

Sure, there's a sidewalk, but I'm too pressed for time to hoof it all the way up there.

She'd read in a borrowed newspaper that Mary Heaton Vorse, that new Socialist-Activist type of woman, had been invited by prominent ladies in Arma to speak, following the womens' picnic.

No doubt, ladies from as far away as Girard'll be there. Socialists over there, anyway, aren't they?

Danika scanned her big upper body in her cloudy dresser mirror. She ran a hand over the bosom of her second best dress, a garment remodeled several times in order to keep up with the changing times.

No use going out looking like yesterday's hanger-on.

She noticed that her hair was beginning to show the hint of gray at the sides, She'd swept it back and twisted it into her usual knot, tightly anchored with combs.

She wished she had something besides a navy sash, held together by an old mother of pearl pin, but decided it'd have to do.

Wonder who'll be there? Myrtice Hester would bust a gut to get to a picnic. And Ophelia Otis? Would a stuck-up mine operator's wife soil herself by sitting with commoners? But she might be interested in a real woman author. What had that Vorse woman written? Neda'd told her about it. A love story, "I've Come to Stay," wasn't it?

Danika was determined to get her mind straightened out about just what this Activist policy was.

How was it different from American democracy and this so-called capitalism?

Not that she understood completely how Democracy actually worked.

Sure, I voted in 1920. Suffrage, they called it. Well, women did suffer their humiliations and limitations set by menfolk, didn't they? If suffrage was enduring the change, I'm glad for it, now let the men twist and learn to live with our newly won rights.

Danika wondered, too, why that Susan B. Anthony woman chose the word suffrage to refer to voting. Nevertheless, she'd cast her vote for Mr. James M. Cox, the Democratic candidate over Warren Harding but the Republican Harding won by a landslide.

But Eugene Debs was an attention-getting Socialist candidate, even though he had to run while he was in a federal prison just for stating his beliefs.

Danika had read some of his thought-provoking columns in *The Appeal to Reason*, published over in Girard, sharing them with Milan after supper.

Course the times boiled with suspicion. Only three years since the Great War. Germans and aliens in the U. S., persecuted then. Wilson failing to get a good foundation under his League of Nations before he died. Rumors of strikes, riots, and newspaper columns expressing fear of alien uprisings.

Since her work shoes were scarred and caked with garden mud, dried on harder than cement, she sank her feet, sheathed in black stockings, into her high-top Sunday shoes, hoping that the scuffs and more-than-slightly run-over heels wouldn't be noticed.

She stepped briskly over to the safe to retrieve the potato salad she'd made early that morning. She'd packed it into a stone crock half-buried in a dishpan of cold water so that it would remain cool for the picnic.

She'd almost forgotten her hat.

A woman needs a hat at a summer picnic, especially when sitting before a prominent author from New York and one who'd been to Girard several times to speak.

Mary Skubitz'll be there, she's the daring type. Head the pack, for sure. Maybe Bessie Septak. Possibly even Clemence DeGruson.

She packed her plate, fork, spoon, and the crock of salad into a basket and folded a cloth over the top. She snatched her "Old Faithful," a little pancake hat of black straw, which sported a narrow brim. She shoved the survivor of many summers upon her head, anchoring it with a hat pin. Her heels clunked as she grabbed her basket and tromped toward the trolley stop.

Her feet thudded upon the path alongside the road ditch. Yarrow, Johnson grass, dandelions, and wild dock nodded as she swished past. A couple of hounds south of her house barked, and the silly baaing of Neda's goat, Burley Boy, tethered by a rope alongside the road, echoed in her ears.

Lyrics of a song being played on one of those new Victrolas drifted from the open windows of the white-painted house across the road. She quickened her steps at the zippy tune and words.

One of those new jazz songs Neda'd been humming. What was it?

> *"Margie, my little Margie, I'm always thinkin' of you...*
> *I'll tell the world I love you?"*

Danika was too rushed to decide whether or not she liked it. She could hear train wheels squeaking on the rails over at the mine southeast of Franklin. The sound was mixed with the clanking of chains and the drift of mine noises, alive, working again with dragged-in miners called "scabs."

Many of them were college "kids," and ex-sailors and soldiers, recently returned from the war and hadn't found work or direction yet.

Her eyes scanned a shabby gray miner's house, thin, grimy chidren, dressed in rags, spilling out of the door. She thought about the pale, frazzled women in such households. Their lives: endless washing, scrubbing, cooking, canning, gardening, sewing, praying not to give in to despair. No time to be sick or rest. Bodies subject to their husbands hard-muscled ones upon the corn husk mattresses at night. The endless cycle of it.

A breeze blew from downtown Franklin, carrying the drifts of sour mash and beer from the not-so-hidden saloons. Danika couldn't help grinning and shaking her head. She needed no one to tell her they lived in the age of bootleg whiskey and speakeasies. She knew she could be walking right by a basement saloon, which everyone called "a Blind Pig."

What did Prohibition prohibit around these parts?

Her frown was automatic as she thought about the Union miners on strike, still protesting the hated Slave Law. Milan, trying to bring in a little cash by helping with the haying on a farm, three miles westward.

She had mingled feelings about Neda with her new job as domestic worker over at Ophelia Otis's big mansion.

Well, three dollars for cleaning that huge house was at least something. Wonder what it feels like, scouring one of those pull-chain toilets and scrubbing the dirt rings on Harvey Otis's bathtub?

Danika focused her eyes eastward, noting that a crowd had already gathered. awaiting the trolley. She heard a mixture of giggles and laughter. She braced herself, ignoring a slight twitch in her shoulder.

Have to risk and push forward in these times. "The times" are pushing us somewhere, and that "somewhere" is still clouded over with misery, hungry bellies, and an unknown future.

****

Danika had to admit that she was having a right pleasant time sitting at the picnic table alongside miners' wives and townswomen. She tried to slow herself down and not fork her food in too quickly, hungry though she'd been.

She noticed that Clemence DeGruson had pierced a fried chicken thigh and was holding it gingerly in her hand, taking small bites. Danika guessed she could do the same thing with the wish bone she'd retrieved from the platter.

She'd relished the three-bean salad with its mixture of sweet-and-sour tastes. She'd even dared trying a slice of those cold cuts Bessie Septak had purchased up at the grocery store.

For herself, Danika could have really smacked her lips over the summer sausage, but she restrained herself, taking proper nibbles, careful not to swallow or crack a tooth on a clove. She passed on the plate of pickled red beets, fearing she'd spear one, and just her luck, it'd roll down the front of her dress.

The womens' chatter had been pleasant so far, and the twitch in her shoulder subsided as she began to feel more at ease with "the ladies." She looked over at the next table and noticed that Anna O'Korn was eagerly poking in Danika's very own potato salad, and Danika felt assured that she hadn't left out the celery seed after all.

She finally figured out that the woman at the third table over with the wide-brimmed beige straw hat and a matching color linen dress was Ophelia Otis.

Sure enough. Let Ophelia shine in her high-priced dress and stick her little finger in the air while she poked in her lettuce. But for myself, if I was a rich lady like Ophelia, I'd use more restraint. Yes. Definitely.

There was no mention at her table of THE STRIKE. It was like ignoring a dangling hornet's nest hanging over their table, with the big question roiling in their minds:

Who will poke it first?

Course, were it the men gathered here, a food fight, overturned tables, and the crash of beer bottles might be overlooked, but since they were expected to be ladies, they'd, so far, followed the voice of caution.

Danika saw one of the Italian women, Mrs. Allino Purgatiorio, turn her head, a small straw bonnet anchored firmly, and stare at the long car which had drawn alongside the road at the picnic site, parked there under the elms.

She turned to look, too, trying not to gawk.

Mercy. What's Sheriff Milt Gould doing, parked there? Is he going to eavesdrop on that Vorse woman's speech?

The six-point star on Gould's car glistened in a flash of sunlight.

When will they stop this spying on miners and their wives's gatherings?

A twitch broke loose again in Danika's shoulder.

They'd all returned their plates and other table gear to their picnic baskets, folding over the linen linings or closing basket lids in attempts to quell the flies. Most of the ladies allowed themselves the advantage of holding on to their iced tea glasses awhile longer as they waited for town councilwoman, Eunice Adams, to introduce the speaker.

Danika cast another quick look at the edge of the park grounds and noticed that the Sheriff had let out his clutch and moved on, gravel crunching as the car slowly eased down the road.

"...and now, ladies, I'm delighted to present a dearly beloved woman in these parts, Mrs. Mary Heaton Vorse. Many of you have read her fine books and her articles in ladies' magazines, like *McCalls*, and a host of others. Others of you may have heard her speak over in Gerard." Eunice's voice, pleasant, and encouraging.

Danika noted that Eunice definitely did not mention that Mrs. Vorse was living with a man without the benefit of marriage, and that it was rumored that she was a tippler.

Sturdy clapping arose, startling a flock of blackbirds lodged in the oak to the left. A stiff breeze drifted from the southwest, carrying the sweet smell of alfalfa hay. A few of the ladies lifted their hands to make sure that their hats were well-anchored. The lonely whistle from a nearby train moaned, the sound driven by the wind.

Mrs. Vorse stood and stepped with long strides to a little shady spot in front of the first row of wooden tables. Her hair, black as a crow's wing, parted on the right.

Danika noted that Mrs. Vorse had a sad look about her, like there was something out of kilter in her own life, or that she was searching for something but had never found it.

Her eyes swept over the dress Mrs. Vorse sported, a beige mid-calf linen dress, more of a loose two-tiered sheaf of the times, except that it did have respectable three-quarter length sleeves. Mary Vorse's broad-brimmed straw hat matched her dress and protected her eyes from the bright sunshine. She held a few notes on a card in her hands.

The solemn-faced, dark-complected speaker thanked the councilwoman and the women who'd obviously come from several outlying mining communities.

"It's a pleasure to enjoy this picnic with you ladies, and, I wish to thank you for the invitation to speak about my recent trip to England and some aspects of the activist government there and, also, here." She smiled pleasantly, after she'd scanned their faces.

Danika heard a low-pitched voice drift from the table behind her. She was sure she recognized it as Myrtice Hester's.

"Well, ain't she something? What's she gonna tell us that we don't already know?"

"My friends, I want to share with you what I learned about Socialism in England and the principle points of emphasis."

"Better watch out for them high sounding words like 'principle points.'"

Again, Danika was certain the words came from Myrtice's ungoverned tongue.

Danika turned to give her a cautionary stare.

Mrs. Vorse outlined her points, mentioning that since the Great War, England had drifted toward a Socialist government and that such a view was knitting the shattered country together after their bitter ordeal with Germany. She pointed out how even more democratic the Socialist view seemed to be with its focus upon equality, justice, and promotion of a sense of togetherness in England.

Next, Mary Heaton Vorse's speech turned to present day America.

"These ways of organizing government have been largely spread in our country by the Progressive candidate, Eugene Debs. He placed a great emphasis upon being responsible for the way we vote. I can remember one of his favorite sayings:

'I'd rather vote for what I want and not get it,
than for what I don't want and get it.'"

Murmurs rose up, smiles spread on numerous faces.

Sounds like something that Oklahoma man, Will Rogers, might say, Danika thought to herself.

Mrs. Vorse continued. "Many persons accuse Mr. Debs of trying to take over the railroads and destroy property rights. They think of him as an anti-war extremist. In fact, after I met with him, I concluded that he was a big-hearted man, deeply loved by many citizens, especially in Terre Haute, Indiana, and next door in Girard. I, myself am a pacifist, I stood almost alone against the Great War, that killed and maimed so many of our boys and left Europe devastated and the people starving.

"Some of you ladies may know Mr. Debs or me through his writings in *The Appeal To Reason*, and how he had to make his candidacy known from a prison in Atlanta, Georgia. A fact that should more than startle us. It shows us how some in our unions and government have a fear of full liberties for the working class."

Again, murmurs of approval rose up and heads nodded affirmatively.

Danika liked those words, "equality" and "justice."

Need more than a little more of both of those around here. Even more, action. We need action!

Danika tasted a bitterness in her mouth as she thought of their poverty and of the ill-famed Slave Law which kept the men out of work and denied them their full rights, and kept their cupboards empty and their children hungry. Supported by Governor Allen, too. Don't even mention John L. Lewis.

Danika remembered a cartoon in a newspaper back when Debs ran for president against Theodore Roosevelt. Debs had been skinny dipping in the river and saw Teddy Roosevelt racing away with his clothes. Another candidate, who was watching from behind the bushes, minus his clothes, says: "Don't be too upset, Gene, he's already taken mine."

Danika was more than familiar with political wrangling and men in high ranking policy-making positions quite willing to snatch their opponents' clothes, their livelihood and their reputations.

She wondered how Mary Vorse could be so poised, standing there without swaying and speak to the women. Especially with the pressures of the 1920s, the upheavals, violence brought on by prohibition and the dreadful conditions of the miners.

Would Vorse visit Alec Howat in the Girard jail?

Danika's hand slid over her mouth. She stared straight ahead, aware that she could not quell the sadness she was certain reflected from her eyes, though she was confident that Milan'd want her to be doing just what she was doing right now, trying to broaden her views and understand the "goings-on."

Maybe even take some definite steps toward....

After her short talk, Mary Vorse's eyes scanned her audience as she asked for their questions and input.

Ophelia Otis raised her chin from her thin neck, encircled by a strand of white summer beads. She stood to ask, "Mrs. Vorse, just how different would a Socialist government be from what we have now under President Harding?"

Mary Heaton Vorse thanked Ophelia for her question, pointing out that the Socialist position would possibly have prevented America's entrance into World War 1. Thousands of lives, both civilian and soldiers, could have been spared.

She outlined how that approach made room for more equality, public ownership of municipal services, water works, and electric companies, and the abolishment of children working in mines and factories by establishing labor laws. She reminded them of the sad Mishmash case, still unsettled. She spoke of consumer cooperatives in order for folks to have quality products at lower prices.

Danika glanced back at Mrs. Otis, her lips set in a straight line.

"You mean, Mrs. Vorse, that when faced with the grievous conditions the miners face here, leaders like our Alec Howat wouldn't be thrown into prison?" Mary Skubitz, a known Socialist, asked.

"You understand quite well." Mary smiled at the tall woman, obviously a miner's wife, but cleanly dressed, sporting an admirable summer hat. "It is the position of the Socialist activists that workers always have the right for address of their grievances. If they are not heard, as so many times happens, even here, they have the liberty to protest and even strike."

Mild clapping, by at least three-quarters of the picnickers, echoed in the air.

Speaker Vorse asked, "Is there another question?"

An intelligent-looking woman dressed in a coarse blue dress raised her hand. "I wanted to ask, Mrs. Vorse, just why is this Mr. Debs in a federal prison in Atlanta?"

"Yes. Well, may I clarify that. You know that we have been through a bitter war, The Great War. Mr. Debs favored other means of settling international conflicts. He greatly emphasized the importance of peace. Since he spoke openly of these views as the war approached, a new law was passed:

James D. Yoder

The Alien and Sedition Act, which made it a federal crime for anyone to speak out against the war."

A ripple of murmurs rolled across the crowd as if they were familiar with the accusations from the Governor's office in Topeka about how they, themselves, were viewed here in The Little Balkans.

Then, from behind, another question. She took a quick glance backward.

Why it's Myrtice Hester. And her voice loud and scratchy like that. Looks like a seventeen-year-old in that stiff polka dot organdy dress, and she's past fifty, at least.

"Why, Mrs. Vorse, I, I wanted to ask just how does this Activism differ from Communism? Seems to me like you've been courtin' something very close to that Bolshevism we read about in the papers." Myrtice stared straight at Mary Heaton Vorse, who'd turned to face her, as if she were proud of pronouncing that word "Bolshevism."

"Yes. Yes, may I address that." Mary Vorse's feet shifted. "We, of course aren't talking about Communism here, though there is an American Communist Party, which Governor Allen opposes openly. They've been trying to organize the wheat farmers over in Butler County."

Danika noticed how the women around her twisted in their chairs, hands raising to their mouths.

"The Socialists oppose that kind of Russian Communism with its Politburo governing from the top down. It is an unfortunate way of controlling the masses. Actually, it limits the freedoms of ordinary workers. We're talking about..."

Suddenly Danika noticed Mary Vorse's eyes widen. Her hand rose to her chin as she concluded her remarks to Myrtice's question.

Danika looked to her left.

Just when had Sheriff Milt Gould slipped up on them again like that? Where had he parked his car?

He leaned against a tree fifty feet away, toothpick wagging in his dark sandpaper jaw, arms folded across his wide chest.

84

What did it mean? He was eavesdropping, wasn't he?

After Myrtice Hester's question, Mary Heaton Vorse drew her session to a close. Danika noticed that a somberness had slidden across her face.

Danika, after having shaken hands with Mrs. Vorse, and not able to keep herself from giving a respectable bow, turned and walked alongside Ellina Purgatorio, who was headed to the trolley stop for her ride back to Frontenac.

They chatted about their families and their welfare during the hard times. They shared words of approval of Mary Vorse's speech as well as from the question-and-answering period, Danika cut her eyes over toward Sheriff Gould's car.

It couldn't be?

Myrtice Hester, making a beeline run toward Sheriff Gould, purse in the air, flagging him down, no doubt, for a chat.

CHAPTER TWELVE

St. Barbara and the Kite

Toma Cratnick glanced up at the mid-morning sky where cirrus clouds drifted high in a wind, a contrast to the blight below. He worked his way through the last ten feet of the Kentucky Wonder bean row in the garden, thankful that, due to a rain three days ago, the soil turned easily as he chopped and dragged the hoe.

Toma wiped sweat from his brow with his shirt sleeve. Neda's goat, Burley Boy, tethered by a rope at the edge of the garden, chewed on the ragweeds and wild dock. The goat had sent him sprawling once when Toma was staking the tomatoes. The ornery critter had worked his tether stake loose and took the opportunity to lower his head and send Toma sailing into the butter bean rows behind the outhouse.

The summer days lagged as dust-laden clouds lingered on the horizon in the stagnate wind.

What was there to do? Pa forbade me from even thinking about coal mining work.

His thoughts turned to his sister, Neda. A sadness moved through him, seeing her return from her work at the Otis mansion, yank the curtain to her nook shut and fall upon her cot.

An unnamed despair like a gloomy summer haze lingered. Her clerking job in Pittsburg had lifted her spirits. He had seen the hope shining from her face. To see Neda "doll up," hop lightfootedly upon the trolley, and head for the city, had given the whole family a boost in spirits.

Toma had a growing awareness, however, of his own developing skills, especially in mathematics, passing on easily into the introduction to algebra. Miss Cunningham had complimented him, though he'd grown hot around the neck and knew his face had turned red at the praise. At an awakening threshold, he had only faint intuitions regarding any clearly defined future awaiting him.

But this afternoon? Who knew?

He must focus now upon the agonizing present without sagging too deeply into despair. He recognized that his mother held herself back from being critical of folks around them and of the hard times. He noticed, also, how her trip to the womens' picnic in Arma and listening to that Vorse woman speak, had given her spirits an encouragement. He could tell she pondered the rock-edged hardness of the situations they faced, even mentioning that "the ladies" would surely have "to do something" if the strike and struggles lengthened.

One could only stretch soup so far.

He grinned to himself, remembering when he was in third grade and Miss Blough asked the class to write definitions to words she called out. Calling out the word "beef," little Celie Snow had written down, "Beef is soup bone Ma makes soup out of."

But what could his ma and other plain old coal miner wives do?

Pa, too, tried to hold his tongue in order not to discourage his family, but it worried Toma that his silence seemed without end. He suspected that it was related to the the increasing violence throughout the coal camps and towns. Papers led with stories:

"Murders in Frontenac." "Body Found Shoved Into Abandoned Well." "Three Women Violated in Arma." "Brawls in Buckets of Blood Saloon." "Eighteen Chickens Stolen From Barn." "Angry Miners Yank Scabs From Mines in Dunkirk."

Well, Pa'd helped him learn how to "put up his dukes" in tough times.

He'd "put 'em up," too, when Turney Pugle, a pimpled-faced bully at school kept shoving a second grader into the mud. Cautioned him first with a sturdy warning. When Pugle ignored him, he lit in. Took his punishment when Miss Cunningham made both of them stay after school, wash the blackboard and bring in five buckets of coal to feed the huge cast-iron stove with the hover around it for the next school day.

Finished with the bean rows, Toma placed his hoe in the shed Pa'd built from scrap lumber retrieved from a ditch. He headed for the back porch and the wash bench. After dinner he had plans. Real plans.

Well, no, I haven't told Ma about it. Pa over at that farm ain't...isn't here to give me his cautions.

Yep, Cecil Otis and I are gonna take a trolley ride down to Chicopee. Cecil said he had an interesting project for both of us to work on over there at his Cousin Otto Grinaldo's place.

****

Toma's hurried steps led him past the elevated Dance Hall, on past the Franklin Theater, an old grayish building,with its broadside painted with the words, "Bowman Undertaking Company," and their telephone number.

Who could even dream of such a thing as a telephone in one's house?

He circled telegraph poles and hurried past the Western C. and M. Company General Store, wishing he had extra pennies so he could run in and grab a couple of jawbreakers. Toma grabbed at the bill of his cap as a sudden gust of wind hit him.

Good day for kite flying.

To the right, the sidewalk led to the imposing Otis home. The house graced with well-trimmed arborvitae shrubs, lilac bushes, and stately oaks. Toma fingered the change in his pocket, checking to see if he still had his trolley fare. He also wondered what Neda'd be doing inside that three-story house.

Does she really scrub out the Otis's toilet? Do they make her eat her lunch on the back porch?

"Hey, Toma."

Cecil sat upon the front step awaiting his arrival. He sported a new corduroy cap, covering all of his hair except the red cowlick poking out from underneath the bill. His pants were a heavy material of a nondescript brown called knickers which every "town" boy or merchant's son wore. Argyle knee socks met the knickers at his knees.

A flash of insecurity raced through Toma as he looked down upon his well-worn and scrubbed denim overalls. Red handkerchief in his back pocket. His cap? - a striped engineer's cotton cap, which his Ma had starched and shaped over a lard can.

Toma could tell that Cecil's father insisted upon his son "dressing properly."

Wonder how much money Cecil's packing?

Cecil leaped from his perch and met Toma at the rose-covered arbor, the scarlet climbing roses in full bloom.

"Hurry, Cecil, we don't want to miss the trolley to Pittsburg."

"Na, we're not agonna be late. Miss one trolley, another rolls along in a few minutes."

"But don't we have to change at Pittsburg? Get another line to Chicopee?"

"Oh, yeah, but that's gonna be easy. Chicopee's only four miles southwest of Pittsburg. Cousin Otto'll be waiting. He's got all the materials we need to put a kite together. We're gonna build the biggest kite the world has ever seen!"

Toma felt his eyebrows raise at the mention of the astonishing plans.

The transfer in Pittsburg had been an easy one, but, surprisingly, the trolley to Chicopee was crowded. The boys managed to squeeze into the second-to-last seat in back.

"Where do you think all these women are going?" Toma surveyed the womens' heads before him, decorated with a wild assortment of hats. Broad-brimmed hats, mushroom-shaped hats, flat pancake-like hats. Hats that Neda would call "cloches." .

"Ah," Cecil added, "these old biddies are going over there probably to meet in the basement of St. Barbara's Church and play bingo all afternoon."

Toma knew a little about St. Barbara and how the miners' prayed to her, at least the Catholic ones.

Wasn't she the Miners' Saint? They pray to her in hopes of preventing a flash and blowout when a miner sets a charge in the mine. They even say that St. Barbara can send down thunder and lightning.

The boys rocked along in silence as the laughter and chatter from the women, obviously on an outing, drifted overhead.

Toma ignored the slag heaps and rusted mining colliers, his spirit eagerly awaiting the challenges ahead. He noted the wind hadn't died down, the tough bushes and trees alongside the track bent in the wind.

Cecil's Cousin Otto was waiting at the Chicopee station. He was taller than either Toma or Cecil, a year older and already in high school.

Whatever the undertaking Cecil and Otto had in store, Toma rested assured that the high school boy would take the lead in their plans for a raunchy, rip-snorting time.

Toma hadn't felt this light-hearted and raring-to-go for months. He could feel his heart increase its beat in his anticipation. Trolley ride, new town, even if it was a coal town. And, their project for the afternoon.

The boys hurried toward uptown. Toma noticed the rows of miners' company houses, shabby and dreary-faced, like the ones in Franklin, as they approached the Santa Fe Railroad.

Cecil stared at a woman with a painted face and a red dress shoved down at her bosom, leaning out the second-story window of a saloon named The Old Soak.

"Look at that? Is that one of those *those* houses?"

"Yeah," added Otto, digging his fists into his pants pockets, his long pant legs reaching the tops of his shoes as he swaggered. "Yea, that's a bawdy house. Ain't old enough to go in there yet, but there's no charge for looking at that thrill dame."

Cecil's eyes bugged as he gawked, almost smashing into a lamppost.

Then Otto, his voice in a deep-drop sultriness of male adolescence, bragged about his goings-on with a girl named Pansy.

Toma felt his own eyebrows raise, his mouth filled with saliva at the he-man tales.

Wow! This is a trip!

Tramping on past more respectable houses, the boys turned into the driveway of a brown bungalow with a shady front porch. "This way. I've already got some of the wooden strips I cut from lathes I laid out."

They passed a bed of red and pink hollyhocks, ducked under light green willow fronds and on into the empty garage.

"Pa took the Buick up to Pittsburg. We got the whole floor here to build the kite on."

"Well, we didn't bring any supplies," Cecil said, glancing down at the narrow strips that Otto had already prepared, along with the cord for binding the wooden strips , a basket of rags for the tail, a roll of paper from the store, and a stinky pot of glue.

"Got all we need right here."

Willow fronds swayed in an increasingly brisk wind.

****

The three boys heaved the fabulous kite, seven feet long and forty-two inches wide, off the garage floor, walking it out into the wind. The kite sprang alive, having a lusty energy of its own.

Both Cecil and Toma were hypnotized at Otto's daring. Upon the front of the kite Otto'd painted in broad red letters the name of that girl he, he, well...the name "Pansy."

"Hold it," Toma called to Cecil. "Think maybe we'd better add another two feet of those red rags to the tail."

"Na," Otto called back, fairly bursting with pride at their success so far. "Drag 'er on out here in the middle of the street. Trees ain't so tall here, we'll get 'er up above them telephone lines." He tugged at his end, holding the contraption at the intersection of the bound cross sticks that provided the backbone for the kite.

Toma and Cecil brought up the rear, dragging the weird, rag-tag tail, made out of old underwear, torn women's garments, and strips yanked from an old sheet. The knotted tail began to lash around Toma's head in the sudden onslaught of wind. He stumbled. "Grab it, Cecil. Grab it!"

On they staggered until they came to a portion of the street where the trees were shorter or absent entirely.

"Here. Now you guys hold on back there, keep that tail off the ground and start running when I do." Otto let out his best Indian whoop and off he galloped.

"We ain't agonna be able to...." Cecil stumbled, but Toma grabbed the slack and raced on. Suddenly his arms were jerked hard. There was a "whoop" as the wind caught the inside of the kite and began heaving it skyward.

"Yeah! Oh, boy, ya see that? Told you it'd...."

Otto's foot caught on an uneven brick. He went down with a thump, striking his chin on the hard red surface.

No one could figure out just how it happened, but suddenly the fantastic kite, named Pansy, danced high above. Pansy zigzagged drunkenly then soared heavenward.

Otto heaved himself up, ignoring his bleeding chin. He let out the heavy fishing cord which he'd wound around a stick. "Look at that! Oh, boy, look at that! Up, up, tail flailing over Stone's Hardware." Suddenly the kite took a nose dive over Big Kate's Saloon, nearly crashing into the brick chimney.

Otto's body jerked like he had the St. Vitus' Dance. He struggled to keep his feet on the bricks below. Again, a knockout wind hit the kite. Otto sailed, feet dragging all the way up to Beulah Bitsy's Boutique. Beulah, standing outside, cursed like a miner with a ton of coal on his foot. A Model T with an ugly "a-uggg-a" sounding horn, stopped in the middle of the street, the driver gawking.

By now townsfolk had begun to cluster, yelling and pointing at the wonder in the sky with the wild whipping snake-of-a-tail.

"Them's women's underthings," old Annie Slocum hollered. "Fer shame, fer shame. What is the world comin to?"

Toma was more than amazed. Spellbound. Then Cecil, coming to his senses, yelled, "Haul it back, Otto, haul it back. We need more weight on the tail."

It took all three of them to reel Pansy, tipsy and sashaying, back down until Toma could grab her.

"Yeah, I see we gotta add more weight to her tail. Know just the right thing." By now Otto's eyes were filled with the gleam of triumph. "Get er back to the garage."

After herculean struggles the three vagabond craftsmen hauled the contraption in, Pansy, now lifeless, her tail dragging in a wilt.

Otto went straight to the wooden box at the back of the garage. He lifted the hinged lid and dipped his head and shoulders into the shadows. "Here they are. Yep."

Toma and Cecil stared, eyes glazed with excitement.

When Toma could focus his eyes clearly, he saw Otto turn. He held three red stick-looking things, each about seven inches long.

Toma stared.

Weiners? Hot Dogs?

Cecil seemed to know what they were. "Blazes, Otto. Put them down. Where on earth did you get those? Why your dad'll...."

Otto, holding the three long red sticks, grinned. My Pa's a foreman at the Klondike Mine. Ain't you ever seen these things before? They sure ain't baloney."

Toma swallowed. His knees began to knock.

Dynamite. No!

****

Pansy, aloft again, though lumbering with her added weight, carried on, undaunted. A sudden gust of extra-strong velocity struck her at her crossbeams. She flashed her pied-and-knotted tail, which wagged like an agitated water moccasin.

Toma, from below, shielding his eyes, mouth agape, shuddered when he saw Pansy's three inserted sparklers sizzling in the sky.

"No. No," he yelled. "Otto, pull 'er down!"

More townspeople clustered around lampposts, pointing to the sky.

A wrinkled old woman, dough still on her stubby fingers, hollered out, "Oh, I'll swan! Would you look at that? Dynamite, ain't it?"

Toma and Cecil stood speechless, feet anchored as if buried to their knees in river mud.

Suddenly Pansy took a dip, then another. She circled in spirals as her "inserts" fizzed, smoked, and sizzled,

Before Otto could drag her into a more steady wind, Pansy hit the tiled roof of St. Barbara's Church, the saint who commands lightning bolts and thunder.

People, aghast, hands at their mouths, hollered, "Pull her down. Pull her down. Oh, them fool boys!" Then they began to scatter.

Toma yelled, his heart nearly stopping, "Get 'er down, Otto. She's gonna blow."

3.

Otto yanked. He yanked again. His eyes bugged with his own fear.

Suddenly St. Barbara must have given Pansy a nudge with her foot. Pansy flopped like a wounded duck. Her tail buzzed and twisted like twisting rattlers. Sparks sputtered in desperate writhings.

Then Pansy blew.

Otto was knocked nine feet to the west side of the street where he lay, stunned. Cecil and Toma had the fortitude to race back up the street, staring open-mouthed as black dirt, rocks, shattered bricks, and tree limbs lifted skyward.

Dust and pulverized bricks and cement dirtied the air. When the cloud cleared, spectators viewed a six-foot hole in the street.

Yep, St. Barbara could sure send down lightning and thunder, couldn't she?

****

Otto's father dug up two hundred dollars to bail Otto out of the calaboose, the steaming sheriff being lenient, since Mr. Grinaldo was one of the leading Chicopee citizens.

As for Cecil Otis, well, Mr. Harvey Otis drove the big blue Packard himself all the way to Chicopee, fat billfold in his pocket, leaving his chauffeur at home trimming hedges. Toma's mother, Danika, still in her home-made dress, hunched in the passenger seat as she rode on the opulent leather, eyes staring straight ahead, a handkerchief in a hand at her mouth.

She looked as dazed as St. Barbara might have been at the boys' calamity. She held her jar, pulled from the hole under a loose board by the pine pie safe, holding all the money she'd been able to save. An offering for Sheriff Putty in Chicopee if she needed to cough up a fine or bail. It contained sixty-seven dollars and thirty-three cents.

The car zoomed past the sunflower-and-ragweed-lined road as she murmured to herself, "Oh, Toma, Oh, Toma, just what have you done?"

CHAPTER THIRTEEN

Milan

The corn shuck mattress crackled as Milan tossed. He knew he was disturbing Danika's sleep but his mind whirled like a twisting mine cage descending into hell. He could hear Danika's heavy breathing, her body sunken into her small portion of the bed, a heavy breast hanging to the side beneath her gown.

Through the tiny opened window, a touch of a breeze from the southwest, slid over his forehead, bringing with it a drift of antediluvian stink of coal. As he took a deeper breath, he savored the faint aroma of sweet clover, from along the roadsides, mixed with a touch of newly-cut Lespedeza hay, drying in some farmer's field west of town.

He tried again to settle his mind from the invasive thoughts that, if he'd list them, would surely fill Toma's Big Chief tablet.

The kite calamity in Chicopee. The fifty dollar fine Danika had paid to the Chicopee court. Toma grounded. Absolutely and firmly.

No! The boy could not accept invitations from the Otis boy to come over and play mumbletypeg with his penknife. *Forbidden.*

The long-faced boy accepted his punishment without outward grumbling, being assigned to womens' work, helping his ma, in addition to the humiliating goat-watching.

He committed himself to garden work and to guarding Burley Boy so that he could graze in the tall, uncut growth along the roadsides and ditches. Extra assignment: shoveling out the dung stacks from the rear end of the two-seater privy.

Burley Boy relished the sour dock, now grown tall. He devoured the green leaves and the tall tobacco-brown heads swaying in the wind. He gulped down honeysuckle vines, clawing beneath fences onto the roadsides. He belched, baaed, and gobbled, while Toma, head buried beneath a frayed-brimmed straw hat, tried to hide his face from the people rattling by in the Tin Lizzies, drivers and passengers pointing and giggling.

He turned his back on the rambling, loose-jointed ice-wagons and delivery vehicles, drawn by tired teams of horses, unloading their biscuit piles along the roadside, steaming and fouling the air.

Burley Boy swallowed half-chewed tickweed and round clusters of evening primroses. Flowers Danika cherished, vanished in a couple of gulps.

Milan had informed Toma that he was old enough to husk corn right out of the field when ripened in September, and thoroughly dry, in farmer Davis's fields, three miles west of town. They'd work together. Good for the boy. Learn skills that would take his mind away from the bottomless hole of mining troubles.

Next, Milan pondered Neda's calamity and her job over at the Otis mansion. He and Danika worried over the girl's dogged look, and her seemingly disinterest in her life. They both recognized that she bore a heavy weight.

What was it?

She hadn't complained about Ophelia Otis making unreasonable demands, nor had she mentioned much about Harvey Otis, though Milan knew that the sharply-dressed mine operator had a substantial amount of freedom. The blue Packard eased out of its parking spot at the mine office, coming and going.

Did Harvey drive home? Did Otis invade Neda's space? Interfere with her cleaning? Catch her in an uncompromising position?

Milan was aware that he had to halt the rumblings surfacing in his mind.

If her job was secure, the pay reasonable, then why did Neda's face sag like that of a hound dog who failed to bring in a squirrel?

Surely, it must be more than losing her job at the Five and Ten.

Her muteness bothered her mother even more.

Many of the miners were infuriated, fully aware of mean-spirited mine overseers. The names of a couple of them came to Milan's mind: men frequently fortified by illegal liquor, available on every block in town. It had been more than a whisper, how overseer, Filus Jablock, sneaked out of his office on Friday afternoons. More than hearsay that he paid surprise visits to miners' wives upon, what he called, "their lonely afternoons," their husbands buried in the safety of the mines. Rage seethed among them when titillating stories were whispered from miner to miner. The rumors stirring up fights and viscous drawings of knives.

Milan knew that state of affairs was a loaded keg of dynamite.

At last he fell into a restless sleep, followed by a dream. In the dream his eyes focused upon a gray hearse, trimmed in black, drawn by two teams of ghostly, dappled horses, their rumps rising, their heads dipping, as the hearse's wheels rolled silently through a thick fog. Startled, he gazed upon the two coffins rocking within the death-wagon.

Who are they? Two coffins?

His mind leaped ahead of the morbid coach. He saw himself waiting by cast-iron cemetery gates where bare oak branches clawed earthward, ready to snatch unwelcome apparitions from the air, and etch the sides of the reeling hearse with undecipherable words. His dream eyes surveyed staggering headstones, moss and lichen-covered. Blackness. A darker ebony than the trim on the dream hearse.

Stove-pipe black crows flapped shroud-like wings, skimming over the hearse, scrawling the names of the dead in the leaden air.

The scene changed. Suddenly he was laboring in the mine, three hundred feet below the surface. Water dripped like the ticking of a weary clock readying itself to announce the approach of doom. The same apprehension prevailed.

He, a brusher (one who blasts and removes rock), and Luigi Caputo, heaved, grasping their picks with hard-muscled hands, their rhythmic blows chipping fragments from a granite wall. They assailed the solid rock in order to make a passage for the team of mules, waiting to enter the opening. Mules, slick, waggly-eared, fed and groomed better than any of the miners.

Luigi and he grabbed their shovels. Backs bending, muscles straining, they heaved the rocks into the waiting cars. Jake Anselm and Ed Busse joined in, their faces greasy with perspiration. The pitiful light of their carbide lamps cast a glow like the patina of Death upon a cadaver. Their eyes glistened out of black circles, faces fixed, enduring the agony in their straining arms, shoulders, and backs.

Milan heard the foreman yell: "Slackers, heave-to down there."

He and his men had loaded over a hundred tons of rock, drawn by the mules to the top, where they were dumped upon the slag heap.

Milan himself had drilled eight-foot holes, placed in the charge, shot it, and lumbered for safety as the avalanche of glossy bituminous coal tumbled and heaved toward them.

Now, load the smutty chunks. Heave. Pitch. Ignore the crooked back, the muscle spasm, the trembling legs -- the pant of a brother miner. Dismiss the fear. Cut grit-filled eyes away from Luigi Caputo, bending over, gasping to draw the stale oxygen into his rotten, coal-blasted lungs.

Gas. Death-laden, silent, ever-creeping, ever-fatal, eagerly waiting to usher a miner into an everlasting sleep.

Again, Milan gazed upon the hearse of death, the wheels silent in the fog. The pale horses waiting.

Why can't I smell it?

Next Milan saw his comrades' picks and shovels drop from their hands in supernatural silence, knees bending as they yielded themselves to the damp, cold, ground, silent as folding buzzard's wings.

****

Milan awakened, gasping. Sweat-drenched. He heaved his hairy legs out upon the rough floor. Sleep, and attempts to sleep, over for the night. Finished. He groped his way in his BVDs toward the back stoop where he sat watching a half-moon sink behind globes of tree tops to the east. Head in his hands, buried in his lap. He could smell the sweetness of Danika's four-o'clocks by the edge of the steps, flowers not yet opened by the morning sun.

Oh, St. Barbara, have pity upon us poor miners.

Hours and days must pass before nightmares and dreams interred in the depths of unconsciousness, have their way. But like a poorly-buried corpse, such dreams, sooner or later, heave tortured bones upon the shores of remembrance, waiting to haunt one in some unpredictable and unforeseen time,

Milan heard rustling and the thud of bare feet. He knew that Danika had risen, after finding his side of the bed empty. She'd thrown a home-made smock made of flour sacks around her shoulders before she stepped through the kitchen door, her black hair hanging loosely behind her. She eased her big body beside him, her arm drawing his hunched shoulders into her own warm and mothering body.

They sat in silence, listening to and watching the awakening of the morning before an onslaught of light would blast against the skeletal coal colliers, illuminate the uneven, weed-lined roads, and expose the faces of the pitiful company houses.

Milan felt the drawing power of her love through her flesh. He reached over and clasped her hand, not as muscular, but as rough-palmed as his, holding it in silence as mourning doves announced the resurrection of the day.

Together their eyes turned eastward following the narrow streak of orange marking the horizon. The moon faded, sinking into its resting place in order that the light might have its way as it struggled to surpass the onslaughts of the roiling pillars of smoke from the collier stacks.

They smiled and whispered to each other, "Another day."

Milan scanned the mist-shrouded outline of the peach tree he'd planted at the south end of their lot. He could see shadowy tops of the turnips Danika'd sown in the rich earth, thrusting their heady stalks upward, waiting to be brushed with light and uncurl their dewy fronds.

"Well," he said to Danika, "at least we know what we'll be eating for a couple of months."

****

To Milan's surprise, that very evening a bouncing, badly-used Model T with patched tires parked alongside their minuscule "front yard."

Milan stepped to the door to greet the visitors. He recognized the brothers, lean and loping, Albert Casseletto, and his brother, Luigi. Before he could step out, the brothers had already slipped around the corner of the house. Milan turned, slipped through the kitchen to greet them in the backyard.

Figure they know where the wine cellar is.

He'd already noted that a bottle tipped from Albert's back pocket, and Luigi carried a brown jug.

Rotgut?

"Hey, you dirty coal miner, you." Albert greeted Milan, attempting an easy, joking entry. "You taken a bath already this summer?" He threw back his head to laugh, revealing yellowed rotten teeth.

The brother, Luigi, bent over in snickers and jerked at the corn cob securing his homemade shine.

Sure, thought Milan. These men from over at the Mulberry mines are rough, but ain't they good fellows? They'd been together at the Miners' Hall, played pool together. Joked and pushed each other in jest.

Plain old loyal miners, ain't they?

Little shooting the bull good for us from time-to-time.

Since he had "company," Milan invited them to seat themselves on the back porch. He noticed Danika attempting to drag out the old bentwood chair.

What had Father Pompeney said one time? "You never know when you're entertaining angels unawares."

"Take seats on the porch, fellas."

"Na, we don't need no chairs, Mrs. Cratnick," Albert said with a syrupy grin, betraying that he had already come "fortified." His lean butt found a place on a porch step. Luigi crossed his long legs as he sat on the edge of the porch.

Milan caught a drift of their definitely unwashed bodies.

After her hesitant greeting, Danika must have realized that this was a men's bull session. She stepped back into her kitchen.

Milan seemed to ease into the camaraderie.

Sure, it'd be jostling and joking. Rough fellas, but they mean well, don't they?

Albert slapped his knee with a calloused hand as he bragged about the benefits of the United Mine Workers of America and their steadfast leader, John L. Lewis.

"Owe him a lot of loyalty. These long strikes gonna tickle his nose one day and we're gonna hear him sneeze." He chuckled.

"Well, yes, Lewis has done a lot for the miners of America. Sure, Albert. The other side is how he has treated such a loyal fellow as Howat."

Milan, not quite secure in his contribution to the conversation then added, "You fellas like to taste my last season's elderberry wine? Ripening up real nice in the storm seller, yonder."

Luigi and Albert, faces lit up like Chinese lanterns at Milan's warm invitation.

Milan brought out three glasses of mixed sizes. He retrieved a jug of his last year's more aged wine and poured each a generous sample.

Luigi Cassaletto gulped his down within two seconds. He smacked his lips and extended his glass for a refill.

Though caution nagged at Milan, he tried to be a congenial miners' friend.

Loosen things up. Let the nagging worries seep away. Times hard enough without being cold shouldered. Otta celebrate sometime.

The hour progressed, punctuated by the pop of Luigi's corn cob stopper and the friendly gesture of "passing it around."

Milan took only one bitter sip. It scoured his throat. Man ought to be decent to fellows friendly enough to drop by and be neighborly.

He glanced at the screen door and noticed Danika shooting a cautionary look his way.

The conversation shifted to the local strike. How fine an orator their local Alec Howat was.

"Yeah," hooted Albert. "I seen your own wife over at that jail speech he give, month ago."

The hour wore on. At times their conversation seemed to Milan to "get edgy," but after all, they'd just had a little "too much." Yeah, that was all. Milan especially tensed at Albert's mention of the 1919 strike and the governor's order to send in the militia.

"Ready for Allen to give em a poke agin," Albert said, swiping his lips with the back of his hand. "Shake the miners up a mite."

Milan decided this was the time to keep his mouth closed.

When would his "visitors" leave?

By the time the brothers had finally noticed the setting sun and wobbled around the house to climb into their flivver, Milan had gnawing concerns about their driving skills on the way over to Mulberry, in addition to their tempers about the strike and the comments about their beloved Alec.

Luigi cranked up the Lizzie, staggered and hooted, while Albert gripped the wooden wheel with one hand, waving the other unsteadily at his Franklin "friends," Milan and Danika stood anchored at the front door.

Together they watched the rust-encrusted back end of the Ford shimmy down the road.

"Well, Danika, we had company, didn't we?"

"That kind of company, Milan, we don't need too often. You know that?"

That's all Danika had said. Not a pushy, nagging wife, his Danika.

"Yeah, Danika. I endured it. But what did Father Pompeney say?

Danika said it with him, her face resolved: "You never know when you are entertaining angels unawares."

CHAPTER FOURTEEN

Mary Skubitz Calls a Meeting

Danika was tired of the nagging indecision. The worry over the life-menacing conditions of the miners kept her and a bevy of neighbor women tossing at night. They had been busy salvaging what they could from their gardens; however, some of the women, broken down and burdened with newborns every eighteen months, scarcely had the time to unbutton their dresses and let their screaming babies suck.

The men, too, were numb and unsettled during the three-month layoff, drifting into nonchalance, others into loss of hope as the strike lingered. They were tired of the repeated names, John P. White, John L. Lewis, Governor billiard-ball-headed Henry Allen, and Judge Curran. Resentment against International leaders smoldered. Some of the out-of-work miners began to doubt the guidance and wisdom of their own Alexander Howat. Jailbird or not.

After all, Danika recognized that a man can sit under a shade tree with his buddy miners and whittle, chew tobacco, swap stories, and play poker (but with what?) only so long before losing interest and simply going through the motions.

And if Alec Howat had been such a wonderful leader of District 14, then why had their lives sunken into such a stagnant muddle? Had they made the right decision by calling out "Alec, we're with you"?

What good did it do?

Governor Allen simply asked the court to order the state to take over control of the mines. Slowly, some of the miners, hungry and destitute, picked up their shovels and lamps and headed into the mines. The miners and their families were caught between the order of the court and starvation.

Danika's lips closed in a firm line as she thought about the scabs, those sickly-pale college boys who responded to Governor Allen's call for laborers. They drove in with their backfiring jalopies to attract attention, chased their daughters, sought hanky-pank liaisons and left heartbroken young women pregnant and no husbands.

What was that song? "Careless love, ...oh, what careless love has wrought..."

Then, too, it was shameful, that college up in Topeka granting those young bucks college credit for working their own husbands' jobs. Wasn't that a scandal?

What about the negroes imported into the community to pick up shovel and buckle on the carbide lamps? Were they innocent? Did they know that with their help keeping the mines open, the regulars and their families were starving?

Wouldn't be so bad if it weren't for all those home stills and wineries steaming, gurgling, distilling and pouring out rotgut and soured, suspect wine, poisoning the impatient tipplers. Sure, they were Europeans and didn't they know how to handle their wine and strong drink? Look at the added wretchedness that Prohibition had brought to their communities.

But when the malaise dragged on through dog days and into the beginning of the school term, the men grew straggly-haired, stubbly-cheeked, ill-tempered, and angry.

It was not at all uncommon to read the sad accounts in the Franklin News: "Knife Fight Breaks Out in Front of Pool Hall." "Distraught Miner Takes His Own Life." "Company House Burns Down." "Miner Suspected of Arson."

What should she do with the invitation from Mary Skubitz?

Danika reflected upon it all morning as she shelled the last of her butter beans from the garden. Toma, off the leash finally with Burley Boy. He'd willingly strapped on that little leather band and hook around his hand, learning to shuck corn with his father over at that Davis farm west of town. And they could use the money!

Now with that invitation from Mary Skubitz to gather with a group of women over in the Union Hall for a womens' meeting, her questions circled.

What'll I wear? Do I have the time? What will I say? Why would Mary Skubitz need me?

Danika knew that Mary Skubitz was able to speak in at least four languages. She was frequently sought out to aid the court recorder over in Girard when the judge needed translations of the grunts of the poor tongue-tied, broken-down miners, who'd been caught in more than just a discretion.

Yes, that woman was more accomplished and better educated than the rest of them. Well, excepting Ophelia Otis, but who wanted to stand around and listen to her brag about her sorority days at that high up Cotty College over in Nevada?

Wonder who all will be there?

****

Marie Merciez, Clemence DeGursen's mother, who ran a grocery store over by Camp 50 just to spite the Company Store there, got to the hall early and brewed tea for the women. With quick steps, the lean woman, ever smiling as if she had a host of secrets, set the steaming cups upon the table.

Danika stepped into the room lighted by two glaring electric bulbs, dangling on cords. She'd hurried to finish sewing up her dress, made from three feed sacks with a pattern of scattered indigo pea blossoms against a dusty pink background. She tried to control the trembling in her hands, finally interlocking her fingers.

Danika saw that Mary Skubitz was busy unfolding wooden chairs, arranging them in a circle. She glanced over at the table holding the cups of tea and saw that Marie had taken off the towel covering a tray of oatmeal cookies, studded with black walnuts, she'd obviously baked early in the morning.

Wonder if my hem is straight? Does my dress bag in the back? What on earth will I say among all these women?

When her eyes adjusted to the light she saw Anna O'Korn and Fanny Schaub over on the right, getting ready to seat themselves on the spindly chairs. She glanced to the left and noted Bessie Septak, another large-boned miner's wife, already gulping hot tea, and surveying the gathering women. Mrs. Allino Purgatorio ambled over to a chair, wearing a black dress of a decade ago, which gave her the appearance of someone awaiting a funeral.

Fanny Schaub and Helen Grisholano traipsed into the room, feet sporting quite nice Mary Jane shoes that showed very little scuffing. Grisholano chatted, interspersing Italian phrases every now and then, like the tapping of a woodpecker upon a hickory tree as if neither of them had a care in the world.

Danika found an empty chair by Myrtice Hester, of all people. When she fully realized what she'd done, she swallowed, nodded and said, "Glad to see you, Myrtice."

Did I really mean that? Oh, Danika, for pity's sake, get ahold of yourself.

Mary Skubitz, a tall plump woman with a friendly face greeted them all as she drew up a chair in the space to the left of the refreshments table. Her dress, a brown crepe, sported the sarong-like uneven hem of the times, and low waist, casual, though probably not new. She cleared her throat, and for a moment, her hand went to her throat where she fingered her brown amber-like beads. She smiled, her face reflecting a warmness. If she had insufferable cares, they didn't show.

"Neighbors," her well-modulated voice greeted them, her smile reflecting her genuineness. "You may wonder why I invited a few of you to gather here, but I think that all of you know that with this never-ending strike, almost all of our mining families are growing desperate." She paused as if considering how to stimulate the conversation and sharing.

Or did her pause reflect a moment of anxiety over whether or not the group was trustworthy enough to attend to the seriousness they faced?

"Well, Mary, I think you did the right thing, and thank you." Helen Grisholano, her staccato-rhythmed voice echoed.

Suddenly, Danika heard the clonk of heels and a scraping sound. Several women turned their faces toward the door, staring. There stood old lady Roberta Schlooscicker, her crooked hickory cane tapping the floor. With bent back and staggering totters, she heaved her emaciated frame into the room. She wore a dirty old brocade dress that must have belonged to her long-buried mother. Beading her cataract-glazed eyes upon them, she scanned the room for a seat.

"Here, Lady Bob," Mary Skubitz said, rising and grabbing another folding chair, making room by her own.

The old woman wobbled over as the seated women attempted to hide their discomfort at her sudden appearance. A few women rolled their eyes toward their neighbors as if to say, "Ghouls have their own ways, don't they?"

Mercifully, though, Mary Skubitz showed proper respect to the crone-like-woman, whom everybody called "Old Lady Bob."

Danika, cutting an eye toward the skeletal woman, knew that Mary Skubitz would show proper respect.

A little spice for the meeting? One could even say red pepper thrown in, as no one could predict what commotion Old Lady Bob would cause.

Mary greeted "Lady Bob," then turned her attention back to the group and the business at hand. "Well, thank you, Helen. It's important that we have a discussion. Even plan on some strategies if the situations around here don't improve. As everyone can see, our men are growing desperate." She waited.

Myrtice Hester was the first to interpose her thoughts. "Well, I don't know what's keeping a delegation of us from taking the Interurban right over to Girard and having an up front talk with that jail warden. We'd demand to see Alexander Howat. I'm beginning to think that he needs to bear the responsibility for this misery." Her look, a "so there," with an "I dare you," behind it.

Several women cleared their throats. Others raised hands to their mouths, eyes shifting over the seated women.

"Well, Myrtice, yes, going to see Alec Howat just might be a good thing, but Judge Curran sentenced him. It takes money to appeal. For that we'd have to work through the Local 14 Union." Skubitz crossed her ankles and sat straighter in her chair.

Danika's head thrust back, her chin lifted, her cheeks hot. She leaped to her feet, though she'd told herself to stay calm and for pity's sakes, don't make a fool of herself. She turned to face Myrtice.

"I want to tell you something, Myrtice Hester. I took the time to hear President Howat speak over in Girard. I tell you the very angels were with him. He wants good equipment for our men, safer conditions in the mines, education for our children, and fair wages. Did you hear that, Myrtice? He sacrifices himself for fair wages and food on tables around here." Danika plopped back onto her chair, which creaked as she tried to settle herself. Her hand, trembling, crept up to check the hairpins beneath her twisted knot in back.

Mary Skubitz's eyes shot toward Danika, appreciation for Danika's contribution evident upon her face.

Then Anna O'Korn chimed in. "Well, I know one thing," she said, "since it's fall already, there ain't no more dandelions to eat, and poke's all growed up into them bushes with poisonous berries on them, my Herman is tired of eating turnips and won't even try turnip greens, even if I boil 'em with salt pork."

Mary Skubitz waited, as if evaluating the heat in the room. "Yes, many of our families can no longer afford meat at all. You're right, Anna. But I'm wondering if we could do something more aggressive, like..."

At that point Old Lady Bob giggled and piped up, "Why, you women. Don't you know what to do? All of you. Course I can't, I buried my Boris twelve years ago, so's I won't be able to cooperate." Lady Bob paused to catch her breath.

"Well," Mary Skubitz said, looking over toward Lady Bob. "Just what did you have in mind?"

"Well, I'm of the opinion you ladies here otta just up and let your men sleep without the benefit of your bed presence. Yep! That'd stir up some action sure enough. A randy goat ain't agonna stand still long!" Lady Bob broke into a sultry giggle.

The silence lasted so long that Danika even thought a strong woman like Mary Skubitz was buffaloed, standing there, trying to catch her breath.

"Why, uh - uh, that is a thought, Lady Bob, but I doubt if it's..."

Mary Skubitz' eyes opened as if she'd seen the Lord on Judgment Day. She rubbed her sweaty palms together. "

Danika thought Mary was going to say a big word like "efficient," but wasn't certain. Then too, wouldn't Father Pompeney come down on them? Right from the pulpit. Surely, some old codger would go over to the rectory and blast the women for the sinfulness of "withholding themselves." Against the Bible, too, wasn't it? And Father Pompeney certainly wouldn't offer them communion.

They broke for a tea break. Danika and Myrtice Hester reached for one of the cookies together. Myrtice turned to Danika: "I seen that girl of yours yesterday walkin home from the Otis mansion. Did you know that one of them young college boys you talk about stopped his fliver? Your daughter, Neda, just a standing there leaning in talking to him. Danika Cratnick. Ain't you takin notice of your own daughter?"

A red hot anger flashed through Danika. She turned, facing Myrtice, light shimmering off of Myrtice's out-of-style dress, the know-it-all smirk on her face.

Danika tried to pull her eyebrows down and close some of the bug-eyedness she was certain reflected upon her face. She gulped a swallow of tea.

"Let me tell you something, Myrtice. My daughter is a good girl. She has a job. A real job. Down on her knees scrubbing floors, polishing silver, waxing furniture, cleaning out sheds and basements. I want you to know that I'm quite taken aback by your hint that Neda is somehow in trouble, or that I'm not being a proper mother to her..."

"Oh, no. No in-sin-u-ation, Danika. Don't get on a high horse. Jest like these women here, bitching about no money and nuthin to eat. Why don't THEY go into town and get jobs? I hear the lead smelters in Pittsburg are hiring."

Danika turned, thankful that Mary Skubitz, who may have overheard Myrtice's crabbed complaints, tugged at her arm. Mary smiled "Danika, let's get seated again. We do have some more unfinished work to talk about."

For the next half hour, Mary tried to lift the conversation to something more constructive. Fanny Schafer had suggested they keep their iron skillets handy to conk lazy husbands over the head, prompting them to at least go fishing.

Helen Christiano's contribution was that everyone in town ought to have a wine-making apparatus in their root cellars, then, prohibition or not, go out on the back roads in another county and market it. Danika's neck grew hot again. She folded her arms across her bosom.

Who does she think she is? Look at the crime Prohibition caused. Never had she smelled so much booze or heard of such lawlessness.

She recognized that such easy access made enforcement of the law almost impossible.

And, hadn't they heard?

"The Law" was scared to come into the mining commu-nities and raid the stills. Timorous and afraid of hot-headed foreigners, ready to flash their switchblades. Why hadn't some of the moonshiners been caught transporting garden hoses filled with rotgut home brew? Prisons were already overcrowded.

Besides, hadn't she seen a number of women (whose names she wouldn't mention) fall victim to strange maladies and with or without their quack doctor's prescription, hightail it over to the drug store and order the "prescription" for their cure?

Mary Merciez chimed in with her suggestion that all the "ladies" should get busy knitting and crocheting shawls, baby bonnets, scarves, antimacassars, and open a store down in Pittsburg.

Still registering shock at Lady Bob's suggestion, Mary Skubitz drew her meeting to a close, promising that if the conditions worsened they would get together again. She wasn't sure just how or where, but everybody "keep an eye open."

To top it off, as Old Lady Bob bobbed along toward the door, scratching the floor with her crooked cane, she turned her bleary eyes, glistening from a light beam from a coal-dusted window. She raised her stick, opened a near-toothless mouth, cackled and said, "Well, I want all you ladies to know that I can fly. Yep, fly. I've known it for sometime, now. In the spring on such-and-such a warm day, I'm gonna climb up on the roof of the Company Store and take a good sail right over toward Frontenac."

Danika realized then that the womens' meeting was over. Good and over.

Head down as she walked home, she focused her eyes upon the wild dock and dandelions along the blackened road; she guessed that she'd just have to dig up some new recipes for cooking turnips.

CHAPTER FIFTEEN

Trials of a Cleaning Woman

Neda tipped the bottle of Old Time Furniture Polish, allowing a small stream of liquid, a mixture of lemon oil and beeswax to dampen her flannel cloth. She was tired of the stink of cleaning soaps, scouring powders, polishing oils and how their odors lingered on her skin, long after washing.

That was another matter. She was forbidden to use the Otis bathrooms upstairs, or the one in the hall by the kitchen, even if it was her assignment to keep the giant walrus-of-a-tub, hiked up on ugly claw legs, sparkling. She wasn't certain that she'd even want to climb up into one of those contraptions.

Her mother had told her to quit complaining and "be thankful," when she griped for the third time about how sore her knees got, when she was down on that biggest bathroom floor scrubbing those little octagonal black-and-white tiles. She'd heard folks say about tough jobs, "Well, it'd make a preacher cuss."

She surely would like to know what one of those ministers like Guy Howard, the Walking Preacher of the Ozarks, who came to Pittsburg to stop the saloon traffic, would say about tough situations. And if it were Father Pompeney, he might have to hightail it to confession himself.

If her own bowels gave her a cramp, she had to lock herself in the stuffy room off the pantry and hump upon that cold, wooden toilet seat.

Even worse, as she sat there nagging her body to hurry, she was forced to face the hideous mop sink anchored to the wall in front of her, scruffy and soured mops soused down into it. Those massive-knuckled faucet handles, which were hard to turn, ruining her palms as she twisted them. And watch out for the scalding water and steam which enveloped her head and made her hair curl.

Not only the icky sink but looking to her side, she faced a rack of brushes, mops, and brooms. She couldn't even turn her face away from the rows of cleansers, soap boxes, and scouring powders. She was weary, watching that Old Dutch Cleanser woman clomp in her wooden shoes in front of her. And just how long can one stare at a sickening-yellow box of Bon Ami?

The scouring agent odors made her sneeze a couple of times, at least, interrupting her business, which she knew she should "get through" as quickly as possible, for Lady Ophelia just might ring for her to race out to the garden to bring in a basket of those new red beets Gardner had just dug for her. So far "the lady" hadn't scolded her for using too much toilet paper, which wasn't the good soft kind upstairs anyway, but so far, thankfully, that hadn't happened.

Today she'd tackle the table and chairs. Huge, tall-backed, woman-killer chairs, more suited for a baron's castle in Europe than this mining town of Franklin. She'd already polished the massive-legged mahogany table, which, when outstretched would seat at least twenty-five diners. It glistened like satin in the light filtered through the sheer curtains on the eastern window, a window at least nine feet tall.

Oh, yes. "Water those giant ferns over there in their wicker plant stands, and for pity's sakes, don't spill any water on the rug."

She'd slopped a little water on the varnished hardwood floor last week, but she'd mopped it up before Lady Otis could discover it and lecture her on how it would blanch the wood.

Next came the other commands. "Now, Neda, when you've finished with those chairs (there were twelve of them) you must wash your hands carefully. I'm having a dinner party tomorrow night with important guests from Pittsburg. The table linens will need to be ironed."

Yep! and my palms rough as a coal miner's. Probably snag a runner in the damask fabric.

Her back already aching, Neda knelt on the French Aubusson Rug sporting the burgundy fleur-de-lis design in the middle. Exhausted as she was, she was tempted to lie down and take a nap. Still she rubbed and waxed the turned rungs of the weighty chair. She gave the polish cloth an extra twist, remembering the chiding she'd received from Ophelia about the heavy bureau mirror frame she'd overlooked a couple of weeks ago in her hurry to finish and get down to the Company Store and wait for Matt.

And Matt! Thinking of him helped ease the ache in her back muscles but she mustn't stop. Keep on rubbing. She reflected upon how they'd met. He had just stepped out of the Company Store, the "Pluck-Me-Store," according to her father as they plucked the customer a third more for a can of beans. Matt sported a new pair of denim overalls and a striped cap tossed back on his fine black-haired head.

She knew he had seen her lean over to hear what that college boy hollered out at her as he stopped his 1921 Chevrolet coupe in the middle of the street. When she recognized that he was one of those Washburn scabs Governor Allen'd ordered to come down and steal her father's job, she gave him a quick brush off, even if she'd have half died to have ridden in that fancy buggy.

Well, when Matthew Enrico just stood there and waited for her to return to the sidewalk, and she was steaming, chewing on her bottom lip, she nearly bumped into him.

"Whoa, there, young lady," he'd stepped aside. When she lifted her eyelids to his face, his Caruso grin lit up his dark, chiseled face, clean as the blue overalls he sported. He chuckled, his voice mellow with a sultry huskiness.

"Oh, excuse me." She stepped back, recognizing him; the tall high school youth her best friend Tillie Lovell swooned over a couple of years back, which might as well have been a million, considering how things turned out.

Salutatorian, wasn't he? Class couple of years ahead of me?

He was a coal miner's son, but he actually remembered her name. It seemed he didn't at all mind walking a coal miner's daughter, wearing a sorry brown maid's uniform, right down the dusty coal-gritted road, lined with ragweeds, wilted marigolds and horseweed.

When she'd shot quick glances toward him in the past, she'd always said to herself, "He may working the mines today alongside his father, but tomorrow? Tomorrow, he's going somewhere."

Sometimes she even fantasized moving to a city like Joplin over in Missouri.

Or how about Kansas City?

Hadn't everyone heard about the tree-lined boulevards and the parkways, circular flowerbeds radiating splendor, fountains shooting streams into the air, water rushing down over naked cherubs?

And wasn't there a place there called The Country Club Plaza?

Oh, she'd die to go there.

****

Through for the day, a week later, Neda dragged along toward the company camp and the shabby rows of shacks. Thoughts crowded her mind: Ma and that bevy of women meeting last week to focus upon all the problems here. Old Lady Bob, and Myrtice Hester making Ma nervous.

Why didn't Ma tell Myrtice to take a hike? Tell her to head for that low land east of Pittsburg where the eerie lights float, sink, and circle around again. Scare the old busybody enough to make her race all the way over to that Bedlam place in Nevada, Missouri.

She hadn't expected him at all, since he'd been filling in at the lumber yard down by the railroad tracks, but there he was with that Caruso grin. Her mind had been so occupied that she hadn't even heard the put-put of the Model T behind her.

When she finally turned, startled, there he was, drawing up beside her, hands gripping that wooden steering wheel. Well, yes, the Model T was an old one, but it sure did beat "shanks mare."

"Get in, Neda. Take you home, or for a little drive up west of Arma."

He'd opened the tinny door and she scrambled up, unable to control the grin on her face. Her heart thumped. "How on earth did you get this car, Matt?"

"Oh, I've been saving. They got a plan at the used car lot down in Pittsburg where you pay on time. Course I had to put some money down."

All Neda could think of was, "Amazing! Can this be?"

"You mean you didn't have to pay it all at once?" She looked around and noticed worn places, and the Lizzy did shimmy to the left, but what did that matter? The wheels rolled, didn't they? And that road west of Arma, tree lined, beautiful. Soothing. A real lover's trail. God, Father Pompeney, and that St. Barbara must be smiling on her.

Neda just couldn't help staring at his muscled biceps.

And wasn't he taking boxing lessons down in Pittsburg?

****

Something she wasn't telling, though. She'd made up her mind on that.

Unless it happened again.

Last week, on a Wednesday, wasn't it? She'd skipped down the long twisting back stairs that led to the pantry and the wash closet with the brooms and mops to get another can of Bon Ami and a clean polishing rag. She' hurried back up the stairs to finish the bathrooms.

Soon be four o'clock, and M'Lady would be driving in in the Packard.

Ophelia had Driver take her down to Joplin to shop for the newest styles coming in for the fall. Real high-up ladies' dresses like the ones Neda'd seen in last month's issue of *McClure*. Ophelia trying to be a genuine Gibson Girl, which she thought was preposterous for a woman of her age.

She was down on her hands and knees in the pink-wallpapered bathroom. Her hand ached from scrubbing the inside of the porcelain stool, which M'Lady perched herself upon, especially ever since she chewed and swallowed that foul Ex Lax, so's she could keep herself boyish-looking and slim.

At her age, too.

Neda could feel her buttocks waggle as she worked, her backside swaying. She drew her right sleeve across her sweaty forehead, then returned to scouring, trying not to breathe in the fumes, which were about to choke her. She knew it was near quitting time and she had to speed up in order to check off everything on the list Ophelia had left for her.

The half-closed bathroom door squeaked. She guessed it was the southeasterly wind blowing in from the partially-opened window above the tub. Then she was sure she heard the touch of a shoe on the tiles. Her head shot backwards over her shoulder, eyebrows raised, mouth half-open.

Mr. Otis. What on earth is Mr. Otis doing in here?

Alarmed, she started to rise.

Am I going to get fired for not getting the job done satisfactorily?

She was still jumpy over her Pittsburg experience. But before she could stand up completely, a hot hand grasped her shoulder and began rubbing it. Heat penetrated fully to her toes.

"Mr. Otis, why, what...?"

"Didn't mean to startle you, Neda. No. Wouldn't want to do that," his voice was husky and had a little quiver in it.

He grinned down at her, hairy hand shifting from her shoulder to her goose-pimpled-arm as he stepped closer. She could smell Bay Rum radiating from his neck and partially-unbuttoned shirt. A vein throbbed in his neck. He seemed to be almost out of breath. A mat of tangled, brown hair sprouted from his opened shirt. He grabbed her behind her head and attempted to draw her face into his chest.

She screamed. The Bon Ami can crashed to the hard tile below.

"What are you doing, Mr. Otis. No! Her right leg drew back and she kicked his shin with the toe of her hard work shoe. When she turned, his hand, gripping the front of her dress below the collar, ripped off two buttons.

Instead of scampering for the other upstairs bathroom, she half-fell down the servant's stairs and locked herself in the mop room, collapsing upon the stool lid, trembling, head buried in her hands.

Oh, God above, St. Barbara, now what shall I do? What does a girl do in a predicament like this? Should I tell Matt, or not?

Neda's head roared, her heart palpitated so strongly she wondered if it would knock itself right out of her side.

What do other girls do when they are put upon like this? I can't tell Pa, or Ma, can I? Oh, God of mercy, help me.

When she'd stopped heaving for air and her brains quit twisting, she lifted her head out of her lap.

Now what?

There was a tap on the door. Gentle enough.

Did Ophelia come home already? Thank God.

Then she heard a syrupy, low-pitched voice.

"No need to hide, Neda. You just got to think about it. Pretty girl like you - no opportunities in the coal towns. I can help you out. Sure. I've done it before. Girls like my help. You don't want to slouch around like this, growing old, no future, teeth falling out, back humped. You're too fine a girl for that."

Neda tried to control her knocking knees.

Get ahold of myself.

"There'll be another time, Neda. I can help you get a nice apartment in Pittsburg. Get you some of those flapper clothes that'd make you shine. Take you up to Kansas City to the theater. Buy you a fur if you'd like, whiskey flask and real Bourbon or Scotch in it for your hip. Silk stockings and high heels. Cigarettes, too, and one of those long, classy holders. Think about it. Didn't take the last two girls who worked here long to decide."

She wondered if she was going to vomit.

"Mr. Otis, go away! You're wife will be home soon, then what'll you do?

If I ever get out of this closet shall I go for the sheriff? Would he just laugh at me? Oh, God. How can I tell Ma?

The voice paused; then a gentle rap. "All you have to do, Neda, is to think about it. Not a hard decision to make. And, I didn't even mention all the fun we can have together."

She waited for another few minutes. She could hear a southeasterly wind pick up in the trees outside. She rose, crept to the door, turned the knob and took a peek through the crack. Gone. He'd gone.

She heard the purring of the powerful Packard motor as it drove in the circled drive.

Ophelia, home at last.

Neda grabbed a cleaning rag. She clawed and stumbled, scraping her knees, until she'd reached the upstairs to finish the cleaning.

Today was pay day.

CHAPTER SIXTEEN

Slave of the Wheel of Labor

The change in his sister was evident. When Toma peeked between the edge of the curtain and the wall, he could see Neda sitting on the bed, knees drawn up, back plastered against the wall, head bent over a book she'd checked out of the library by that German author, whose name he couldn't pronounce, Hergesheimer or something. Book titled *Linda Condon*.

He had sneaked in and scanned a few pages when she was working over at the Otis mansion. Story on the back cover described her as a "woman made of alabaster," and "the most sterile woman alive." He pondered just what Hergesheimer meant when he used those words.

Alabaster woman? Sounded cold, like the Arctic, didn't it? Why did Neda balk when Ma nudged her to go to confession? Turned her back on Ma. Neda stormed into her room and yanked the curtain shut. Was his sister turning into the "stone woman?"

Didn't talk about her job at the Otises anymore, either. Stopped bringing home small gifts Mrs. Otis had given her from time-to-time: a little green vase that looked nice with wild violets in it, a compact for face powder Ophelia said she didn't want anymore, a book with an interesting title, "A Girl of the Limberlost."

Course he hadn't read it. Book about girls, men, engagement and sticky love problems.

He wished she'd have brought him a book like *Man of the Forest* by Zane Grey.

Now that'd be reading that'd whip the brain into a fever, wouldn't it?

Anyway, whatever life was like at the Otis place, Neda held on to her job like a dog gnawing on an everlasting bone. He understood why. Saving her money. Opened her own bank account in the Company Bank in town. Of course she only put in half of her pay as she gave the rest to Pa and Ma. Nevertheless, she says she's going to college someday.

Wouldn't that be something for this family?

Still, she has those angry spells and silent moods. Toma believed Father Pompeney could help her in that little confession booth.

"Bless me Father, for I have sinned...and so forth."

Everybody needed to say words like that from time-to-time, didn't they?

Well, maybe I need that, too, after those pictures Cecil slipped to me. Sure helped me unload after the Chicopee kite episode. Father Pompeney said the blessing over me and asked me to say the Novena for nine Saturdays. I know it strengthened me. Didn't need to be told that I'm a sinner and in need of the grace of Christ and his forgiveness.

I still say that prayer:

> *"O, most Holy Heart of Jesus...*
> *I adore Thee, I love Thee and with a lively sorrow*
> *for my sins, I offer Thee this poor heart of mine...."*

Now I have to work on forgiving Cecil.

And Cecil? Well Cecil hasn't come over with other exciting fun suggestions; not even finding a good space of hard-packed ground for playing mumbletypeg.

Toma had seen him down at the Company Store looking at the penknives but Cecil ignored him. Toma could see that he'd grown a few inches, too. Strutted in his long pants, sauntering like Captain Easy in the funnies, flashing his

James D. Yoder

dollar bill to pay the clerk for the pearl-handled one he'd picked out.

Well, O K if he didn't want to speak to me.

Toma recognized at some place deep within himself, that he wasn't sure he had squeezed out all the anger he felt about getting trapped in that Chicopee predicament.

He did meet Cecil by the Dance Hall in town, week ago, leaning against the east side in the cool shade, bottom of the wall green with moss. Cecil's hands busy sorting through a stack of cards. He slipped a couple of cards over to him with an odd grin and a wink in his eye. Toma glanced down and saw that they were pictures of scantily-dressed women in the strangest poses he'd ever seen. And one of them was wearing nothing at all.

He shoved them back, noticing two town women clutching basket handles as they turned the corner and headed toward them on the sidewalk,

"Gotta go, Cecil," he'd said. "Ma wants me to pull up the old tomato vines since the frost."

Cecil's upper lip curled into a sneer. "What's the matter, ain't you a man yet, Toma Cratnick? Come over to our basement and I'll show you some real pictures I pasted on the ceiling behind our furnace."

He wasn't certain about all the last words, but he realized that they would make Father Pompeney's forehead sweat and his bones quiver. He headed for home, the Fatima prayer overshadowing his mind.

He noticed that Pa worried, too. He sighed a lot, air coming from deep down in his chest. Sometimes stirring up that stuff in his lungs he coughed up from time-to-time, running to the kitchen range, lifting one of the cast-iron lids and spitting.

He'd listened, his parents' voices vibrating through the thin wall.

"Milan, do you want to break the strike and go on back to work? Governor Allen ordered it. Bill Blessant, and Albert Buche have gone back. Said their children were starving."

Pa's booming voice vibrated along the thin studding and Toma heard every word.

"No! Woman, you otta know better than to say words like that."

Toma knew when Pa talked to Ma like that, he'd feel badly afterward. Sometimes, he would ask her for forgiveness for hollering. Other times he'd grab her around her waist and give her a squeeze.

No, Pa wasn't cut out like rough Adolph Simon, or mean-spirited Fox Harris, who'd split their wives's lips if they mouthed words they didn't appreciate.

Ma understood, though. He knew that. He knew she was worried about the food on their plates with winter coming. Ma was getting, what do you call it? Agitated about the long strike.

Ma talked about that Socialist woman, Mary Skubitz, too.

Weren't they going to get together again? Figure out how to help?

Ma had canned jars of green beans, red beets, tomatoes, pickles, peas, and peaches from their own tree, along with some Jonathan, and red Winesap apples for making pies, come winter. He knew that women with bigger families and sucking babies didn't have the time to tend a garden, nor the strength to put away food like Ma did.

They hadn't butchered Albert, their pig, yet. Wait until after frost for that. But Ma'd empty and soak those guts, then grind up the hog meat, season it, and stuff it into the cleaned entrails. Course she'd scald them first in lye water. Next, she'd pack the sausages in lard and put the crock in the coldest place in the root cellar outside. He saw her down there one day, pushing aside Pa's wine-making apparatus, jugs, hoses and stuff. Course, even if she grumbled a little, Ma did like a touch of Pa's elderberry wine on a cold winter evening.

Cabbages? Well, when it was a little colder, she'd have him help her dig a big hole in the garden, line it with straw and put in a dozen fat cabbage heads, more straw, then dirt on top to keep them from freezing.

He had helped her make sauerkraut back in August. Had to grab the kraut cutter off its nail on the back porch. Cut those Flat Headed Dutchman heads into quarters and heave them back and forth over that slicing slot. Careful not to take off a slice of a thumb or hand.

Use a hammer handle to stomp the shredded cabbage into a five-gallon stone crock. Salt each layer. When the crock was nearly full, top it off with broad grape leaves, cover them with a flat sand rock and a wooden lid, leaving it to fizzle and ferment. Roll the crock down into the root cellar where the kraut would mature.

Toma thought about high school coming up. Freshman, over in that big brick two story building.

What will it be like? What kind of clothes will I wear? Don't have a year older brother to pass down his "used pants."

He'd seen Ma sort through the boys' corduroy trousers in the store, glance at the price tag, shake her head and grab her purse handle with both hands, her knuckles white. He didn't like to see the sorrowful look on her face. He guessed most of the boys his age would wear overalls and chambray shirts, anyway, wouldn't they?

And how about getting roughed up by the older bucks? Juniors and Seniors? More than a few "tough nuts," for sure. Pimple-faced Turney Heavener, six foot tall, biceps bursting his shirt sleeves and that look of contempt on his face.

And that old Myrtice woman who comes over here and bothers Ma when she's shelling dried butter beans, yapping about how the big bucks at school load up the freshmen "sissies" in the back of a Model T truck and haul them over to Frontenac where they make them strip and climb a greased flag pole, while they laugh and hoot down below, holding canoe paddles and snickering about your privates?

Pa did insist that Ma take him back to the store to try on better-fitting shoes since his old ones wore out at the toe, sole leather flapping. Course some of the fellows, when the soles of their shoes gave out, drew around the soles with a pencil onto pasteboard, cut out the copies and shoved them inside, making them do for another month.

Needed the new brogues, brown ones called Wolverines, supposed to be tough and long lasting.

Bless St. Barbara! Pa bought them for me.

Toma reflected upon how his Pa was pleased with him about how he hadn't complained, and built up muscle in his arms when they were over at Davis farm with those corn schucking hooks strapped to their palms. Together they slung the plump, golden ears, reflecting the bright sunlight, up against the bangboard on the opposite side of the wagon box. Horses, tails swishing, heads nodding, waiting, moving on faithfully at Pa's clucking tongue.

What about Pa and Ma's hero, Alec Howat? Guess he's still over in Girard in jail. Maybe they moved him and that Vice President fellow, August Dorchy, up to the jail in Columbus by now.

Well, if the miner families around here were down to eating watery soup every day, at least they weren't in jail cells, staring at moldy bread and cold gruel poked through a little opening in the iron bars.

****

August Dorchy, former Vice President of District 14, leaned against the jail wall in Columbus, Kansas, feet outstretched on the upper bunk. Alexander Howat reclined on the lower bunk, head and feet opposite Dorchy's in order to carry on their conversation.

"Don't you wish, now, Alec, that you'd have obeyed the injunction from the International in Indianapolis? You probably would be courting Agnes, forking in fine pheasant in that dining room in the Stilwell Hotel down in Pittsburg."

The very thought of Dorchy's suggestion of dining in such opulence made Alec's mouth water. He was tired of weak bean soup and cornbread. He'd gagged on boiled cabbage and tough corned beef on the off days.

Coffee? Don't even mention it. Ground peanut hulls would make a better brew.

"Lewis and his pack of lawyers can push the law all they want to. Sure, I violated the National Union injunction, but I'd do it again. I did it for the common man, the down-in-the-hole miner. I couldn't get that Markham poem out of my mind."

"Poem?

"Every kid in our school memorized parts of it. About broken down laborers like farmers and coal miners. I know what it's like. I, myself, have suffered the slavery of the wheel of labor. Down on my knees, breathing dust, bones bending and aching."

"I know what you're talking about, Alec. Too much agony. Stifling air, explosion ripping through tunnels. Cave-ins, measly pay."

Alec continued. "The words haunt me at night, restless as sleep is here with the drunks thrown in every other night. And that's another matter. That wouldn't be happening if it hadn't been for that Eighteenth Amendment, Prohibition, which they call a noble experiment. Scandalous, the problems it brought on. Ripped the German communities apart. Made felons out of them, spoiling their culture and customs."

"Well," added Dorchy, "I have to agree. We've never had such liquor violations and so much under-the-table drinking. A few years ago, nobody heard of a speakeasy or so many women drinking. But let's get back to the laborers, the miners."

"The words go through my very soul, every night, August, like someone saying the rosary over and over again:

> *Slave of the wheel of labor, what to him*
> *Are Plato and the swing of the Pleiades?*
> *What the long reaches of the peaks of song,*

The rift of dawn, the reddening of the rose?
Through this dread shape, the suffering ages look;
Time's tragedy is in that aching stoop
Through this dread shape humanity betrayed....

"That's quite a poem, Alec." Dorchy shifted his legs, jiggling the bunk.

"It speaks the truth. You and I know the aching stoop. And it's been going on ever since King Solomon's mines. Humanity betrayed."

Both men were silent as a cardinal outside their tiny window perched upon the ledge and began a song to its mate: "Sweet cheer, cheer, cheer, cheer."

Alec watched the redbird fly toward a tall cedar in the distance. "Fly little bird, and we need it, the 'sweet cheer.'"

"We were betrayed," Alec continued. "All the Dean and Reliance Strip Mine operators needed to do to avoid all this pain was to fulfill their duty, abide by the District rules and their own constitution."

"Maybe, though, Alec, it was too big of a price to pay for standing up for principle. There are hundreds of mining families about to run out of food, winter coming on."

"Don't you think I worry about that? The men declared it themselves: 'We'll all strike, we're with you, Alec.' You know the stand they took; like soldiers holding a line in a field of battle." Alec lifted his feet from the thin mattress, planting them upon the cement floor. He sat up, ran his fingers through his tousled hair. "All they had to do was to pay that boy, Carl Mishmash, his money. Less than two hundred dollars. Think about it?"

"Well," added, Dorchy, "someone wrote, 'for want of a nail, a shoe was lost' -- and finally, a horse, and the whole battle, I think."

"We're talking about more than horses' feet, here, August. Feet rotted from standing in cold water. Feet with smashed toes or blown off altogether. Men bruised and permanently crippled. Lungs rotting inside, stifling their breath."

As the shades of evening dimmed their cell, they sat in silence, listening to the howl of the outside wind. Somewhere within the chilled walls they could hear the forlorn, perhaps forgotten prisoner, weeping.

Alec turned his head toward the fading light. The cardinal had returned, blessing them with an evening benediction.

CHAPTER SEVENTEEN

The Leech

As Neda drew on the dishwater brown uniform M'Lady insisted she wear, she noticed that after three boilings in the copper-bottomed boiler and a dozen scrubbings over a metal washboard, that it was too tight at her breasts. Nevertheless, she twisted her torso and squeezed herself into it.

She could hear the rumbling from the Jackson Walker mine, staffed by a mongrel group of scabs imported from the south along with a few slap-happy college young bucks from those schools in Topeka and Pittsburg. She pushed the curtain aside and stepped out of her room. Before she realized what she was doing she was humming the tune of "K-K-K-Katy, beautiful Katy, You're the only g-g-g-girl that I adore..."

In spite of the smokestacks from the working collieries, the sunshine spilled through the window with morning brilliance and the growls from the machinery hadn't drowned out the trilling of a mockingbird in the peach tree, leaves slowly turning autumn orange.

She glanced at her mother who was frying slabs of cornmeal mush and eggs in an iron skillet for their breakfast. "Morning, Ma." The smell of fried mush made her taste buds swell. Her mouth watered.

After she'd washed her face and brushed her teeth out on the back porch, she slid through the screen door into the kitchen.

Noticing that the table was set for two, she quickly poured water, retrieved from the water bucket, into a beat-up tin cup. She saw that her mother had boiled coffee for herself. "OK, Ma, if I pour your coffee?"

"That'd be fine, Neda." Danika turned to face her. "About time you're smiling, I was beginning to worry about you."

"No cause to worry, Ma. I gotta tell you something, though."

Her mother pivoted on her worn shoe soul, placing a plate with two slices of the crisp mush and a fried egg, sporting a sunny golden yolk, before Neda. She set her cracked plate on the table, drew up the bentwood chair and seated herself.

"Where are Pa and Toma?" Neda waited for her mother to settle herself.

"They're cutting and shocking grain milo out on the Davis farm. Bright October day for it, too. Nice if they'd bring home a pumpkin or two."

Together they repeated the table blessing:

> *"Bless us, O Lord and these Thy gifts,*
> *which we are about to receive from Thy bounty,*
> *through Jesus Christ our Lord, Amen."*

In unison they made the sign of the cross.

Neda picked up her wooden-handled fork, cutlery common among "poor folk." She sliced through the crusty mush, then took a bite, savoring the mellow taste.

"Troubled me, you shuttin yourself down, Neda, ever since you lost that job at the Five and Dime," Danika said.

"Well, I finally told myself I gotta get over it. You know life isn't easy, Ma. You've often told me so, especially for coal mining families. I'll find something again. I'm ready to start hunting. In the meantime, I'll work for Ophelia Otis three days a week. She's going to raise my pay ten cents an hour."

"About time."

Neda saw her mother's mouth set into a straight line as if she had more words pushing at her lips, but she restrained herself. Danika reached for the aluminum pepper shaker.

"Well, the work's hard, Ma. Cleaning powders and soaps are tough on my hands. Ophelia did give me a half of a jar of lotion for my chapped hands."

Should I tell Ma about...?

She decided at present to let sleeping dogs lie, but these were growling dogs, bloodhounds with their noses to the ground.

Mr. Harvey Otis did hint that he'd be "around" again, didn't he? Like I'd cave in and let him buy me.

Neda forked a slice of her fried egg and chewed slowly. She looked into her mother's rust-colored eyes, noticing the gray had crept upward at the sides of her hair.

Her hands, oh, her hands!

"I guess I'd ought to tell you and Pa about Matt, Ma." Her smile spread across her face. She felt her cheeks growing warm with a blush.

"Well, I figured something was comin. I thought that there might be things you'd want to talk about." Danika took a sip of water.

"I've met a young man, Ma. Nice fellow. Good looking, too. At least I think so. Matthew Enrico. Yeah, he's a miner's son, so we're kind of a match." She couldn't help smiling as she mentioned his name.

Her mind lingered on the bumpy ride day-before-yesterday when Enrico took her for a drive over to Mulberry near the Missouri line. She'd been impressed with the three or four mansions similar to the Otis house.

Nice main street, too. Someone's raking in the money over there.

Matt, hair so black when it caught the light it seemed purple. And those white teeth. Almost tongue-tied, so overcome with pride of being seen with him.

Top it off, the sarsaparilla he bought me!

And the scenery. The twisting road, leaves hanging low, slowly turning into yellows and oranges; black-trunked oaks, stalwart and everlasting.

"Enrico? Italian. From Frontenac, then?" Danika leaned back in her chair.

"Yes, from Frontenac, now, but earlier they lived here. He was two years ahead of me in high school. His father was transferred over to the Reidville Mine, south of Frontenac. He's an overseer in the mine there."

A robin hopped upon the window sill, pecked the glass and looked in.

"Matt works in the Frontenac bakery when the mine is shut down. Good cook, too, Ma. But he wants to study mathematics, maybe be a teacher. Who knows?"

"Na," her mother replied. "I'd never hold being a miner's son against a young boy. Fella can learn a lot in the mining industry. Builds up muscle, too, but it sure isn't for the long haul."

Neda smiled, laid down her fork, forgetting the last bites of her corn mush.

"He's got his own car, a second-hand Lizzie."

"Then you've taken rides with him? Guess I just over-looked my daughter not getting home after work on time." Danika grinned, reached across and pated Neda's arm.

Neda felt a slow blush creep over her cheeks.

"Bring him around, Neda. Maybe to church some Sunday. I still have a couple of fryers out there. Gotta get at em before they get too tough."

Neda could tell by the warmth in her voice and the lengthening smile that she was pleased.

And that other subject? That leech, Harvey Otis?

Neda decided to hold her tongue. Wait to tell Ma about Matt Enrico's boxing lessons and what a wonderful dancer he was, swirling her in the Too Fat Polka..

Yeah, wait for another time. Pa always said, 'don't spill your beans all at once.'

Neda decided that with the continuing strike, she'd better hang on to her Otis job, like it or lump it. She recognized the conflict over the fact that several mine operators ignored Alec Howat's order to strike, and the Local 14's almost unanimous approval.

She realized this caused factions between the John Lewis supporters and the loyal Alec Howat followers. The struggle rumbled.

Where would it lead? Many folks were already wringing their hands, eyes wild and anxious.

She couldn't help noticing how the hollow-eyed Hoback children next door, five of them, stared out the doorway of their shack. Mother inside, torn apart by worry, an eighteen-month old hanging onto her soiled apron, and another baby pawing at her breast. Father probably south of camp, drunk and fallen into a ditch.

"God, help her," Neda whispered.

Course Ma had taken over a dozen jars of her canned green beans. She'd even dug some pork chops out of the lard in the five gallon crock in the cellar, insisting that Lizzie take the food. Canned tomatoes, too.

That was Ma. She couldn't stand to see starving children, barefooted and in rags. Ma'd shake her head, groan and pray to St. Barbara. Pray for the bleary-eyed alcoholics, and staggering out-of-work miners who'd lost their way.

That Prohibition was a laugh, wasn't it?

****

Up at the Capitol in Topeka, Governor Allen leaned back in his swivel leather-upholstered chair. His pouty lips pursed in annoyance over John L. Lewis, haranguing him almost every day on the telephone.

Wouldn't be so bad if old Lewis would realize he comes across like an army sergeant, boisterous and demanding. Egging me on to send in the State Militia down to the Kansas

135

coal fields like we did back in '19 when the strike continued in spite of President Wilson's and my orders.

Don't want to be a Nervous Nellie, but to be honest, it crosses my mind daily.

Division among the miners. Near insurrection in those two counties. Thought it'd simmer down with Howat in jail. Let Howat and Dorchy rot in Columbus. Deserve what they got.

Like I always said, biggest conglomeration of Eastern European immigrants in those counties in the U. S. of A, wasn't there? Such names. Most of them I can't even pronounce. And, what country are they loyal to? Those foreigners running after good, white American women, marrying them. What kind of children will they have?

***Then** you've got the Socialists and the Debs lovers, waiting to take over the government. We all saw what happened in Europe, didn't we? Our Doughboys helping the English and French stomp out that war in a hurry.*

Read in the Topeka Journal about that Vorse woman stirring up the women around Franklin and Arma. Loud-mouthed and her own life out of control. Claimed to be a writer. At least Old Lady Mother Jones hasn't come back, yet. Oh, yes. She'll fly in on her broom, soon enough.

Then nobody's following the Prohibition laws. I know the Law is staying away from those mining towns. Talked to Sheriff Matt Gould, myself. Don't rightly blame them. Never know when a switchblade'll flash and someone's throat'll be cut.

You got men out of work, their own fault, sitting around, lazy, drinking their own moonshine, tempers flare at the slightest provocation. Oh, those hot-blooded aliens love to fist fight, anyway. Have to give some of them credit, though, some good boccie (lawn bowling) games going on down there. Like to see one, myself.

Read in Pittsburg Daily Headlight there's a drive to get the wheat farmers organized in the counties further west. Communist Party. Think of it? Already infiltrated the oil

136

drilling sites around El Dorado. Next, you got the Ku Klux Klan moving in eastern Kansas. There've been some negroes lynched, and I hate that. I gotta look into it one of these days.

As my dear departed mother used to say, 'Son, when it rains, it pours.'"

CHAPTER EIGHTEEN

"We Need the Whole Experience

Well, now, there was surely something else Danika would have to confess to Father Pompeney. No doubt about it. Danika wrung her hands and shook her head as it trailed through her mind. She'd told Milan about it last night when they were in bed. Held off going until eleven-thirty. He'd laughed so hard that Toma came to their door and wanted to know what was the matter. Still Milan hooted and giggled.

For another half hour, too.

That was a good thing, seeing him come out of his despair like that.

But at what cost? Had she and Fanny Calobis made enemies? Hadn't they had enough to reckon with without lying to someone? Deceiving them?

Even thinking about it today made Danika slap her thigh and bend over in hysterics.

And, wasn't that a contradiction? Sinning, then laughing about it?

She was weary of Myrtice Hester coming over, at least two mornings a week. Dragging up a chair and sitting there dishing out dirt. Even asking for a cup of coffee.

These days, too, when most people couldn't even afford to buy coffee.

She hadn't realized she had said it, but she couldn't restrain her tongue when she looked out of the kitchen window and saw Myrtice swinging her little black purse, taking mincing steps, heading right over to her place.

Neda had heard Danika's words, too, which was a shame, and another sin she'd have to confess to Father Pompeney. The words slipped out like a frog's tongue flicking to catch a water spider.

"Dear God above," she'd said. Neda standing there in the front room doorway.

"Here comes that nosy Myrtice Hester. I wish the floor would split and swallow me. "

Nothing Christian about that, was there?

Course, Neda giggled and grabbed her book, raced outside to sit under the peach tree to get out of the kitchen. Reading that book called 'The Sheik," by Edith Hull. Love story, girl being seduced in the desert somewhere in a foreign country.

Myrtice finally settled herself at the end of the kitchen table so she could yap at her and take a sip of coffee, every now-and-then. Her words still sullied Danika's brain.

"You know, Danika. I think the miners around here are making too big a stink about things. No need to be out of work. The Governor and President Harding both ordered the strike to stop."

"But Myrtice..."

"Selfish, ain't it? Carrying on so. They getting good pay for a good day's work. Mining ain't the worst job in the world, is it?"

"Myrtice, let me tell you about when I worked in the mines in Southern Illinois. Down by Carbondale by the Mississippi. Yes, I did. When I was seventeen. Pa died of cholera and Ma had those twins. I took up the shovel and..."

"Why, I never! Danika Cratnick, you? You working in a mine?" Myrtice put one hand over her mouth, head bent, eyes closed, while her other hand clawed at her thigh.

"Why, Danika, that's just a scandal. Down in a mine with all those men?

"Four of us girls, all of us facing hardship bound our breasts, grabbed shovels and picks, and strapped on our

139

carbides. Yes. We did. Put on overalls and men's shirts, and hard-clodhopper shoes and descended into hell."

"You don't need to use cuss words, Danika."

Danika felt flames burn her throat. She knew her cheeks were reddening. She swung her old chair back and plopped down, her head leaning in toward Myrtice.

"The operator of that mine allowed it. He knew families were starving, all that cholera and death. Pa died. Yes, Myrtice, four of us girls. Aline Shortworth, Beulah Butler, and Parthenie Hodge. We worked in the mine for eighteen months until I met Mr. Cratnick, and Ma could get a pittance-of-a-pension to live on."

"I still say, Danika, that it is a scandal and if I were you, I wouldn't be telling about it. Shameful. Why, with all those men?"

Danika thought she'd seen a lusty little gleam in Myrtice's eyes at the mention of four maidens in a coal mine with all those men, as if she, herself, might have relished such an opportunity.

"Well, I got to ponder that situation, Danika. I'm telling you, it makes my throat tighten just to hear you tell me about it."

"There's a principle involved, Myrtice. President Howat clarified that. There's a reason the men are ignoring Governor Allen and the president's orders. That Slave Law Governor Allen passed is illegal. Takes away the workers' freedom. You ought to know...."

It had been a futile effort, a ruined morning. Danika looked down and saw that her arms were trembling from restraining herself. How she wished the old Biddie would shut up and go home.

Myrtice didn't stop. She sloughed on, her tongue flapping.

"That's all one hears from the women around here. 'Our men just not getting the pay they deserve. The mine will close in three years and we'll have to move again. These shacks we live in aren't fit for a ...'"

"But Myrtice, that's the truth!" Danika hadn't meant to raise her voice.

"Not only that but the drinking. Lots of the miner's making moonshine; staggering around on the sidewalls half soused."

"You gotta understand, Myrtice, these men work under the worst of conditions. Many of them just don't know what to do."

Doesn't she have any pity?

Myrtice cleared the phlegm from her throat and stared at Danika. "Then they grumble about the mine conditions, how dark it is down there, and the bad air. Well, they've got electric fans blowing down those shafts somewhere, don't they? For myself, I'd really like to go down sometime just to prove to folks it ain't all that bad."

Danika felt a hot anger burn up from her throat. She could feel her heart thumping.

Oh, I wish I could drag her into one of those cold, lonely shafts. Let her stand there in utter darkness, wondering if she's in hell.

Danika opened her mouth again. "The truth! Three dollars a day? Think of it. Joe Rondella crushed to death last week in mine Number 6 of the Mount Carmel Coal Company. Why, a whole mass of slate and rocks fell on him. There've been twelve ..."

Myrtice set her coffee cup down in front of her and beaded her greenish eyes upon Danika, her mouth drawn. "You don't have to raise your voice at me, Danika Cratnick.

I'm talking about people having opportunities for regular work these days ought to be thankful for it. They came to this mining field on their own, didn't they? Nobody dragged them here. "

Danika realized that she'd better just button her lips and change the subject.

"Myrtice, I gotta get the dinner started." She hadn't even considered it, yet, what she'd fix.

Dig out a couple of the pork chops from the lard in the crock? Stir up some red eye gravy?

Myrtice Hester didn't take the hint. She bellyached on until she had unburdened herself, whether it insulted the mining families or not.

****

Fanny Calobi first brought it up when Danika let her outrage at Myrtice Hester's blaspheming leak out. They'd met just outside of the Miners Hall. Danika had taken a cake over for the Red Cross Benefit to help struggling families and the ones who'd suffered mine casualties and were seriously injured.

Fanny brought up the subject first. "What are we going to do with her, Danika? If she isn't hogging up your time, she is bothering me. And what she says? Scandalous!"

"Well," Danika replied, hand on her hip as she shielded her eyes from the sun with the other one. "Wish there was some way we could get her down in a mine, Fanny. That just might do the trick."

Fanny's eyebrows lifted. "Why, Danika, I just thought of something. Myrtice told me that she loves persimmons and here it is October, already. There's a persimmon grove just beyond the Breezy Hill Mine. My uncle Joe Wimler's the Manager in that mine."

"But it's closed due to the strike, isn't it?"

"Uncle Joe opened the mine. According to the law he had to do it if one third of the miners returned. Those and the scabs make it profitable. Machinery's running over there."

Danika pondered the possibilities as they coursed through her brain.

How? What?

"Go on, Fanny, this is interesting, for sure."

"Well, I got a horse and buggy. We could invite Myrtice to hop in and take a ride over to shake one of those trees and gather up some persimmons. They otta be ripe by now, late

October like this. That is if the possums haven't eaten them all by now."

"Yeah. Then what? You suggesting that we visit the mine there? Isn't it closed due to the strike?" Danika stared.

"Well, yes. Mine was closed. But Uncle Joe goes over there and works in the office, filling out reports and stuff." Fanny grinned impishly.

Danika's mind grew dizzy with the possibility.

Really? Could Fanny and she....?

****

Fortunate they were. There stood Myrtice Hester by her mailbox, her feet shifting in the dust, waiting for her ride over to Breezy Hill. Her outlandish orange dress of some kind of crepe with swags and overlay skirt flopped in a southerly wind.

Fanny Calobis sat on the right side of the buggy seat, reins in her hands as Old Dink, the swaybacked sorrel, plodded along. "Giddyup," Fanny hollered, giving Old Dink a slap with the reins.

Danika's shoulders rocked back and forth next to Fanny. They had agreed that she would have to step out and let Myrtice climb up and sit between them in the one-seated buggy. And it would be a tight fit with Danika's bulk.

"There she is, Fanny. Right by her mailbox, standin in those ragweeds."

A cottontail scurried across the dirt road pursued by a mangy hound which had leaped out from under the Haggler's porch.

"Compose yourself, Danika. Let me work out the details." She brought the buggy to a stop at the mailbox. The buggy tipped to the left as Danika disembarked.

"See you got your basket and straw hat, Myrtice." Danika pulled her face together.

"Well, yes. I waited here in the hot sun for twenty minutes." Myrtice's face scrunched into a 'why did you neglect me?' look.

"Sorry, Myrtice. Old Dink is slow. Then I had to drop by Danika's place but there's plenty of time. Rest yourself and enjoy the ride. Blissful day, ain't it, Myrtice," lines in her face struggling to set themselves into a pleasant grin.

"Well, Fanny, I always say, if you're gonna do something, do it, don't dither."

By the time Danika resettled herself, the seat definitely tilted toward the left ditch along the road where wild marigolds still showed their faces through the coal grime and dust.

"Well, let's share some of our recipes." Danika tried to focus upon something constructive, while Fanny kept slapping Old Dink's rump in order to keep him awake.

"I want to get enough to make two pies for the Methodist Ladies' Aid supper coming up next week. I want you to know that my persimmon pie won the blue ribbon at the county fair last year. Yep, it did."

"Well, congratulations, Myrtice, next time save a piece for me," Danika said.

Myrtice leaned outward to be certain she looked into Danika's face. "Would you believe it, Danika, all these tall ragweeds and sunflowers and sumac sticking out into the road. I'll bet I'll have a fit of sneezing. Why doesn't someone call up the county commissioner and tell him we need the weeds mowed? Ain't they any prisoners around here?"

"Well, Myrtice, neither Danika nor I have a telephone. When you go over to Girard next time, march right into the courthouse and give em your mind." Fanny sniffed and guided Old Dink into the narrow road alongside the railroad that led to the Breezy Hill Mine and the persimmon patch behind it.

Yes, there was smoke rising from the stacks. They could hear the thump and rumble of the big steam engine providing power. Fanny's Uncle Joe must have gotten it all stoked up.

He's probably asleep in his chair this time in the afternoon, anyway.

"Would you look at that persimmon grove? Why, Danika, those leaves are such a pretty violet in the sun. Reminds me of the color of the dress I want to wear when I'm all laid out in my coffin." Myrtice gripped her basket handle.

"Well, that's not going to be this afternoon, is it, Myrtice? I'd say, the way you get around town you'll have to wait awhile for that dress." Danika could hardly contain a giggle.

They stepped out of the buggy. Fanny tied Old Dink to a sapling in a shady spot. His legs spread and his head dropped.

"Oh, Danika. Oh, my. Look at these! Big persimmons." Myrtice reached down, snatched one up from the bluegrass, removed the stem and popped it into her mouth.

Myrtice chomped. You could see her tongue circling inside her mouth as she separated the seeds from the flesh. She spat the brown seeds upon the ground. "My, Fanny, that was good. Now you gotta look at them real close. With your eyesight you just might pick up a green one. You know what that's like, don't you?"

Well yes, Danika knew. Just like a spoonful of alum emptied into your mouth.

"Well, I wasn't born yesterday, Myrtice. Get busy filling your basket and Danika and I'll see if we can shake the tree." Fanny marched over to the tree.

An angry jay kept circling and scolding them. They ignored the bird. In a half hour they decided that everyone had gathered enough, both from the ground and those they pulled off the low branches.

"Gotta leave a few for the possums," Danika cautioned.

"Tell you what, " Fanny said. "You keep telling Danika you'd like to go down into a mine shaft sometime, that right, Myrtice?"

Myrtice straightened herself, her face shifted into a half smile. She gripped her basket handle. "Why, Fanny, why, who told you that? Did I say that?"

"Yes you did, Myrtice. And Danika here," she pointed to the stalwart smiling Slavic woman.

"That's right, Myrtice. My husband, Milan, always says, 'ya gotta take your opportunities when they arise.'"

"Well, yes. I wouldn't argue about that, Danika." Myrtice toed the ground with the tip of her shoe. A trail of smoke from the smokestack behind them circled down. They batted the floating soot.

"Well, let's move away from here, Fanny. Get your horse woke up and let's ride over there and have a look inside that colliery." Myrtice glanced over to the mine buildings.

"Na, I'm not disturbing Dink. We can step the few yards over there, Myrtice. Good for us. Ain't we tanked ourselves on persimmons, anyway?" her laugh, sultry.

They sauntered up the rise leading into the mine's main entrance. It was pleasantly cool inside the cavernous building. To the left was the door with the sign, "Manager." Fanny tromped over and rapped loudly. They waited. Myrtice's eyes shifted left, right, then up to the rafters as if she was checking to see if there were any bats anchored upon the ceiling. Scraping and rattling noises erupted to their far right in the sorting room where grimy-looking men sorted through the bituminous coal chunks, sorting it from the brown shale, rocks, and debris to be emptied upon the slag heap.

Uncle Joe finally awakened, opened the door, shifted his pants up, ran a massive hand through his wiry gray hair. Seeing Fanny and the other two women, his face broke into a look of surprise. "Well, I declare? You ain't scabs, are you?"

"No, Uncle Joe. No, we ain't here to ask for work, though I see the mine's operating today. You got scabs on duty, now, huh?"

"Well, yes, Fanny. Strike's been going on for so long, the men needed the work. A third of the men coming back are regulars, though."

"Well, we women rode over here to gather persimmons back of the mine. Fine persimmons but I want to chat with you about a matter. Could I just step inside your office, there?"

"Well, guess you got family business, Fanny. Grandpa die this afternoon or something?"

They were gone for only a few minutes while Danika and Myrtice wandered in a circle in the gloomy interior. The air was saturated with the oily stink of newly dug coal.

"Danika, would you look at that mixture?" Myrtice pointed to a "buggy" (a small mine car) to their left on the tracks. "You'd think the miners would be able to see they dug up a lot of rocks, wouldn't you?"

"That's often the way it is, Myrtice. Blast a seam of coal and load up what falls, you gotta take the rocks and all, sort it out later up here on the sorting table."

"Well, I never...." Myrtice's face tightened into a knot, lips turned down.

Fanny returned, big grin on her face. "Uncle says we can have some time to celebrate our outing right here in the mine, girls. Have a little fun." She sniffed to draw the grin into something genuine.

"Really?" Myrtice leaned forward, shuffling her feet.

"That'd be a real treat, nice afternoon like this. Just what did Uncle Joe suggest, Fanny?" Danika bit her lower lip to keep it from twisting.

"Would you believe? Real opportunity. Since the mine's not fully operating, he suggested that we hop into the cage and take a ride down. Now, wouldn't that be nice?"

"Won't there be too many men down there?"

"Oh, Myrtice, the few men working will be down a long shaft half-a-mile away. Might hear a mule heehaw, little clanging noises. Maybe the echo of a shot."

"Shot -- they going to shoot guns?" Myrtice stared at Danika.

"Just a blast of dynamite, Myrtice. But it'd be far away, wouldn't feel anything but maybe a gust of air."

Myrtice's eyes bugged open. "A gust of air, my goodness, will my skirt..."

"No, Myrtice, your skirt won't fly up." Danika giggled and patted Myrtice's shoulder to steady her.

Danika's sides were shaking by the time the three of them edged into the cage, anchored upon its supporting rails. "Like we said, Myrtice, this is kinda like visiting a museum, isn't it?"

"Well, yeah, well..." Myrtice's hand reached up to twist at her carbide lamp anchored to her forehead. "And these lamps, Danika, ain't they pretty? Why, I never expected to descend into a real coal mine. You do think it's safe?"

Fanny chimed in. "Oh, yes. Not many miners have been killed by a sudden drop of the cage or a cable breaking." She cleared her throat as the cage squeaked and rattled on its guiding rails, descending.

"We want to see what's down there, Myrtice. Wouldn't want you to miss anything." Danika tried to avoid looking at Fanny. Besides, the light was dimming as the cage lowered.

"And those men, will they be there when we get off?"

"No, as I said, they'll be using their picks and heaving coal far away." Danika clasped her hands in front of her as they continued their descent.

"Oh, Fanny. Maybe you otta push a button and stop this. Are you certain you want to see what's at the bottom?" Myrtice's eyes, wide open as a startled cat's.

"Oh, we can't do that. Nope. Manager up there'd think something bad happened and get all upset. His blood pressure, you know." Fanny swiped her mouth with a hand.

The cage hit bottom with a convulsive thud.

"My goodness, don't they ever oil this thing? Cracked my noggin against these rails here."

"No cause to worry, Myrtice. You get your wish today. Not everyone has a chance to get a wish fulfilled."

Fanny took Myrtice's arm and dragged her out of the cage door, quickly as possible before she froze.

"Why, uh. Oh, my. These bluish lights." Myrtice giggled like a girl seating herself in a new outhouse. "Why, uh, - -- Ain't, - oh, my! Well, ladies, I can't see much down here, and I do think it's a little chilly."

"Part of the experience, Myrtice. We need the whole experience, you know. Then you can tell the ladies at the Aid about this outing. Betcha they'll ask you to present a talk."

"You think so, Danika? There was a tremble in Myrtice's voice. One could hear her feet shifing in the gravel and coal particles below her shoe soles.

Then the unexpected. Myrtice Hester's carbide lamp flickered two or three times, then went out.

"Oh, oh, my. Fanny. What's happened?" I can hardly see you women."

Both Danika and Fanny had stepped aside, unloosing their grips upon her, giving Myrtice the space for her "experience" in the mine.

"We're here, Myrtice, on each side of you." Danika's voice had a ghostly echo. "Would you like to take a few steps into one of those tunnels?"

At that point it seemed like a spirit had whispered a message to Fanny and to Danika at the same time. They glanced at each other, their eyes locked. Simultaneously their hands reached up and turned out their carbide lamps.

Eternal night, damp, enveloping inkiness. Witch-cloak blackness. Deeper darkness than midnight, emptied of moon and stars.

Myrtice's scream split the air. The sounds ricocheted and bounced off invisible granite walls and coal seams.

Fanny fumbled for Myrtice's arm so that she wouldn't lose her. Danika grappled until she, too, had a clutch of Myrtice's upper arm, flesh which was jerking spasmodically and trembling like a convert at a Pentecostal meeting.

"We're here, Myrtice. Your light just went out, that's all."

"But yours? You, you --" She panted like a heifer at first calving.

"Part of the experiment, Myrtice. Real museum don't present visitors with fake stuff. You got the real thing. That's why..."

Just then, a few sleeping bats, anchored to the ceiling were startled by the noise. They flapped their viscous wings, emitted shrill cries, and descended in sweeping circles a few feet above their heads.

Danika could feel the air stirred by their whipping wings.

"Eeeeeeeeeee!" Myrtice's voice, that of a specter lost forever in a haunted house."

"What is it? Not bats are they? Ohooooooooo!"

"Don't step away too far, Myrtice. We wanna keep together." Danika reached up and turned on her carbon lamp. There stood Myrtice, feet stomping in a circle like an Osage Indian doing a war dance, arms flailing above her head. When Danika saw how far Myrtice had actually wandered, she felt a touch of apprehension. Shame and guilt below it.

"Do you want to walk further, down that tunnel there?"

"Don't ask me any more questions, Danika, I can't see your 'tunnel there.'"

"Then you ready to go, Myrtice? Or do you wanna stay here and meditate about it awhile?"

"Where's that cage contraption? Are we far from it? Oh, God help me! Them bats up there, ain't they poisonous?"

"Over, here," Danika said. She grabbed for Myrtice's arm, turning her so she would be facing the open cage.

By then Danika found out that her lamp was working after all. She shoved Myrtice onto the cage platform. "Where's the switch, Fanny, or are we gonna have to holler to have Uncle Joe turn it on up there?"

Fanny's hand reached across and shoved a button. The cage door rattled shut and they began the ascent, cage wobbling, pulleys groaning above them.

Myrtice was silent most of the journey back to Franklin. She sat with her head thrust out into the sunlight and her knees hunched up in front of her, basket of persimmons clutched by white-knuckled fingers.

"Giddayup, Dink." Fanny slapped the reins on Dink's dusty rump and the buggy rolled along. "Well, Myrtice, I'll bet you'll give the best talk at the Ladies Aid program that they've ever had on your visit to the coal mine." She dared not look at Danika.

"Yes, I think you should write your relatives about it and tell everybody about how you got your wish. Not everyone gets to go down into a coal mine." Danika's face, frozen as a slab of salt pork left outside on a zero day.

Myrtice descended from the buggy and staggered across the road ditch, wobbling on toward home without once looking back.

Dink moved on as Fanny jostled her reins. "I can tell you what she's gonna do, once she gets home."

"What's that, Fanny?"

"Well, her husband left quite a few quarts of Bourbon whiskey in their cellar. She's gonna knock the cap offa one and pour herself a good half cup to settle her nerves, that's what."

Danika's shoulders rocked as they clopped along. She then remembered the Bible reading from Father Pompeney's own mouth two Sunday's ago:

"Sufficient unto the day is the evil thereof."

CHAPTER NINETEEN

Father Pompeney

Father Joseph Pompeney rose at his usual five o'clock. Glancing out of his stark window toward the east he could see the morning light, traced by an invisible finger. The trilling of a songbird echoed through the half-opened window.

After his usual libations, shaving, and donning his garments, he reached for his cassock, which he would later, at the hour of morning mass, exchange for his alb and stole in order to serve holy communion.

He expected only a few, even though the people of his parish were oppressed with cares and woes almost too heavy to bear. Faces ever before him: the hollow-eyed children and crying babies; the trail of toddlers clinging to their mother's skirts; eyes filled with pleas for nurturing and something to stifle their hunger due to the seemingly endless strike.

Dear Jesus, how much water can a poor soul put into a stew pot and still call it soup?

Then, too, the men. Maybe a third of the miners had returned to their dungeon-like conditions, some to be demeaned by callous overseers, others consistently under the influence, so to speak.

He could not overlook the anger building up. An explosive air grew stronger as the laborers drifted back to the shafts. With this danger, there lurked the real possibility of rupture within the various tribes and tongues.

Difficult enough to weave the fabric of community with folks of the same ethnic background. But in this town, a dozen or more nationalities faced the confusion of language usage and the changing terms and conditions ordered by union bosses, executives, and politicians.

He'd recognized the growing rift, a chasm ever-deepening as the strike continued and more and more miners who could not look upon the drawn faces of their children, grabbed their picks and shovels and trudged back into the pitch-black caverns. Who could blame them?

The community was fragmenting.

Oh, Jesus, who will save them?

Compassion pressed at his heart as he stared into faces of pathetic men who'd gathered behind buildings and in basements to roll dice in crap games; faces unshaven, bodies emitting the sour smells of the unwashed. The paltry surveillance by the sheriff or his marshals troubled him. Sure, he knew the reason why. They were afraid of the knife-flashers, the angry, hot tempered eager-to-fight aliens, an air fostered by the governor of the state himself.

O Lord Jesus, the pleas and confessions of their women.

At times he had to stop the mumbling words and wait in silence for the Spirit of God to bolster him.

"Father, he knocked me off the back porch."

"Father, he is so tired of eating roots and greens. He threw my only stew pot into the weeds in the back yard."

"Oh, Father, how do I deal with the drunkenness?"

The latter plea, most usually, whispered by a hunched penitent with blackened eyes and hair half hanging down her back. Bruises on her arms, hands wringing in unbearable anxiety.

And, their bodies. Human bodies, their ever-challenging hit-and-miss struggles with their baser urges and drives. How many times, Oh, Lord?

The young female confessor. "Father I have sinned. It was my first time. I knew it was a sin but I was so lonely.

And now, *this*...," the penitent breaking into an uncontrolla-
ble sobbing.

At times he wanted to scream: "Jesus, where is Jesus?"

And so, he prayed for pity. Prayed for a heart filled with
love, not judgment. Sometimes he slipped from his tiny seat
in the confessional to kneel and pray and weep, and offer
forgiveness and merciful penance.

In the morning light, Father Pompeney fell to his knees
upon an old prie-deu given to him by a kindly bishop in his
younger years. In his rugged hands, he held his beads as he
began his morning prayers.

He made the sign of the cross: "In the name of the
Father, and of the Son, and of the Holy Spirit...."

They flashed before him as he prayed, the face of the
crazy drone called "Old Lady Bob," pleading for him to
reveal the time for her to fly.

The sweating, hairy and harried giant who could barely
fit into the confessional booth, fumes from his home-made
brew drifting through the lattice.

"Father, I poured white lightning into the partition of my
lunch pail where we carry our water. We have to carry our
own water, you know. I spiked it heavily, Father, a good
healthy dose. I set the charge, Father, and when it come time
for me to light the fuse, the charge exploded and Bussel
Hitchcox was blasted against a bench and I think he's gonna
be addled the rest of his days....."

There was a boy of tender age who had discovered a fire
in his own body members and was confused and embar-
rassed and threatened to drown himself in an old strip mine
if....

"Oh, Father, tell me what to do...is it sin?"

The father of six children who wept on his knees. "I
need her, Father. She removed herself from my bed in order
that we not...you know what... I lost control and dragged her
into the back yard in the middle of the night and I guess
you'd have to say that I..." And the account of what he'd done
was not repeatable.

Other venial sins erupted from the penitents squeezed into the cramped quarter, pleading for mercy and not to be regarded as straw to be cast out and burned.

Last of all a big-boned woman of Slavic descent, named Danika Cratnick. She breathed heavily, the smell of fried mush upon her. He could feel the trembling of her body as she unloaded her burden.

"Father, I, I, I tricked an old loudmouthed woman. I set her up, Father. I managed by deceit to crowd her into a mine cage. Me and another woman left her to wander about in the dark at the bottom of the mine. Oh, forgive me, Father. I took pleasure in it..."

"Is there something else, my daughter?

"Yes, Father. Yes. My own beautiful daughter works where she is exposed to the lusts of her employer. She's a nice girl and I don't know what to do, but I can tell something happened and I hate him. I hate the man, Father."

On and on the confessions erupted, onslaughts upon his spirit as well as his ears. Six confessors that morning. Then, after he had time to compose himself and put on his cincture and surplice he'd step forth for the morning mass.

The prayers would flow from his lips and the congregates, few in number this day, would mumble their pleas and entreaties. He would pray and lift the chalice.

"As we prepare to celebrate the mystery of Christ's love, let us acknowledge our failures and ask the Lord for pardon and strength."

And the shabby, straggle-haired people responded in broken dialects: "I confess to almighty God and to you, my brothers and sisters, that I have sinned through my own fault, in my thoughts and in my words...In what I have done, and in what I have failed to do..."

Such was the portion of the life of a priest, one serving under the call of God. This morning it was the full measure of his strength, soul and body, extending itself for his people.

"You bring pardon and peace to the sinner."

The broken voices of the penitents: "Lord, have mercy."

James D. Yoder

And as the truth of life resided among the people, there also lay mercy. Mercy toward one another. Shared kindnesses. Forgiveness for their sins against each other, for they knew they were the downtrodden, the prodigals. They remembered a Father's call, but not all of them knew how to rise and go home.

CHAPTER TWENTY

Old Dutch Cleanser Rocks

Neda had finished removing three heavy leaves from the massive table, resting them against the arm of an upholstered chair. Next she heaved the heavy boards, one by one, toting them to a storage closet off the kitchen pantry, her back aching, her fingers strained.

A part of her felt like whistling as she shoved the table halves together and reached for the Scottish Lace tablecloth. She gave it a unfurling shake then dragged it over the fine-grained wood, stepping hither and yon around the table to center M'Lady's table linen perfectly. She reached for the Autumn Elegance doily and anchored it in the center, smoothing out the edges. Next, she replaced the polished brass two-and-a-half-foot-high candelabra.

Now where did Ophelia say I should look for the new candles?

She began to doubt if she'd finish all the work by five o'clock. Already her neck had broken out with perspiration.

Swing music swirling through the room from the spanking new cabinet radio inspired a zip within her spirits. She swung her dust cloth in a rhythmic beat.

What was that tune? "It's Gotta be Love"?

Once in awhile she allowed herself the liberty of hiking a calf in the fashion of the Charleston but she realized she mustn't be sidetracked.

Matt coming tonight to take me for a drive after work.

At the recall of his name, her lips spread in a smile, a warmth filled her breast as his name bounced into her mind, bringing a cleaning maid comfort and encouragement.

Since the strike, Matt was working five days a week at the Frontenac bakery. Kneading dough. Flattening dough with his fist and palm. Pitching dough. Watching dough bloat in big tubs. She wondered if it was a calling he'd follow through with.

However, he'd surprised her by telling her that he had sallied down to Pittsburg to that college and enrolled for the second semester. Well, with the energy he displayed, he'd be like a fired-up steam engine with a fully-opened throttle. Hadn't dropped the boxing lessons, either.

The music changed to Jelly Roll Morton on his coronet playing *The Kansas City Stomp*. Neda couldn't help but stop her work, kick up her heels, throw out her chapped hands and shake her bottom.

Sure good thing Ophelia Otis is over in Chanute today. St. Barbara above! Old Otis himself off somewhere, too. Probably climbing the carpeted steps of Millicent's bawdy house down the street from where I used to work. Yeah, that'd be like Harvey Otis, for sure. Maybe St. Barbara would send down one of her famous flashes of lightning.

She swished her hips and hopped until she looked through the kitchen door and saw that she still had that floor to mop and M'Lady had expressly said in her whiny voice, "Now, Neda, this time I want you to scrub the baseboards."

She headed for what she called the "slop room" with its beastly trough-of-a sink that wouldn't scour white, no matter how much she poured on the scouring powder and blistered her fingers.

She began to sweat heavily, realizing that she'd fallen behind in her work.

Down on her knees on the floor she swirled and shifted her brush, arms aching. She raced for a mop to finish, a bucket of soapy water dragging down one shoulder.

She thought of her life and where it was going. She'd made an appearance at the Woolworth Five and Dime in Pittsburg but the old biddy there surveyed her from top to bottom through her pince-nez glasses, pinching her nose.

"No, hon, we have a full staff here now, and I'd need references, anyway. Do you have a letter of recommendation from a former employer?" Her look, haughty as a red tailed hawk's sitting on a fence post.

By the time she finally glanced out the western bay window upstairs, she saw that it was getting along toward four o'clock and she still had to put the sheets on one more bed, a high one where she'd have to step up upon a stool to reach across.

Just when she had tucked in the bottom corner of the sheet, she sensed a presence. Now what? Her head swiveled to the right.

She only saw a shadow on the floor. Even before she turned, a man's hand closed around her mouth. She kicked backwards. She jerked her body. She tried to reach his face with her free arm until suddenly he'd bound it to her side with his own muscled arm.

Harvey Otis's chuckles and hot body made her shiver.

Dear Lord, how am I....?

He'd released her mouth and grabbed her around the waist, holding her on the bed.

"Shhh, now. Shhh. Don't want to raise the neighbors. We got this time completely to ourselves. With one hand, Harvey dragged a green bill out of his pocket, flashed it in front of her eyes, and laid it upon the lamp table beside the bed.

"Ya see this, darlin? Not every gal in your situation gets to take a look at and pocket a hundred dollar bill. Now, how about a little kiss?"

When she finally could turn her eyes fully upon his face, she saw that it was flushed, cheeks red from excitement and expensive Scotch. *Or, was it Bourbon this time?*

Neda tried to scream as he pressed her down onto the bed. "You're a feisty little filly, didn't I tell you that you and I could have real fun together? Hush your screaming, nobody's gonna hear from this side of the house and the sheriff's over in Girard today. Honey, we got the next hour and the whole room to ourselves."

****

Matt Enrico's trainer, Buddy Polsak, stepped aside in the practice ring. Matt grinned, knowing that Buddy was more than pleased with the foot work of his new trainee.

"The best in Pittsburg," he'd heard Buddy brag to a colleague, standing by the ropes.

Matt relished his training and, like kneading dough in Frontenac, he gave it his best blows. Today he'd worked standing in front of the punching bag for a good twenty minutes, swinging until the sweat rolled down his sides. Lean, dark-skinned and fast, Matt concentrated upon his pounding until his arms ached.

He was smart enough to know that in the ring "avoid a dogfight." That is only a distraction.

Work on one's jab. Always stick to a game plan and never change.

An opponent, becoming confused with the steady and fast punches, often changed his plan, lost his rhythm, and usually lost the fight.

"Never stand in one place," Matt had told himself. He practiced another forty minutes with the jumping rope, then switched to the medicine balls, all in the process of building up his body core, trunk, arms, legs, and shoulders.

He had become "fast with his jab." Especially his swift right hook that caught the unwary opponent under his chin.

"Crack em with a good right hook," was his motto. And, Matt kept in mind, keep smiling, it confuses the challenger.

He had showered after his practice and donned his cord pants and chambray shirt. He hurried out to his Tin Lizzie, reached in to set the throttle, grabbed the crank and, with his muscled arm, hardly felt the resistance of the motor turning over.

The tiny motor shuddered with its "put-put chickalaka, put-put chickalaka" sounds, echoing across the roadsides on his way back to Franklin. He began to whistle, thinking of his blond beauty as he guided the frail car past the deep green of the Osage Orange hedges, steering clear of the ditch on his left.

Tonight they'd visit the park down in Scammon where, under the shade of a giant oak, he planned to give her the little package with the amber necklace nestled within.

He began to sing that new Al Jolson song,

"Let me sing a funny song/ with crazy words that roll along/. And if my song can start you laughing...."

The October late evening glowed with shadows cast by the sun, motes beaming through the hedges and into the western fields.

A perfect evening just for "Me and My Gal."

He guided the Lizzy down the slab past The Company Store. A couple of miner's wives, their steps dispirited, dresses hanging like worn sacks, stopped to stare with haunted eyes as he shimmied by.

The Lizzie bounced as he guided it onto the street where the Otis mansion loomed. Neda had told him she'd be ready, soon after four. He guided the car past the arborvitae into the driveway, coasting toward the back and the "servants" entrance.

As soon as he'd turned off the ignition switch he heard a wail.

An animal caught somewhere? A cat fight?

Next, he heard a piercing scream, high-pitched and wobbly, followed by a muffled crash.

Neda? Was it Neda?

He leaped from the Ford without any conscious thought, his body smooth, automatic, his steps rapid leaps until he grabbed the handle of the back screen door, nearly tearing it from its hinges.

He bumped a kitchen work table sending a couple of pots scattering as his legs, without breaking rhythm, found the servant's staircase. At the top landing he saw the heavy bedroom door.

Closed. Probably locked.

"Stop it! Didn't I tell you no? Get out of here."

Another scream.

Matt's shoulder hit the door. Flesh and bone thudded against the varnished door, but it hadn't moved. He backed up a few paces, this time throwing the full weight of his body against the oaken wood, it splintered and flew open.

A bug-eyed Harvey Otis turned to stare at the intruder.

Matt's eyes caught on Neda, crouching behind the left side of the bed, holding her torn dress together at her neck. Her face, pale, eyes bulging.

"You little upstart. Get out of this house, who do you think you...?"

Before Harvey could mouth "you are?" he felt the electric punch of Matt's upper right on his cleft chin. Otis staggered, nearly losing his footing.

"You Italian idiot. What do you think..."

Otis struggled to gain his posture, threw back his torso, chin up, eyes narrow angry lines. He drew a right fist, catching Matt with a glancing blow on the side of his face. Matt staggered, dukes up.

He pivoted, regained his balance. Before Otis could draw back for another blow, Matt's doubled fist caught him squarely on the chin. He went down with a "plomp." Out cold upon the floor. The oriental vase on the shelf to the right crashed, shattering, as Otis fell.

Matt leaped to Neda's side, lifting her to his chest. She clung, weeping and silent. Her body gathering itself, shivering in broken-rhythm.

Together they made their flight down the stairs. The Bon Ami can spilled a gritty streak upon the expensive carpet, like an old dog who'd lost bowel control. Its companion, old lady Dutch Cleanser, rocked drunkenly upon the floor from the aftershocks.

CHAPTER TWENTY-ONE

Growing Dread Clouded His Heart

Toma lay curled in bed due a sore throat, fever, and a hacking cough, which Milan prayed wouldn't turn into pneumonia. He shook his head at the memory of the scores of marches to the cemetery couple of years back in '18, when thousands of poor souls all over the world died. Thirty four thousand folks. So many dying that the children made up songs.

How did that go?

I had a little bird
His name was Enza.
I opened the window,
And in flu-Enza!

Danika had made a mustard plaster for Toma's chest which stank up the room. Next she stoked up the kitchen stove with a shovelful of coal to keep him warm.

Milan's steps led him to the Davis farm, the smells of late autumn mixing with the drift of smoke from a coal collier south of town.

At the farm he'd grasp the corn knife and tackle the Osage Orange hedge marking the western edge of the pasture. Unless the tough growth was trimmed regularly with the swinging knife, the limbs would fight their way into the sky, hard as iron. In due season they'd drop croquet-ball-sized hedge apples upon the pasture, and as farmer Davis said, "flatten my cow's bags flatter than an old woman's purse during a depression" if his Holsteins gulped down the green knobby apples.

Milan's mind circled as he planted one weathered shoe ahead of the other. He drew his denim jacket, to which Danika had stitched on two new patches, closer to his chest.

Frost glistened on the fuzzy mullein leaves. He could hear the thuds of his run-over-heeled shoes, his walking rhythm triggering the wanderings of his mind. He marched past leaning sunflower stalks, most of their petals having already dropped, exposing the hard brown seed heads. Finches hopped, and meadowlarks flitted from stalk to stalk.

A growing dread crowded his heart and seeped into his brain, the same dread that spread poison among his miner companions. Their work, always hit-and-miss. Bowed down by servility, and unable to talk about it. Ears dulled by the barks and harangues of labor leaders. John L. Lewis's shenanigans. Henry Allen's school-girl flitters. Even their own Alec Howatt's nose-thumbing at Attorney General Hopkins only made things worse.

When thinking of his fellow miners like Perry Burgar or Arne, he realized that few of them ever had more education beyond the second or third grade. Many who couldn't read depended upon their wives to puzzle out how to exist on their meager company script.

Neda's job at the Otis place finished. Now she sings like a canary fresh out of its cage. And that Matt Enrico fellow? Italians in Frontenac are hard-working people. Most of them owning their own homes. Stripe above the rest of us beaten-down mules.

He thought of the floppy-eared half-donkeys in the gloomy, damp mines. Stable, seemingly content with their lot, though they never saw the light of day in the constant seventy-degree temperature.

Groomed and well-fed by three miners who were assigned to their care, the hennies and mules fared better than their masters. They had their second feeding at the end of a morning drag of pulling loaded buggies (coal carts) and scoops, filled with rocks, shale, and newly fallen debris. Hooked by a doubletree to a stack of fallen shoring timbers, one hefty pull and they'd done their job.

Course the miners all stank of mule and mule dung which would have to be scraped up and shoveled behind a shelf of rocks somewhere, the smell of their piss lingering wherever it splashed.

Good mules. Easier to work with than horses and even some of the men. Stronger, less given to complaint, that is, if they were treated right. Loyal beyond a best buddy when they'd singled out the miner kindest to them. Several miners had their own "pet" mule who'd nuzzle their necks, causing them to turn and pat their mossy noses and lips.

When Danika told him why Neda quit her job, he'd have marched over and knocked Harvey Otis's block off himself and rolled it like a billiard ball down the steps into the parlor, but he held himself back. Knew he'd just be shoving a row of dominoes, bringing on never-ending consequences which would be taken out on the miners' hides.

A part of him felt hangdog and helpless as if he needed to find the energy to drag a sand rock over the voices of accusation:

Am I a coward? Do I have to admit that miners are more helpless than brute mules? Am I betraying my family by not taking justice in my own hands?

Going to the sheriff? What a laugh. Hadn't Matt Enrico taken care of the situation for him? Knocking old Otis cold? Young man, involved in boxing lessons. Who would have thought of it? A regular Jack Dempsey.

Course Sheriff Gould knew where the political power lay, the pay-offs and under-the-table deals.

Matt enrolling in college, too. Well, the young'uns do find their way, don't they?

He hated it. The times when they buttoned their lips and swallowed their gore. Despised it when insults were hurled

and they felt beaten down like slaves upon a plantation
ninety years ago.

Have we really grown so powerless?

"Yas, Massa. You'se right, Massa."

Milan's mouth watered. Sure, he'd liked to have forked
one more slice of cornbread, dipping the end of it in red-eye
gravy this morning but he knew that Toma needed it.

One egg for himself as the hens were into their off
season. He and Danika debated, with the lengthening strike,
whether or not to coop them up for the winter or butcher
them next week, can them and shelve the jars in the root
cellar to help them through the winter.

Guess it depended upon when the strike ended. Worried
him that about half of the miners had returned, bent over,
dragging their heels, whipped before they even sank a pick
into a black coal seam.

Milan, though, believed in his budding children.

*Neda soon old enough to marry. Heard her talking
about enrolling in college,too. Think of it! How can I stretch
my brain around that? Well, that beats working at a greasy
spoon restaurant.*

What was it she mentioned? Art? Clothes designer?

He'd cut his dark eyes over at her in the evening in the
kerosene lamplight, watching her scan some cast-off
newspaper or magazine given to her by Mrs. Otis. Her eyes
locked upon an advertisement of women's dresses, the way
they hung; the sashes, the uneven hems, all that women stuff
that changed so quickly, men like him could only sit back
and ponder. She'd take a flattened piece of a brown paper
bag and pencil an exact copy of the dress featured in the ad,
the model's face, body, legs, shoes, everything.

Sure, he liked to see a well-dressed woman stepping
along a sidewalk down in Pittsburg, head silhouetted by one
of those broad-brimmed hats, lifting her arm to hold it in
place in a stiff wind, gauzy dress plastered against her
breasts.

Course that was another thing. Women of these times didn't own them properly, their breasts. Tying em down with bands so's they could slip into those ugly sack-like dresses, swing their beads, galoshes unbuttoned, flaps flopping. Men whistling and calling them "flappers" while they lusted, and grinned at one another, joking with each other about how far they'd have to reach to snatch their whiskey flasks.

Yep. Father Pompeney's ears surely burned when one of the miners was bold enough to squeeze into that little confessional box and spill his guts.

Lust. Wasn't that one of the big sins?

Milan turned into the Davis lane which was outlined by a wire fence anchored to sturdy hedge posts. Here and there milkweed stalks bobbed in the wind; pods emptied of their seeds exposed their silvery linings. He could hear the honking of a flock of Canada geese heading southward high above, flying toward the *Verdigris River* over west.

CHAPTER TWENTY-TWO

"Yeah, What If?"

At the Joe and Mary Skubitz home in Ringo, Mary emptied the last of her wheat flour, mixing it with some shortening and water. She rolled the dough out upon the enameled cabinet top, preparing to make noodles to stew with the chopped onions and a half-dozen chicken livers. She hummed, then began to sing the words of that new song she'd heard on the radio down at the Company Store:

"There's nothing surer, the rich get richer and the poor get poorer."

Well ain't that the truth?

She reached for her rolling pin and began to roll out the mixture. Mary worked swiftly, grabbing a knife, she began to slice the dough into narrow strips which she'd leave on the counter to dry, then toss them into the bubbling broth on the stove.

Sure. the Skubitz family was better off than many of the other coal camp folks. Gotten their sled runners under themselves and accomplished enough to think about buying an abandoned coal shack close by and have it moved smack up against her own hen-house-style house, and bless Pat, if she wouldn't have three extra rooms.

Actually she could take in a boarder for increased income when Joey left for college, but he was still struggling with geometry over in Gerard High School. He hadn't decided upon college, yet, and they'd have to figure out some way to pay for at least part of the tuition.

Scrape up a little extra to get him some proper clothes and a suitcase. Something beside pasteboard.

Don't want to whistle onto a college campus with a pasteboard suitcase in your hand, for sure. Forget about the coonskin coat.

Mary glanced into her tiny living room, admiring her oval braided rug on the floor and the angelwing begonia blooming pink in the east window. Proud, too, of the upright piano on the west wall, a few framed family pictures resting on the top of a white lace-trimmed runner she'd crocheted last summer.

Think of it. Her own boy a piano player.

Course some of the neighbor women in Frontenac talked about her extravagance behind her back, but who cared? Jealousy was no respecter of persons. For herself, she had to hold it back from time to time when her neighbor, Beulah Butler, got herself one of those perculating coffee pots.

But when Joey played the neighbors listened. Joey could bring folks out on the front steps when he played *Yes We Have No Bananas*. And she actually saw that dreamy-eyed single woman across the street raise her arms and take a swirl or two on her porch when Joey played The Blue Danube. Shame, though the way she disgraced herself the evening he zipped out *"I Wish That I Could Shimmy."*

Those days were almost over, now, with the prolonged strikes. Seems like since 1919 folks could no longer take ahold, times so tough.

Course, the piano made her front room floor sag, but that was a small matter since Joey had already been asked to play for the dance over at Capaldo. Earn a whole dollar-and-seventy-five cents. Think of it!

The noodles boiled in her Dutch oven. She stirred them around with a wooden spoon.

While her supper cooked, she sank into a rocking chair and picked up her crocheting. Working on a long antimacassar for the new horsehair couch she hoped to buy someday. She'd already decided she'd want a wine-colored

James D. Yoder

couch. Put the crochet work away in the small trunk in the bedroom, waiting for better times.

Her mind wandered.

Alec Howat over in Columbus in jail. How that man has suffered, paying the price for all of them.

Mary wondered about John L. Lewis and what he was up to these days.

She thought about neighbor men, sneaking back to the mines. Well, not actually sneaking, since the mine owners had ordered it. Those orders and the gnawing stomachs of their families sent them staggering up the grit-laden road, gripping their lunch buckets, probably holding little more than water and lard sandwiches.

What could the women do? Any woman who can have a baby ain't powerless.

No, she'd aligned herself with the Socialists and hoped to help level things out. No problem with that. Spent extra time talking with that Mary Heaton Vorse, didn't she? Mother Jones, too. That old lady could stoke a fire in the belly.

She chuckled thinking about Alec Howat at that debate months ago with that big cheese John P. White stumbling over himself and losing his way up against Alec.

Ended up looking like a possum hunting a tree limb, didn't he?

Then her mind caught on Danika Cratnick, Slavic woman like herself. Big boned. Sturdy woman.

Why, I remember Ma telling me that in the peasant village in the old world, the Slavic women could even pull plows.

That Danika surely interested in settin things right or she wouldn't have met that time over in Arma when Vorse gave her speech.

Maybe she and I should spend more time together. Nickel or a dime to take a trolley over to Franklin. Big bunch of miners' wives wringing their hands in desperation over there.

What if...? Yeah, what if?

170

CHAPTER TWENTY THREE

Tragedy in Mulberry

Milan had hesitations about going to the event in Mulberry at the Buche's. He, however, knew that, with his low spirits, it might be a good thing to jar loose, forget about his troubles and mingle with friends. Still, there was a nagging part of him that resisted. Even to think of a get-together in these times seemed "off" to him.

But, who knew?

"We need a break, Milan," Danika still had on her church dress. She anchored her old knitted hat upon her head. He could see that it pleased Danika to have an opportunity to swing up on the trolley and rock over to Mulberry to Perry and Agnes Buche's place. Of course he anticipated that the men would cluster in the back yard and play boccie. He was certain, too, that they would blow off steam about the conditions in the mining communities.

Danika mentioned that the Lewis and Loretta Grinaldo would be there to share the comradeship. Course there'd be another couple, at least, to keep the game balanced. Enough men to kick up their heels, while the women sat in the shade and sipped iced tea, catching up on lean-time recipes.

Be plenty of home-brewed beer to loosen things up for the men. Drag out a jug, too, in all probability. Milan didn't doubt that.

Still, a part of him held back. "Danika, I'm not sure that we otta go. I try not to talk about the strike and the miners'

James D. Yoder

problems with other people around here, at least not fellows I don't know very well."

"We wouldn't be going for a quarrel about Howat or John Lewis, Milan, and the Buche place isn't exactly public. Agnes is an old friend of mine from back in my Illinois days. We'll stay away from hot topics. Had enough wrangling over politics, strikes, and company store managers cheating everybody."

Milan, sensing how much it would mean to Danika, donned a freshly scrubbed pair of cord pants that weren't too frayed at the cuffs, noting the slackness at his waist when he reached for a worn belt. His arms slid into the denim shirt sleeves. He tucked in the tails and tightened the belt in a hole closer to the buckle.

Well, you can't fatten a hog on peanut shells.

Milan eased into the trolley seat as they rolled along eastward toward Mulberry. He'd always admired the way the hills rose up and the character of the land as they approached the Missouri border. He noted the last of the late October leaves and the dull redness of the oaks contrasting with the yellow leaves of the hickories. The dogwood embedded under the oaks along the tracks splashed a flashy red, leaves shuddering in the wind. The sumac, too, abundant this year, displayed reddish-brown heads, marking their importance as they poked at their window. The trolley rattled across a trestle over a creek. He noted that, here, the water rolled over the stones below, rippling and clear.

He was aware that Danika had relaxed. Her chapped hands were folded in her lap, a half smile graced her broad face. Her soft flesh overlapped, warming his side.

He could imagine Danika picking out a little knoll with just the right trees, limbs curving in an interesting twist, pondering something like: "Wouldn't it be pure heaven to have a little white house right there?"

Soothing, after all, the ride together. He reached over and took Danika's hand in his.

172

The Buche place was only two blocks up the street from the trolley stop. Together they stepped up the sandstone sidewalk. A couple of mangy dogs barked as they passed. In spite of the morning frost, a few dandelions thrust yellow blossoms upward.

They saw the Buche place ahead, a building much like their own miner's house, thrown together so that it could be quickly knocked down, pitched upon a freight car, and hauled off to a new location.

Milan noted that Perry Buche had tried to slap a little white paint or whitewash upon the front of the house but the dreary gray boards, studded with knotholes, showed through, an ever reminder of a miner's status.

Gray, like our skin. Black-edged, like our fingernails, if we are fortunate enough to still have five fingers on a hand.

****

Sure enough, boccie in the back yard.

A tickle of nervous energy raced up Milan's back.

He tried not to show his surprise at seeing the Buche's had invited the Cassaletto brothers. Memories of their rough edges, bottle-tipping, and outlandish hoots, flashed through his mind as he recalled their backyard visit at his place couple months back.

They'd separated into two teams. Milan, Albert Casseletto, and Perry Buche on one team. Gabriel Anderson, Luigi Cassaletto, and Lewis Grinaldo on the other. The native bluegrass backyard was still green; the October air, refreshing.

Milan had tossed the wooden ball called the "jack" (boccino). It rolled near the end of the court. The teams took their turns, one at a time in their attempts to throw their balls (four) as close to the jack as possible and win points for their team. At the end of the first game, Milan's team scored, having all four balls closest to the jack, thus scoring one point for each of their balls.

They joked. Shoved each other's shoulders. Looked up into the blue sky at the huge V, shaped by a flock of Canada geese, headed to warmer climes. Their honks drifted toward them, carried by the wind.

Milan glanced over toward the mimosa tree and the gathering of the six women on the back porch. His heart warmed, seeing Danika sitting there, chuckling, slapping her thigh, trying not to spill her tea as the women "got into things."

She was right all along. This is good for us.

Perry Buche approached Milan to get his opinion regarding an unusually large hackberry tree that was leaning at the back of his yard. They pondered the whys and wherefores of the problems of cutting it down as it did shade their garden and sap the ground of nutrients and water.

Milan and Perry were interrupted byAlbert Casseletto, stubbly-faced, one jaw sagging, due to a generous tobacco cud. Albert shoved himself into their conversation, wrinkles lining his forehead.

"Hey, Cratnick," Albert gave Milan's shoulder a push. "August Findly, down at the pool hall in Franklin told me you're spreading tales about me."

Now what?

Startled, Milan turned, his mouth half open He stepped back a pace.

Albert trying to get me into trouble? Haven't my lips been sealed? Why would folks in Mulberry accuse me of spreading tales?

His mind raced back over recent conversations and the miners he'd met. It hooked upon absolute zero. "Why, Albert, I don't know what you're talking about."

Cassaletto trying to stir up trouble? I warned Danika....

Suddenly Albert's muscled grip clasped his shoulder, spinning Milan around.

Now what? This man digging for a fight?

Perry Buche, startled by Albert's crude intervention, stepped toward Albert. "Albert, this isn't the place to..."

Before Perry could utter more intervening words, he, too, received a blunt shove from Albert's paw; Albert's eyes, red, narrowed.

Milan suddenly realized that he was the object of Albert's belligerence and frustration, real or not.

Singled out.

Now, what'll I do? Not a brawl in this backyard, Danika and those other women sitting there?

To make matters worse, Albert's brother, Luigi, spat his tobacco cud, swiped his unshaven chin with the butt of his hand and loped up, shoving his face into Milan's. His breath, hot and sour.

They've been drinking bootleg before Danika and I got here.

Milan attempted to step aside. He stumbled. He braced muscles in his legs when he felt a sudden twitch. To his confusion both Cassaletto brothers crowded him. He could smell the stink of rank sweat.

"We've taken our break," Milan called out, trying to focus upon all the players. "Let's get started on the second game."

His attempt at a grin faltered.

Albert ignored his words and continued pecking him, thumping him in the chest with a dirty forefinger. "You're one of them Dagos can't keep their lips buttoned. Can't trust a Dago, either. Just like Gypsies. Hafta watch your chickens," his sneer, accompanied by a braying laugh.

"I'd say we got us a *chicken* right here," his brother hawked.

Milan turned and stared Albert fully in his bleary eyes. "Look here, Albert, I don't want any trouble. No trouble at all. You've been hitting the bottle, I can tell. Why don't you just take a walk?"

Milan turned, his hands had a new tremble but he threw his boccie ball to establish the position of the jack for the second round of the game.

Gabriel Anderson, a man of medium height, followed suit, his ball missing the jack by a couple of feet.

Luigi Cassaletto socked a heavy brogue beside Milan's. "Listen, you low-down-dog, you goin around insultin my brother? If he says you blabbed about him behind his back, then you did, fer as I'm concerned." His uncivil shove sent Milan stumbling, falling face forward over Gabriel's blue ball.

When Milan struggled to his feet, humiliated, heart pounding, he glanced over at the porch. The women were all standing. Danika's hand had crept over her mouth. She stared, eyes wide open.

Here I am being shamed before my wife and all these men. What on ...?

Albert, who'd marched forward to stand beside Luigi, struck at him, missing his chin by a hair's breadth.

"Albert, if you don't' back off, I'm going to throw this boccie ball right at you. I said, back off!"

Milan realized the words had rushed out without his caution holding them back. His blood rose in heat. His heart thumped. He could feel the sweat on his neck and forehead.

"Now fellas," Perry Buche intervened, "stop this! We don't want no trouble here at our place, and we sure don't want the sheriff coming out here."

Hearing this, the half-sotted Albert sneered, "Shut up, Perry. You a pussy too, and besides, who'd be afraid of a fella named Perry, anyway?" His laugh, diabolic.

Albert Cassaletto lurched toward Milan again, arms extended, a fist balled, sneer twisting his face. Milan drew back his arm and threw the ball toward him.

The ball missed.

The four game colleagues stood frozen in their shoes.

Why had Albert Cassaletto turned into such a devil?

The players stared in shock as Albert's hand reached inside a dirty-edged pocket, grasping. When the hand emerged, their eyebrows arched. They stepped back.

No! Not a gun?

Albert leered, lips turned downward, his face, satanic.

Three of the players yelled. Lewis Grinaldo started running toward Albert Cassaletto to shove him aside but didn't make it before there was a blast from the pistol. Milan Cratnick staggered backward, his hands thrust into the air. An acrid smell of gunpowder drifted.

Crows, settled upon a dead tree limb on the other side of Buche's garden, flopped up, cawing rakishly. The October wind grew colder. A dark-bottomed cloud crept over the sun.

By this time Danika lumbered off the porch, her thudding lurches leading her toward Milan. Perry Buche reached her before she made it, grabbing her around the waist. "No, Danika. This is too dangerous, you must..."

"He's shot." Danika's eyes focused upon Milan's chest where the shirt stained red.

Milan swiveled, leaping toward Albert Cassaletto. Cassaletto raised his pistol and shot again. Milan fell and Cassaletto was upon him.

Rolling upon the bruised bluegrass, the two men writhed and pummeled each other.

Lewis Grinaldo and Gabriel Anderson leaped into the fray, separating the two men.

The women's screams pierced the air, arms raised, hands at their mouths.

"I'm running for the Sheriff," yelled Agnes Buche.

"No! Don't get the Sheriff or police involved in this, Agnes, it'll...."

At this time two of the Cassalettos' cousins leaped from a tinny truck that had driven up. They loped around the house like angry hounds, eager to tree a coon. Mean and lean brutes, toughened by fist fights.

Milan, realizing that he had been shot and bleeding badly, looked up at Danika and started heaving himself toward the porch. The Cassaletto's cousins, Matteo, and Papeo, bounced in. Papeo grabbed his Cousin Albert's gun and fired five more shots at Milan, the shots missing.

The frantic women on the porch parted as Milan wobbled toward the door, Danika following, tears streaming. "Oh, my God. What have they done?"

Milan fell upon the living room floor, his blood pooling.

The cousin, Papeo, who'd followed Danika, grabbed a poker at the side of the stove, raised it above Milan's head in an attempt to jab down with the point and pierce Milan through the throat or chest.

Danika, acting upon impulse, grabbed the poker and wrenched it from Papeo's grip, saving her husband from another catastrophe.

Agnes had run for the police, after all. Two Mulberry policemen burst into the room. They witnessed Danika, a heavy wine bottle she'd grabbed from a nearby table in her hands, ready to crown Papeo.

One of the policemen clasped Danika's arm, twisting it, preventing the strike.

****

What is happening to Milan and me?
Danika staggered backwards.
How had they entered this household of vipers?
Officer Blassant, a bloated-faced man, threatened Danika. "You'll go to jail for an attempted bludgeoning, woman." He reached for handcuffs.

The second officer seemed to size up the situation, ordering his colleague to let her go. It was obvious that he and his fellow officer, Frederick, did not share the same opinion of Luigi Cassaletto or his brother, Albert.

Before Danika's startled eyes, Officer Frederick shook hands with Papeo Cassaletto. She realized that they were bosom buddies.

Justice had flown out the back door.

Danika stood fixed. A million questions raced through her mind in a confused medley.

I should have known. It was these Cassaletto brothers who, two months ago came to Franklin and spent time with Milan on our back porch, sharing his elderberry wine. Slapping butt and joking. They'd even taken out their pocket knives and played a round or two of mumblepeg. It was the mine troubles, after all. They were John L. Lewis loyalists.

Our communities are crumbling. That Bedlam they talk about is right here, not in Nevada, Missouri.

The lurching ride in the ambulance to Pittsburg seemed endless, Danika sitting beside Milan, holding his hand, praying the rosary.

Milan, a genial and good man, an everlastingly-loyal miner, trying to stand for justice, died that night. Men, who'd been his friends a few months before, killed him. Justice itself had become a fugitive.

The horror of what had happened seeped into the very soil of Danika's soul.

I'm forty-three and a coal miner's widow.
How can I tell Toma and Neda?

CHAPTER TWENTY-FOUR

"Where is Comfort?"

What awaits me now? Even the clouds and this coal-dirtied earth meet on this November day.

Who was it? The Blessed Jesus on the Cross who said, "Father, forgive them, for they know not what they do"?

Oh, oh, my God, how shall I put my shoulder to this wheel?

Toma had returned to school. The jarring murder of his father and the event's residue had not yet filtered to the deeper levels of his being. Danika realized life had to go on, but all she wanted to do was sit in her chair by her kitchen stove, holding her cracked cup, staring but not seeing.

"Routines. Keep up your routines," Father Pompeney had said to her

"We have to remember those words Father Pompeney read, Ma, the words from St. Matthew:

'Blessed are they who mourn, for they will be comforted.'"

Danika barley heard Neda's words. Instead, she heard a Niagra-Falls-roar in her ears and head.

Comfort? Comfort?

Where is comfort when the very skin is stripped from my body? Where are the angels who bring release to the sorrowful? Oh, what does it mean when Father Pompeney read, "They shall be comforted"?

And those words of Job. How hollow and meaningless they sounded. Yet am I to believe them? My faith is a bird, flown from its cage, never again to sing here, never to return.

That other verse? "I know that my Redeemer lives and that He shall stand at the last day upon the earth." What does it mean?

Her groans were unutterable. Her muscles, leaden, yet duties awaited her.

Duties?

I can scarcely rise from this near-broken chair. Milan, Milan, oh, Milan?

Her inner eyes could see the opened grave, the gaping hole. The beggarly-looking gravediggers reeking of moldy earth, sorrowful as Job, pity in their eyes. Pity. Holding onto their shovel handles in the fog and silent rain.

Nature herself, weeping.

And that song, which they said was composed of St. Simeon's words: "Lord, Bid

Your Servant Go in Peace"?

Let him go in peace, Dear God. Let Milan rest in peace.

Danika's hands slipped from her cup to her lap, like leaves finding their place after a storm.

Resting? A portion of me, resting?

Her mind caught on a fleeting memory of folks who were there. They'd put on their best in respect for a fallen miner and his family: Joe and Mary Skubitz, among the better dressed. Myrtice Hester, clutching her missal. Helen Grisolano and Anna O'Korn. The members of other families already fading from her memory.

She thought she recalled Clemence DeGruson and her ever-faithful hat. Even Mrs. Allino Purgatorio from Frontenac came. Bessie Septak, too.

Danika remembered meeting Perry and Agnes Buche and Agnes's kiss upon her red, wet cheek. She faintly remembered Loretta Grinaldo's voice.

And how did she forget? Old Lady Bob, bobbing in at the last minute, hobbling to a pew near the front.

In spite of her numbness, Danika made her muscles shove her body from her chair and reach an unsteady hand for the iron skillet. She bent over to the bottom drawer of her cupboard, searching for the bag of corn meal.

Life goes on. I realize that. Toma. Neda. Oh, my God!

There had been many words of comfort, whispered condolences spoken with tears and choking voices. Warm arms had held her, held Neda, embraced Toma, who'd stood anchored in the shock-throes as pulverized as she.

Oh, hours, days, months, years must pass before this calamity can be understood.

That song! "I Know That My Redeemer Liveth."

If there is any faith still in my heart it has no voice. Not even a whisper. It must have its hiding place. Oh, God, a hiding place.

Come, Lord Jesus! You called Lazarus from the tomb, call me forth, too. Call me from this sepulcher, darker than the deepest mines.

"Mama, do you want buttermilk for the cornbread? I've gone ahead and opened a pint of your canned sausage. You've got to eat, Mama. You've got to eat. We gotta think about Toma."

****

Neda reached down to wipe her tears with the hem of her mother's borrowed apron. She hated mining towns. Despised the town of Mulberry where her father had been shot. Detested the lies in the newspaper. Screamed when she had read the brief report.

There could be an inquest by the District Attorney.

Could be?

Neda knew within her deepest self that in this community, in these times, there would not even be an inquiry.

They "couldn't reach the coroner"?

Sure, that was the usual justice here, the look-the-other-way sheriff, the ho-hum coroner, limp as a corpse released from rigor mortis.

Prosecuting attorney? Haw! What a laugh. Like the Colorado Ludlow Massacre, the authorities charged with conveying justice, turned their backs and fled.

Lies. All lies. Papa shot in cold blood. Ma, and witnesses. A half-dozen witnesses.

Oh, God, take me out of here. Out of this hell where the miasma from the mines seeps into every home.

Neda heard echoes from the netherworld, the place where witches stir poisonous brew. She could hear their cackles.

For a charm of powerful trouble,
Like a hell broth, boil and bubble....

The listing of the foul ingredients weighed like witches' rags dragged across her mind.

Fillet of a fenny snake...eye of newt and toe of frog...tongue of dog...blind-worm's sting....Boil and bubble, boil and bubble....

And the lies. The distorted misinformation. Ma'd said that Pa did not hit Albert Cassaletto with is boccie ball, he had missed. Yet that filthy scoundrel had shot her papa anyway.

Oh, God. Who is the God of the poor and the put-upon?

To make matters worse than the words in the hags' chant was the fact that the Otises were there. At the funeral. Had the gall to show up.

Sleazy Harvey Otis.

Simpering Ophelia, dressed in beige and lace, trace of pricey perfume trailing.

Big shot Harvey Otis grasping her hand. His other, the paw of Satan upon her shoulder.

She'd shuddered and closed her eyes, ducking her head. He'd grabbed her hand anyway, a hand surging with the

James D. Yoder

witches' baboon's blood, electric, overheated. His words, sweltered venom!

"Oh, my dear Neda, accept my regrets. I'm so very sorry."

She'd caught the drift of expensive Scotch on his breath.

Surely it must have been the sanctified Jesus standing beside her who'd kept her from vomiting upon his shoes.

After the funeral dinner, Danika, seeing Neda's afflicted face drew her to her side, her arm around her. "Go with Matt. He's standing over there, those sad eyes staring at you. Move on out of here. Take a drive with him but come back this evening to Toma and me. I'll be all right till then."

So Matt, following the dinner, took her for a ride west of Arma. The drizzling rain had stopped, the sun bright in the afternoon. There in a secluded place, he parked and held her. Held her. Held her. Her body accepting the love expressed through his hard, disciplined muscles.

CHAPTER TWENTY-FIVE

A Time and Season for Everything

"We'll do it!"

Mary Skubitz spoke the words out loud to herself as she raised herself from her desk.

Waited long enough. Our striking men are loyal miners, faithful to the union. The fellows following Van Bittner's orders think they're faithful union members, too. Who will challenge the governor and his Slave Law?

Mary Skubitz's "what if?" awakened from its dormancy, arming itself for action.

Action!

Time for a march, protest or something.

She grunted. She pondered.

Get on your feet! Do something. We Women aren't powerless. Not these women.

Not us!

Aren't we disciplined too? Beaten like plowshares into a fine-honed steel of resolve. Don't we know how to manage where others would faint?

Cramped living quarters. Many of us moving every three or four years. Mine calamities, the afterdamp, the explosions, faulty equipment. Pittance for wages. Crooked foremen and weighmen. Absentee mine owners in New York, Chicago, San Francisco, St. Louis, all millionaires. Showing their ruddy faces and gold watch chains draped over their pompous bellies in the dining hall at the Stilwell Hotel in Pittsburg but never here.

We're the ones who know the bare bones of miners' lives. We know when the kettle boils and bubbles and when the stew pot is empty.

Mary Skubitz had had enough.

Only yesterday at the Company Store she'd seen Danika Cratnick attempting to deal with the store manager over her meager script and a few staples She bit her lip when she saw Danika remove three items out of her basket and place them back upon the shelf.

She witnessed haunted-eyed children.

Thin. Used to watered soup.

Mary had said to herself as she watched Danika: "There's strength in that woman. Mule strength. Weighed down in grief, but she's gonna make it."

What had someone said about a decrepit arch? "Put more weight on the top in order to strengthen it."

She decided to talk to Danika. Speak to Clemence DeGruson, and Maggie O'Nelio, too. She'd seen the determined looks in their eyes.

Could we rise against stool-pigeon Bittner? Challenge him?

John L. Lewis? Governor Allen?

Waiting for them to change is like waiting for the end of eternity. Fraternizing with the operators, owners, and corporate executives. Sure, Lewis'd done a lot for the United Mine Workers of America, the owners, the investors, the executives, but he ignored the down-in-the-mine worker.

Isn't there a time and a season for everything?

Though I'm not much of a religious woman, it's in Ecclesiastes, isn't it?

...a time to break down and a time to build up...

...a time to keep silent and a time to speak...

Mary had wearied of reading the newspapers. She was aghast at the daily reports of the widening chasm between the factions. Tired of reading of the explosions, the falling coal shelves, the inexperienced scabs without the knowledge of disciplined miners, risking entire crews.

Weary of sick men whooping up chunks of their lungs.

Twelve miners dying already this season. Over a thousand injured.

Hadn't District 14 received letters and telegrams of support for defying the despised Court of Industrial Relations Law, which turned honest men into slaves? Support from members in Illinois, West Virginia, and....

And UMWA President Lewis, snickering at them. Defying them.

Governor Allen shaking in his boots because he thinks "we foreigners" will bring on a Bolshevik revolution.

Yeah, calling our corner of Kansas The Little Balkans as if we don't have anything else to do but blow up mines, grab arms and take over southeastern Kansas.

Maybe we can show these executives and merchants who stand against our men. Show em that we are peace-loving people.

Sure we come from Ireland, Scotland, Germany, Slovenia, Yugoslavian, England, Wales, Italy, France, and a host of other countries. But that doesn't mean we can't be united. Work together. Put our shoulders to the same wheel.

Dictator Lewis has a Welsh background, doesn't he? Well, we'll give him something to wail about!

Lady Liberty welcomed all of us equally, didn't she? And the Catholics here, they have their faith in St. Barbara's help, don't they?

Our blessed Alec Howat was right, standing up for a principle. The Mishmash case, a scandal.

Sure, the strike makes us tighten our belts and worry about getting through the winter.

The time has come. Yep! We women ain't powerless.

Mary sat down at her cramped desk and began to make a list, planning, grunting audibly now-and-then.

****

The news spread from one mining camp to another. Passed on in hand-written notes.

"Miners' wives, and all women of the coal camps: Meet at the Franklin Union Hall December 11 at four o'clock in the evening to make plans to take action in behalf of our desperate men and starving children."

The word went out in notes, by tongue, neighbor whispering to neighbor.

The announcement was shared on sandstone sidewalks in Scammon, West Mineral, and Roseland.

Women abandoned boiling pots on their cook stoves to rush out and catch passers-by on the way to the company stores. "Have you heard? Can you come? Who has a car? If you have a Lizzie, can you drive? Do you live close to a trolley or the Interurban?"

As women descended from the train cars, buggies, and Model Ts, they clustered, open-mouthed and gasping at the call to duty. Others stood stolid and pensive.

The word went out.

A time and season for everything. To tear down, to build.

THE WORD. And what is The Word?

Mary remembered the reading from St. John's Gospel, "In the beginning was the Word and the Word was with God and the Word was God."

Well, no Catholic herself, but if she ever ran across Father Pompeney she'd ask him more about what it meant. But right now, it meant a call to justice. Balance things out. Didn't the Bible say that "the crooked shall be made straight"?

Dear Papa used to recite it in the Slavic tongue:

"Every valley shall be exalted, and every mountain and hill made low, the crooked straight and the rough places plain."
That old prophet, Isaiah, wasn't it?

In Cherokee on the street behind an opulent executive's mansion, three wash women clustered, sending their children on ahead of them.

"Can you come? You got a driver? Got extra change for the Interurban?"

Another chimed in, "I'm four months along, but I ain't done in. Count on me."

A woman, weary and careworn, uttered in a thin voice, "I ain't got no coat fer winter weather but that ain't agonna stop me. Where we meet?"

In Weir, Dutch Hollow, and Hamilton, the news spread. At The What Not Club, each member gave her commitment to tell and bring five other women.

Like a crow scoping the countryside, looking for a resting place, the news flew from Langdon to Hamilton, Little Italy to Chicopee.

If St. Barbara was looking down, she must have clapped her hands. Pleased to see miners' wives, lowly of the lowly, arm themselves with faith and fortitude.

Let the Catholics appeal to the Saint to "overthrow the mighty."

The Methodists, the Baptists, those of other faiths or of no faith. Lord, help em hear this message:

"We women are coming."

Burned-out restaurant cooks from Frontenac and Franklin, having "heard the word" stepped down from streetcars and headed toward their shacks, sharing the announcement with every woman, young or crone-like, whom they met.

In prestigious Pittsburg, the salesclerks, feet sore in their cheap fashion shoes, calves aching and beads flopping in the wind, raced down the sidewalks to tap other salesclerks on their shoulders as they recognized them as union members.

"Sure."

"Lordy, yes, two days yet and in the afternoon? Ain't that a Sunday? You couldn't hog tie me and keep me away."

Over in Gross a group of women caught up in butchering the family pig, threw their scalded hog guts into a tub and raced across lanes and ditches to announce the blessed news.

The news arrived in those other funny-sounding little places, hardly noticeable on the map, names laughable but where real sweating folks lived, hearts beating, praying for hope.

The words were pronounced in comical little camps like Dogtown, Crowberg, Red Onion, Frogtown, Grasshopper, and Ringo.

Their women listened and dispersed the message. They wrung their hands and giggled together as THE WORD from Mary Skubitz reached their ears.

Myrtice Hester snorted upon hearing the announcement from neighbor Hattie Comely.

"You actually think that women can change things?"

Old Lady Bob cackled and vowed she'd be right there if her stick wasn't broken.

"What did you say the time of meeting was?" her hand at her ear. She guessed she'd have to postpone her flying lessons a few days.

Like the blessed Jesus sending out the twelve, wasn't it? Proclaim the good news in every town, every village.

They hadn't concerned themselves, yet, about "What if their actions and their words were not heard?"

If that was the case, they'd be back to "boil and bubble, Kansas trouble," wouldn't they?

CHAPTER TWENTY-SIX

"Tell it, Mary!"

Danika and Neda tromped up a broken walk toward the Union Hall on a dusky December evening, December the eleventh, to be exact. Hosts of women were marching in from every direction. Like ants in a row, their steps showed their resolve. Their heads bobbed, arms swung. A few faltered but found their paces again, assisted by walking sticks.

Danika hesitated when hearing the news of Mary Skubitz's meeting, debated within herself as to whether or not she should go.

Though still in the throes of grief, and her spirit battered, she and Neda made a resolve that they should help.

"Support the women, after all. That's what Milan would want us to do."

Buggies and surreys loaded with wives and daughters pulled up at hitching posts. A shabby Chevrolet truck, back end sagging nearly to the ground, backfired, then rolled to a halt.

"Must be a dozen women crowded in there, Ma, dangerous, isn't it?" Neda held Danika's arm.

Three trolleys rolled in at the station from Mulberry, Rosebud, and Ringo.

"Did you ever see so many women dislodging?" Neda asked.

The sounding of a two-seated Tin Lizzie's horn startled Danika but when she saw the car was packed with women, some waving small flags, she waved back.

"Maybe that spring in my soul has started to trickle," Danika thought to herself again.

"Mama, isn't that Mary Colabo from Frontenac?"

"Hurry, Neda, yes, and that was Clemence DeGruson crowded against Annie Stovich in the back seat."

Danika increased her steps to keep abreast of Neda, her eyes fixed upon the open Union Hall door, women pouring in. By now they both could hear murmuring, chuckling, laughing, and words of welcome as the women greeted each other. Two women, coat tails swinging behind them pedaled past on bicycles.

"Ma, this is exciting! Mary Skubitz sure has guts. I'd like to sic her onto Harvey Otis."

Neda and her mother had fallen in behind a line of women within a hundred feet of the hall door.

Danika could see that many of the women "came as they were." Didn't matter.

Important thing, they found a time and way to get here.

Mary Skubitz stood in front of the hall under the electric light bulb, arms leaning on the podium. "More chairs over toward the wall" she pointed, her eyes gleaming, smile tracing her lips. Her navy dress gave her a solid, dignified look.

Danika could see that, already, Mary was pleased with how the women streamed in.

Why there must be at least five hundred women here.

The spring within her trickled wider. Danika crossed her arms, smiled at Neda, then nodded at Myrtice Hester, who'd turned her head around to see who was behind her.

Oh, she knew lots of the women. Neda knew them too. Anna O'Korn, Marie Goske, Maggie Bellezza, and even Matt Enrico's mother, Ada. She could feel an electric current in the air. Something alive. Something like Moses getting ready to strike the rock with his staff, water about to pour forth.

"Yep," Danika said to herself, "the word went out. It surely did."

The murmuring had risen to a roar until Mary Skubitz tapped a gavel upon the oaken podium. "Ladies, ladies. Friends and neighbors."

She tapped the gavel again. The cacophony of voices simmered to a low ebb. Backs straightened, necks stretched. Hands found resting places, waiting.

"Friends and neighbors, thank you for responding like this. Why, I'm overwhelmed by your response. I guess the word did get out, didn't it?"

There was a roar, mixed with applause:

"Yeah, Mary, the word got out," a dark complexioned woman from Arma said.

Mary allowed the women a minute of laughter before she proceeded.

"I guess you don't have to be told why I asked you to gather here tonight."

Heads nodded, smiles broadened. Women leaned forward.

"You know the conditions in our camps. Our husbands, sons, divided into two groups. Van Bittner ordering the men back to work, which conflicts with their loyalty and commitment to our deposed Alec."

"Tell it, Mary, tell it," a dark Italian woman on the right front said.

"Too many strikes. Too prolonged. Our men's work taken over by scabs. College kids. Men recruited from Arkansas get off the train in Pittsburg and are shuttled into a chute that leads directly into the mine shaft. Some of the negroes probably don't even know they are violating an agreed-upon strike.

"We're not blaming them, but they need to know the truth."

Someone called out, "You got it right, Mary."

From the back, a coarse-voiced woman yelled, "Pull em out of the holes, the rats."

"Like I said, some of the scabs are innocent but the others? We can no longer allow them to collect wages while our families starve."

"You right," the words from a bent-backed woman.

Skubitz continued. "You all know what Van Bittner said when the men rallied around President Howat, committing themselves to stand by him when he called for the strike. The cause was just. Just. Withholding wages from a boy. Company Stores robbing us."

A slender woman in a faded flower-sack dress on the left lifted her head to say, "You got those word right, Mary. Robbing us."

"Why, after they expelled Alec, that Van Bittner sized it up this way. This way, my sisters.

"He actually said, 'I don't take this matter seriously. As a matter of true Christian charity, I say 'Father, forgive them, for they know not what they do.'"

Groans rose up. Feet shifted, mouths turned down.

A woman by the name of Lizzie Drenik near the front stood up, arm in the air. "Forgive them? You mean he thinks our striking men are in the wrong?"

Someone from near the back piped up, "Why sister Skubitz, don't ya know the blessed Jesus himself would be standin with the striking miners? Yep. If he weren't fer justice, then there ain't any."

A strong applause followed.

"He called our sons and husbands who went on strike anarchists. Anarchists, like they were waiting to overthrow the government down here. Think of the ridiculousness of it.

"Well, we have news for you. Is Annie Wimler here? Annie Wimler?"

An obvious miner's wife, worn by the years, raised a thin arm, her wrinkled face beaming a smile.

"Well, we otta thank Annie Wimler. All of us. She saw through the pretense and puffed feathers. She stood up and called him a stool pigeon right to his face."

Annie chuckled. The audience roared and clapped their hands.

"Let's remember that we're gathered here to protest the Industrial Slave Law, supported by John L. Lewis and other snitches of the international organizations."

A rangy-looking woman in the middle of the crowd spoke up: "Tell us our duty, Mary. Our duty."

"As I see it, our duty as miners' wives and daughters is to put our shoulders to the wheel, the same wheel rolling back, now, over our miner men."

Someone yelled: "We can do it, Skubitz. Tell us how."

"I've prepared a statement of resolve, friends. May I read it to you?"

Voices chorused, "Read it, Mary. Read it."

A woman named Julia Youvan near the back called out, "Well, I'll swan!"

A generous-spirited woman hollered, "You ain't got any spectacles to read, take mine."

Mary held up her resolution page, surveying the eagerly-waiting women. She began to read:

"We the wives of the loyal union men of Kansas assemble in the mass meeting unanimously adopt the following resolution: Whereas, our husbands are striking against a law to enslave our children which is known as the "Alien Industrial Slavery Law," supported by John L. Lewis, Van Bittner (she named four or five other men of authority, calling them all 'stool pigeons')... We feel it is our duty to stand shoulder to shoulder with our husbands in this struggle.

Skubitz looked up at her audience, surveying their response.

"Read it. Put it in all the papers, Mary," a woman from one of the southern camps by Cherokee said.

Therefore, be it resolved that we unanimously endorse the action of the district officials and the miners of Kansas who are loyal union men and have not returned to work through the misleading statements of the international organization, which is trying to lead the public to believe that the strike is against the national over the controversy of the Dean and Reliance strip mine; that the district officials carried out the instructions of the international convention.

"You got it right, Mary, plenty of lies written about our men," a woman on the right shouted.

Mary continued:

"Be it resolved that we will ignore the misleading statements that appear in the public press by the officials of the International organizations; that we will continue the fight against the industrial court, and ignore the camouflage of Lewis, testing the constitutionality of the industrial court. For if he was in good faith he has had eighteen months to prove his spirit as a union man and, be it further resolved that we extend our sincere thanks and appreciation to the Illinois miners and all other organized labor who are assisting us in the fight for our democracy that we were to receive after the World War."[1]

Skubitz read the names of the five or six other women who had helped write the resolution.

A tremendous applause ascended, followed with cheers and a standing ovation.

****

Danika and Neda wound their way home on the street, sidewalk, and dirt road in the company of "their kind." Hard-

---

[1] *The Pittsburg Daily Headlight vol. XXXIV, December 12-16, 1921.* Note, author's editing. Also see http://www.franklinkansas.com/amazonarmy.html - Knoll website

working women, careworn women. Women faltering with canes. Women dragging small children, some carrying babies.

They traipsed by men gathered on the sidewalks and in front of the Company Store, legs crossed, butts against the board wall, hands in their pockets, wondering at the spectacle.

A miner standing by the Post Office with his cronies, spat his tobacco juice, wiped his bewhiskered chin and chuckled: "Well, ya try, but you jes cain't keep a woman down."

Comrade hands slapped him on the shoulder. Men snickered.

"Skubitz says that we should try to meet in front of the Company Store by four o'clock in the morning," Neda said.

"Well, I don't sleep too good after three, so that won't be much of a problem for me, Neda. But you gotta come along."

A rough-looking dog slunk through the homeward-bound women, nervous, seemingly afraid of such a crowd.

"Glad it's not too cold, yet, Ma, It's gonna be bad enough. It's December. Better pray that it won't snow."

"Well, yes. Some of them women haven't got no heavy coats at all. Bet we'll be a spectacle in the morning," Danika added.

"And bring pots and pans, tubs, even. Wooden sticks and spoons to bang on em. For pity's sake, it sure'll be something. We'll be a bobtail army fer sure, ragtag and determined," was Neda's reply.

"Well," Danika said, "I just don't yet know what to think of that order she gave us, 'Yank the scabs up out of the mines.' How we gonna do that?"

"Well, Ma, maybe we'll have to cheat a little and call on Matt, he's had boxing lessons." Neda chuckled.

The moon slid from under a cloud. Ahead, their "cottage," squatted, gray and leaning. The shrill call of a screech owl pierced the air.

Danika focused her eyes ahead, the sagging roof-line of her house barely visible.

"I sure glad to get home, but I do think I've found a bit of hope for tomorrow."

"Look, Ma, Toma lit the lamp for us," Neda said. "I'll bet he has a bite to eat on the stove for us."

"Thank the Lord. Then we can get some water heated up and soak our feet and make a cup of hot tea."

CHAPTER TWENTY-SEVEN

The March Begins

"Ma, would you look ahead! Did you ever see Franklin lit up so early in the morning? The schoolhouse, the store, the street?"

"Why, no, Neda, ain't it a wonder? why..."

"And look at the trolleys and the Interurban pulling in. Hundreds of women, and the sun isn't even up yet, Ma."

"Well, one thing, you could tell Mary Skubitz meant business last evening at the meeting. We'd better step faster, they might be giving our orders right now."

Ahead, women and miners, who were on their way to the Walker Mine Number 17, were pouring out of the cars.

Rumblings of overloaded cars and occasional backfiring Model Ts echoed, frightening the dogs who had sneaked between legs. Eight or ten women poured out of each vehicle.

"Why, look at that! Must be eighty or ninety cars coming down the main street," Danika said, turning to Neda.

Motley-clothed women, carrying washtubs, dishpans, boiler pots, sticks and wooden spoons, streamed toward the central gathering place before the Company Store; eyes wide open, cheeks ruddy from the cold air.

"Look at that," Danika said, some of em women ain't got nothing on but old knitted sweaters."

"Well, most of them did remember to pull on stocking caps or old felt hats. Aren't some of those coats something?

Near freezing today, too." Neda caught a toe in a crack on the walk but regained her footing.

Danika's heart thumped. Her breath caught short as she lifted a run-over shoe to lift herself up on the walk and join the crowd.

Suddenly their ears were blasted by the quick upbeat of marching music drifting in the wind toward the crowd.

Anna O'Korn, standing by Neda's shoulder, hollered in her ear: "Why, here comes the girl's band from the Arma High School. Who woulda thought it?"

"Well, yes, it surely is something, fer sure. Who would of thought to arrange that?" Neda's mouth hung open.

"Sure gives all of this a real American spirit," added Danika.

She was bumped by a hefty woman crowding in and tried to move over to make room. A slice of cold wind cut at their necks. Women yanked up coat collars, arms clinging to their buckets and tubs.

"And, Ma, look at that. Annie Stovich riding in on the fender of that car carrying the biggest flag I ever saw."

Annie, a fourteen-year-old daughter of a miner, smiled as if she'd already won a victory, stepped off the running board and unfurled her flag.

"Why it must be six or seven feet wide, and look, I'd say fifteen feet long. How can she carry that?" Danika pondered as she searched over heads for Mary Skubitz.

Her eyes found her in front of the store, hand up, beckoning.

"Did someone say orders?" queried Clemence DeGruson, who'd crowded in next to Danika.

"Well, yes, somebody's got to take command, otherwise we'd be like those Israelites standin by the Red Sea and no Moses. This is going to be a helter-skelter thing for sure." Danika held tightly onto her dishpan.

The band ceased their rendition of *The Stars and Stripes Forever.*

"Can't say we're not loyal Americans," Bessie Septack chimed in, standing to the left. Her face filled with wonder. "Ain't never seen women doin something like this."

Mary Skubitz stepped upon a soap box which someone had dragged up for her.

"Women! Women! A great day, my sisters. Oh, what a day! What a gathering...."

Women roared in affirmative response, many beat upon their pans with their wooden spoons, showing their eagerness to begin.

Danika noticed dozens of American flags.

Let that bald-headed Governor Allen see that, then he ain't gonna complain about us aliens. Why a lot of us voted last year. We can get this over with and vote Governor Allen right out of office.

Skubitz brought the crowd to a near silence. Her words carried in the brisk morning air:

"I want you to march by Marie Mercy over to the left on the sidewalk. As you go by, scoop up a cup of red pepper she brought in kegs from her grocery store. Each of you put a handful in your bucket or pail."

"Red pepper? What'll we do with red pepper? You don't mean we'll..."

Danika's words were lost in the murmurs as the women slid by Mercy, scooping up smidgens of pepper into their containers, then stepped aside.

Someone to the left said, "You'll know what to do with it, when the time comes, Danika, when the time comes." Sounded like Myrtice's voice, but she wasn't certain.

Wasn't this supposed to be a peaceful march?

They tromped, their bodies easing into rhythm, four abreast, Skubitz and other women who were acting as "leaders" raising their arms, now and then, beckoning them onward. The tromp, tromp, tromp of their feet shook the ground and the sound rose to their ears.

Neda looked behind her. "Ma, the line. Must be over a thousand women, I can't begin to see the end."

"Watch where you're going, Neda. I hear a car coming. Fast, too. We'd better get over to the left there among those half-frozen smart weeds."

"Well, didn't you hear Skubitz say that not only can she understand the different languages but she knows Sheriff Gould and that he's gonna help us."

With unbroken steps, Danika muttered, "Don't count on it, Neda. Don't count on anything from Sheriff Gould."

Then Danika cast a look over her shoulder.

Who would have imagined it? First day of the march, too. Why, surely must be over three thousand women. I don't believe I ever....

Her thoughts were interrupted by the hoots of a horn from a rather opulent car weaving alongside the marchers, the driver, uniformed, leaning forward, leather-gloved hands gripping the big wooden wheel.

"It's the mine superintendent, Neda. Ain't that Buford Lipton? Big shot, lives in one of those Pittsburg mansions over on the east side."

"Get over, Ma, he isn't going to stop for any woman." Neda shoved her mother over to the left by dead sunflower stalks as the car rumbled by, tires kicking up dust, which caught in the wind and stung their eyes.

"Did you see the look on his face?" Danika asked.

Helen Grisolano, behind Danika, yelled, "Well, you didn't expect him to tip his hat and smile at you, did you? Can't expect a big shot to stop for a woman. Can't expect it."

"Well, we'll see. We'll see before the day is over," Danika replied.

Blackbirds awakening from their sleep in Osage Orange trees alongside the road, flapped up, cackling, screeching. Crows, disturbed from their perches, cawed raucously.

"This is truly a wonder." Danika thought "I simply can't believe I'm caught up in such a thing."

Her shoes kept thudding on the gravel, skirts flapping at her legs. By now the women were thumping upon their pans and tubs with sticks and wooden spoons.

What would Milan think? Surely us women going to have sore heels and toes come tomorrow morning.

Danika, without breaking stride, smiled.

Well, maybe Milan's sitting along St. Barbara up there on that morning cloud and they're both giggling at us. Maybe St. Barbara'll send down one of her famous thunderbolts if that superintendent runs over a couple of women.

Word was passed from marcher to marcher down the line. "Don't worry. No cause to. Mrs. Skubitz up ahead speaks several languages, she'll guide us through. She says Sheriff Gould is gonna help us dig out the scabs."

"Ma, look beyond the curve up yonder. See that? That superintendent's driver is slowing down. I can't believe it. Four or five women have lined themselves across the road and they are holding up that big American flag Annie Stovich waved. Holding it right up."

The marchers had stopped. The mine collier, dark, threatening, hunched ahead.

Now what?

The grand automobile ground to a halt.

"Oh, no!" Neda's hand went to her mouth, a wash basin clutched in the other.

Danika stared through the shoulders in front of her and saw the women who'd been holding the monstrous flag, drop it upon the road. There it lay stretched before that luxurious car.

Surely he's not gonna....

The head-capped and eye-goggled driver ground the gears and let out the clutch. He stepped upon his gas pedal and drove the superintendent right over the flag of the great old U. S. A., the powerful motor groaning.

Shrill cries, gasps, outbursts in Italian, Irish brogue, German, and other languages riddled the air and ear at the shame of it.

They were nearing the collier of Johnson Walker Mine Number 17. Danika could feel the rumble of the steam-powered engine in the engine house, gearing up for the morning shift.

Up ahead a train filled with scabs slowed down and stopped. Black smoke drifted back as the engine puffed, smoke burning Danika's eyes. Neda coughed.

Scabs, intent on work, descended in their jackets, overalls, and shirts, and lunch buckets, heading for the changing room where they would don their mining clothes, slip into their work boots and attach their carbide lamps.

A rush of fifty or so women headed for both open doors of the train car.

"Oh, no you don't. Not getting off here! You've taken all you're gonna take from our husbands." Some of the women forgot to bang on their pans and instead, began to flail at the scabs with their sticks as the men scurried back into the car."

"You get in there and stay there," Stella Overstreet hollered, hand digging for a sprinkle of red pepper in her bucket. Eyes burning, the half-blind miners turned around, groping for their seats.

When another group of scabs feasted their eyes upon the hordes of women who'd again started banging upon their pots and tubs, they froze. Then, seeming to understand what was about to happen, they scurried across the railroad track, out into the field, arms flailing.

Women at the front of the line stopped beating their buckets and galloped after them, yelling, "You cowardly dogs! You get back here. You'd better run. We're gonna strip off yer overalls if we catch you. We're finished with you scabs taking our husbands jobs. Our money. You hear us?"

Behind, Danika could see that a group of women, including Julia Youvan, had halted a Chevrolet sedan loaded with miners.

Fingers reached out like witches snatching toads for their brew and yanked the side curtains off the car, exposing the stark faces of men, pulverized by the overwhelming odds. Those who could scramble out ran westward, jumped a fence and hightailed it into a wheat field.

Danika heard the sharp cries of outrage. Red pepper had reached the eyes of the sluggish ones. They circled and pushed, aiming for a water faucet or hose.

"Don't tarry, we got others pouring out of the mine ahead," called Eunice Zerncast. We gotta stop em."

A few women stumbled while going down the road bank after scabs but they gathered themselves up and raced after them. A husky voice yelled, "Pass it on down the line, 'Grab their lunch pails.' They can't work if we grab their lunches."

Lunch pails flashed in the streak of sunlight at the horizon and the electric lights from the mine tiller. A number of women already clutched the two gallon pails and when they bumped into scabs, they emptied the contents in their faces, including the hot coffee.

Danika could see that three of them were racing for a haystack in the field eastward. She chuckled. "Get em, ladies, get em!"

What am I saying?

Danika had made it nearly to the front and was going to approach Mary Skubitz when she noticed a mine foreman, whose name she didn't recall, had found a huge hose connected to a faucet.

"You women stand back! Gonna turn this thing on and it'll blast you clear back to Franklin. Now you hear me..."

Before he could finish, three women had hurried over to the faucet and turned off the water but not before the icy blast hit their bosoms but they seemed to give it a no-never-mind.

When they saw the multitude of women, the line seeming without end, men stumbled, fell, grunted and crawled upon their knees, got up and loped away.

Danika could see that a woman she knew as Silicia Hammond was holding a frying pan by the handle in one hand and was bringing it down upon a man's shoulders, his arm flailing behind him as he tried to escape.

"I thought we were not supposed to use violence," Neda said, stopping, momentarily. "What is going on, Ma?"

"Well Sheriff Gould has several deputies up ahead. They're gonna stop any violence and protect our women. I'm sure he will."

"Who's that woman in the dark skirt ahead, yellow bandanna?" Neda stared.

"Why, ain't that Myrtice Hester?"

"Why, it sure is, Ma. Look at that. She pushed herself right over there and is talking to the sheriff. What do you think?"

"Think? I think she's getting to him. Telling him not to pay any attention to us. You just watch." Danika quickened her steps.

"Look at that." Neda marched ahead. "The deputies have made a line to protect the scabs, Ma."

"Well, I always knew, underneath, that Myrtice Hester was a turncoat. Yellow a good color for her headscarf, fer sure!"

The tipple (machine for loading coal cars) hung suspended in morning fog, steam, and smoke. The tailing pile hunched like an antediluvian monster, getting ready to awaken and roar.

"Better pray to St. Barbara, ladies," Annie Wimler piped. "Looks like Miz Skubitz was plum wrong about her sheriff. Why, he's up there pertecting the scabs. Sicking his deputy-dogs on us."

When Mary Skubitz found out that she and her women were alone, unprotected by the law, she seemed to find her second wind.

"We've just started. Mr. Delaney," she hollered to the foreman, standing by the tipple door. Bring the scabs up out of the cage hole! Get them up here! We're not going to tarry. We've got news for them."

Delaney stared at Skubitz, stroked his chin, looked down the road and saw a cluster of angry women tearing the sidecurtains off a car, sending them flying, and other women busy filling stalled Model Ts with stones.

Neda had turned to look at the women at the car. Why that's Otis Harvey's big blue Packard. He's coming out here, why,..."

Before she could catch herself, she leaped from Danika's side and shoved her way through to the back seat of the stalled Packard.

Her eyes bugged. There sat Harvey Otis, his fine black homburg, smashed and tilting on his head, his arms up as a group of hefty women, who'd yanked open the door, clawed for a hold on an arm or shoulder.

Seeing the opportunity, Neda yelled, "Wait for me. I want to grab the tail of that rat."

Her fingers clutched around his flailing arm and helped three women drag him to the edge of the ditch where they tossed him into the frigid water. They could hear the crunch of the thin ice as he rolled in.

"Fill the car with them rocks by the culvert," someone yelled. The driver, having sized up the scene, was last seen taking speedy strides across a ragged field of corn stalks, heading for a lonesome barn.

Neda grunted and grabbed a heavy sharp-edged rock, bending and staggering, she lifted it up and let it drop upon the opulent leather where Mr. Otis's warm butt had rested. She saw the leather split as she stood back to let the other women heave in their stones.

Back at the mine, Danika could see that operator Delaney stood like a deer caught in a rifle sight.

Surrendering to Skubitz's authoritative voice, he obeyed her command, sending someone down the shaft to call up the morning scabs and any who had lingered from the former shift.

Scabs, young and old, blinked in the awakening light and glare of the electric lights; several were negroes, eyes wide open, shocked. They flinched at the roar of voices. When they saw "weapons," the wooden spoons, walking sticks, pans, tubs, and wash basins, and collected lunch pails, they wilted, waiting for tongue-lashings and threats to come.

One, named Amos Whipple, threw his hands up around his ears. "Why, lady, I don't know who you are. You gonna hit me?"

The other bedraggled fellow, Elija Benning, bowed his head, staring at both of them, stunned.

"What's y'all doin? We jest followin orders. They shoved us in the mine, here, saying we could have these jobs. Our families are hungry, too."

When he saw the furious crowd of women, waving flags, banging pots, shoving miners, yanking others from the hole, screaming commands, his eyebrows flew up, his mouth fell open. His look, boggled and dumbfounded.

Before Danika could control her arm and hand, her fingers had clasped a handful of red pepper, flinging it into the black men's eyes, her effort aided by the wind.

Too late. Mary and Danika realized that the men were, indeed, innocent -- did not at all know about the strike and the history of their struggles.

The men bowed their heads, tears streaming. "Oh, oh, lady, whatcha done to us?"

CHAPTER TWENTY-EIGHT

"Calm Down, Henry!"

Miss Cleva Crawshaw, Governor Allen's secretary, knocked timidly on his office door. She steadied her feet in her shoes in order to stop the tremble in her legs.

She rapped again.

"What is it? Didn't I say I didn't want any interruptions?" the voice, muffled by the door.

She turned the brass knob and entered, stenographer's pad in her hand.

"I'm so sorry to interrupt, Governor, but I knew you would want to know. I have President John L. Lewis on the phone. He insists upon speaking with you." She swallowed, then brushed back a wisp of hair at her temple.

"Yes. Yes. I expected it. Shut the door, Miss Crawshaw. I want to be alone when I talk to Lewis."

She thought she heard him mutter, "Oh, God," as if he was desperate for a redeeming prayer.

Tiptoeing back, she closed the door as silently as possible, making sure she heard the lock click.

****

You can't postpone an earthquake that's doomed to happen. Oh! Why didn't I stop at the Rexall for an Alka-Seltzer?

Pain raced across Governor Allen's forehead, one hand fumbled at his temple while the other grasped for the telephone. He made an attempt to clear the phlegm from his throat.

"Calm down, Henry," he muttered to himself.

His voice wavered. "H-hello? That you, John?"

A voice boomed. "YES, IT'S ME, Hennnrrrrreeee!"

Allen winced at the the pronunciation of his name.

"YOU SEEN THE PAPERS THIS MORNING, HAVEN'T YOU, HENRY?"

There was a long pause. *How could he forget those headlines?*

A coughing fit shook his shoulders and he had nearly strangled when he tried to read *The Topeka Journal.* Headlines in *The New York Times*, *The Pittsburg Daily Headlight.*

His throat constricted. He tried to swallow.

"Why, uh, uh, John, we, uh, the attorney general and I and, uh, uh..." Allen caught his breath. "We're hearing from the Counsel for District 14 Board that the board members are innocent. Not at all involved. We're sure that Howat's angry as a poked hornet over this."

"Innocent! Not involved? What are they, then, putting on aprons and dust caps and running out to join the crazed Red women? Women, Henry, women!"

"I don't think it's spreading, John. Local thing. I'm going to deputize a few more..."

"Deputize? You get your (here he mentioned a portion of Allen's anatomy, impolite to mention) down to Pittsburg."

Allen shifted the receiver away from his ear as the roaring-bear voice accosted him. He could see the shrub-like eyebrows pinching as Lewis scolded.

"I read here, that after the convulsion at That Franklin Walker Mine those foreign heifers hightailed it on over to Central 51, that right, Henry?"

Henry's Adam's apple bobbed. "Uh, yes, they did scramble on over there, but, John, no serious damage. No collieries blown up. No dynamite, yet." He realized he'd said the wrong thing by adding the last sentence.

Lewis'd be out of his chair, now, stomping and jumping up and down.

"Says, here in the paper that the alien cows, old cows, Henry, galloping all over Southeastern Kansas. Attacking the men at Edison 7, Central at Number 48, Ringo, Sheridan 9, and 19. That right, Henry?"

God, above, how did You create such a monster?

"Well, yes, but, but it's being subdued by Sheriff Milt and his deputies."

Allen realized his words sounded like he was offering Lewis milk toast.

"Subdued? What are you, Henry, eighth grade English teacher?

Subdued?

"I'm gonna subdue Milt Gould and his deputies and that counsel-of-the board fellow, Callery. Give em their walking papers like I did to your Howat. Let em study what color to paint their jail cells, Henry."

"I think it's about over, John. Surely a passel of women not agonna take over the mines."

Now I've started using Lewis's English. *Get ahold of yourself, Henry. How do I get off this phone?*

Governor Henry felt pressure at his bladder. He twisted, the leather of his chair, squeaking. Sweat ran down his neck. He attempted to drag a handkerchief out of a pocket to mop his head.

"Says, here in The New York Times that those insane women were 'a picturesque spectacle.' That what you got down there, Henry, 'picturesque spectacles?'"

Henry Allen laid the receiver down upon his desk, crossed his legs. The phone echoed, crackled, the receiver hot from Lewis's searing words. He dared to pick it up after a pause.

"Well, John, I, I, I'm planning on getting down there to Pittsburg, tomorrow. Yes. Setting up my governance there. Right in the Stilwell Hotel. I'm...."

"Setting up governance? What's that mean? We ain't hatchin duck eggs, here, Henry. You call in the National Guard. State troops if necessary. You get down there without back-up of the army, Henry, then you'd better be investigating your old Red Cross job with those women back in Europe."

Allen wanted to order secretary Cleva to take a pair of pliers and cut the line.

How much brow-beating can a fellow take?

He realized that he'd long lost his dignity.

Lewis ranted on. "Says here that the women threw red pepper in the miners' eyes. Is that what the world is coming to? Red pepper?"

"No real damages, Lewis. No real damages."

Oh, for an aspirin. Two of them.

"And, says here in the paper that them women filled expensive cars with boulders and rocks. Tore off the oiled canvass side curtains and isinglass. Turned some of the cars over. Busted springs. Dented doors, ripped seats. You sit there and tell me there was no real damage? That what you just said, Henry?"

"Like I said, John, soon's you hang up, I'm calling my chauffeur, taking my secretary, and other staff as needed and heading down there." He knew he sounded weak.

Call in the troops. Yep! That'd show strength.

"Reads here in the paper that Van Bittner, that District president I appointed, believes Howat and the strikers themselves are behind all this. Anarchists, fanatics, all of them. Put their women up to doing the dirty work for them. Well, we'll see, Henry. We'll see. Get your bags packed and your girlie secretary all readied and GET DOWN TO PITTSBURG before that dynamite you mentioned goes off. You hear me?"

****

When Agnes showed Alec Howat the New York Times headlines, his eyes flew open. Then he laughed.

"Didn't you expect something like this to occur, Alec?" Agnes leaned forward, her husband holding on to the bars of the cell.

"Well, yes and no. Can't blame the women. Strong women around here. Survivors. *Amazons* they called them?" He chuckled.

"I'm not sure why they use such a word as 'Amazons,' Alec, tell me."

"Oh, long ago. Mythology. Greek myths. Big, strong women. Went to war in the Trojan wars. Rumored that each one cut off a breast so that they could better hold their bows in battle."

Agnes's eyes widened. "I don't believe it."

"Well, anyway, the myth carried down through the years. Now the papers pick it up. Agnes, this is an honor. Our poor, beaten-down miners' wives elevated to the same level as Amazons. Who'd of thought it?" His smile spread.

"Honor? I don't know how it's an honor. Sheriff Gould has deputized over two dozen deputies, already, and is asking Van Bittner for more. Some of these women are going to have to serve time over this, Alec. Look for it in a day or two."

Alec's grin slid from his face. "Well, from what I'm hearing and reading there is cause to worry. Headlines calling the women Red Bolsheviks. But, I don't like it when I read about 'bellicose women bombarding the miners.' What's that mean?

"Why, they grabbed the scabs' lunch buckets and pitched their lunches in their faces. Threw coffee on them. Some of them beat the lunch pails over the heads and shoulders of the scabs."

Again, Howat smiled. "Oh, Agnes, the poor women. Naw, they probably shouldn't have done that. A starving miner's wife empties a scab's lunch bucket, poor fellow's lunch nothing more than a two-day-old soda biscuit split in half and loaded with lard. A turnip pitched in. Water portion of the bucket a mixture of moonshine and water. Poor suckers."

"Another thing." Agnes continued. "Said in the paper that at Number 51 Foreman John Murray was forced to get down on his hands and knees and kiss the flag. Think of it!"

Alec hooted.

"It's the issue, Agnes. In America they can't pass a law and get by with it that prevents honest workers from negotiating or from striking. Just can't do it. That's why I'm in jail, here. That's what makes me angry, Agnes."

"Yes, some of the columnists say that you are provoked, Alec. Furious that the women behave so." She searched his face.

Her husband raked fingers through his thick hair, shaking his head. "No, Agnes. I'm not angry at the women. I understand it completely. In fact, part of me wishes you'd have been there chasing some of those scalawags yourself."

"Did you know Allen is sending in troops?" Agnes hesitated.

"Troops? Troops again? Didn't we have enough of that in '19? Nothing miners hate more than State or Federal troops tromping into their communities, forcing compliances. Backing Allen's horrific slave law."

"Well, I read in *The Headlight* that Governor Allen is going to set up his office in the Stilwell Hotel in Pittsburg."

Alex turned, pacing, as he pondered this news. "I'd expect that from Allen. Yep. Not surprised. John Lewis and Van Bittner behind it, pulling the strings. Bet Allen'll hunch and cower in one of those spiffy hotel rooms. Troops, you say?"

"Pittsburg citizens are demanding protection, Alec. I tell you, it's a frenzy there. People running in circles. They really do think the women will attack violently, that war might break out."

Alec hid his face in cupped hands. He hesitated. "Well, that's quite a mistake. Only fans the flames. People on edge, some of them probably hoping that war does break out. Only increases the agitation and fear. No cause for that at all. No cause for it."

"Well," Agnes said, "I'd certainly agree with that."

"And, I can see why the folks in Pittsburg are up in arms."

"Up in arms? Well, most of the reports say it's a wild frenzy. Fanned up a lot of fear. Calling our area the Little Balkans, Alec. I guess, well, they expect it to catch ahold and the whole area go up in flames or something."

"It's the press, Agnes. You'll read a different story in *The Appeal To Reason.*

Correspondents have to make a living. Poor suckers. You know the old saying: 'if it bleeds, it leads.' That's the way newspapers go."

CHAPTER TWENTY-NINE

Sounded Like Those Witches

Third day of the march, already. Toma knew that his ma and Neda were sagging.

How long could they keep it up? What'd they say last night when they fell on chairs and soaked their feet? They'd gone to thirty mines, already?

Pulled a hundred and twenty miners out of the cages the very first day?

Two hundred the second day?

And the funny stories. Women scrambling after scab miners, running over slag piles, jumping fences, raising broomsticks. Throwing red pepper into men's faces. Sounded like those witches Neda told him about in that McBeth story he'd study next year.

Of course Ma had told him that there were hundreds of strikers standing on the sidelines rooting for them. Not a one participating.

Bet they gave them some real whoops of encouragement, though.

A part of Toma reveled in all the excitement.

Like to have seen those wild women tearing isinglass curtains off those big cars. Pouring hot coffee into men's faces. Pretty bad, wasn't it? Bet Neda and Ma didn't do that.

What else was it? A superintendent of a mine forced to kneel down and kiss the American flag? Can't even imagine that. Bout as bad as what Cecil and I, and his Cousin Otto did down in Chicopee.

Neda, that big grin on her face when she shoved him into her corner to tell him how she'd helped pitch Harvey Otis into a road ditch filled with water. Think of it!

Toma hated it that he was relegated to keep the home fires burning, and boil some beans, while Neda and Ma plodded on with their beat-up pans, having all that fun.

Pots and pans probably ruined.

Despised it too, that besides keeping the fire burning by adding a little coal now and then, he'd had to be bothered by supervising Burley Boy, staked out beyond the front of the house by the water-filled ditch, where there was still some real green grass growing underneath a protective overhang of honeysuckle.

But that was the way with Burley Boy, he'd eat anything, wouldn't he?

Made him nervous, too. Horse and wagon drawing by, Burley Boy pulling on his rope and stake. Twice, had to put down my Little Big Book and race out and drag him back to our place. Wouldn't want him to wander down to the Company Store. That'd be real trouble, fer sure. Worse than the bull in the china shop. Bad as what Neda did to that salesman down at the Five and Dime in Pittsburg.

Toma wondered how it would all end. Women, marching, battling it out with sheriffs, deputies, mine superintendents, and overseers. That Van Bittner screaming his head off in Pittsburg. President Howat still over in Columbus in jail.

How'd he be taking all of this? And when would the police start arresting the women? Surely, they wouldn't arrest....

The events, all the swift changes made him dizzy, weary. The heaviness of his pa's murder. Pa, buried in the cold ground. Two months, already.

That thought was too sorrowful to ponder right now. He wanted to pull a screen over his mind so that he couldn't see the pathetic little plot of land, the leaning metal stand, holding up a bit of pasteboard with his pa's name and dates on it.

He made himself concentrate on his algebra book on the kitchen table. About out of tablet paper, but there were some brown grocery bags that he could figure on if he needed them.

When he moved over to the table and took a look at the textbook, he felt a pride welling up. Proud that he was able to solve these equations without a hitch, while other classmates grumbled and struggled. It fascinated him by the way his mind could grasp and work its way through to the answers.

Only one in my class who got an A on the first quarter report card. Miss Nickerson, encouraging me like she did. Smiling at me. Ma, proud, too, though she didn't say any words, her big smile, enough.

Sure glad Neda and Matt Enrico getting along like they are. Real lovers. Guess they'll marry soon. Ma said they both were going to take college classes in Pittsburg after Christmas.

I'm gonna go, too, to college. Yep. How about being an architect? They brag about the big buildings in Pittsburg. Well, maybe, some day I'll just up and design one myself. Wouldn't that be something?

Life changing around here. Ma, gonna take a cooking job at the Maude Tremble Boarding House. Full daytime job. Be at home at night to supervise the home base.

Neda, after this march business is all over, going to take on a half-time job down in Pittsburg at that other five and dime. Woolworth's, wasn't it? Woman there, quite impressed with her. Stash up a little cash for that college tuition.

Ma, crying at night on her corn husk mattress.

Toma wished that right now, he could leave Billy Boy and race over to Frontenac to that furniture store and have them bring over a real mattress for Ma.

Wait'll summer. I'll find me a job. I'm agonna get Ma that mattress.

Or maybe we'll move out of this shack.

That was more than he could think about, now.

One of these days the mines will play out and the Company will come and knock it down, anyway. Load it up on a boxcar and haul it off to some other dreary, newly opened mine.

Toma realized that he'd better stop his mind's wanderings, get back to that fascinating problem calling to him. He took out his penknife and began to sharpen his pencil.

****

Mary Skubitz, wearing a red print dress and a baggy blue jacket, head half covered by a rag hat, waved an arm. "This way, women, on to 40 Central up ahead."

Her eye caught on the massive line, at least two miles long. She yelled at Danika and Neda, scrambling up the incline, "Keep it up. We're almost there."

A flock of women struggled, heels slipping on the chat and stones. Women surged forward. Some of them threw their dishpans and spoons aside to dart after the scabs and miners who dared return to work, obeying Van Bittner's orders.

Skubitz could scarcely believe the overwhelming response: Women, plain, ordinary women, down-and-out in their poverty, charging forth for their idea of democracy. Standing up for freedom. Freedom to have a say in working conditions.

Down with the slave law.

Paper said that there are six thousand of us women. The Lord has answered the prayers of the Catholics aimed at St. Barbara, for sure. I never dreamed of success like this!

Cars stopped at crossroads, disgorging women in baggy dresses, shawls and shabby coats. They scrambled toward the entrance to the colliery. Mine superintendent, McGhee, threw up his arms when he saw the endless stream of females, definitely "out of their places," flailing broomsticks and sticks they'd picked up along the hedge rows. The din they made, earsplitting.

"Call up the scabs, the ones that disobeyed Howat's strike order. Get em up here," Skubitz's voice, commanding. McGhee obeyed, ordering the cage operator to do the womens' bidding.

The miners, amazed, halted, rubbed their eyes and tore out running when they saw the tree-limb weapons, ears deafened by the incessant drumming of wooden spoons upon metal. Some of them threw down their lunch buckets and made a bee line toward a pasture fence.

"Get em! Blame scabs. Otta know better. We're marching because our children are starving. Get the message?"

Undaunted, the Amazon war whoops circled in the air, bonding the women in unity of cause. Their words and sentences drifted from ear to ear.

"Wages. Decent wages for our husbands. Something besides twelve-hour days, six days a week from dark to dark. Working in the eternal blackness. Lung diseases. Dreaded afterdamp. Scalding flames melting flesh. Roofs and shelves falling in, the blow-outs and poisonous gases. Husbands coughing up black chunks. Don't even get us started on the children in the mines. Robbing us at the Company Store. Forced to live in shacks unfit for dogs."

Their bodies and their words were one. Pushing forward, an army. Undaunted. coattails flying, hats falling off or knocked askew. Shoe leather giving out, a shoe lost. Feet bleeding, heels blistering. Their shanks lifted, they hiked on.

"Yeah, the paper was right. Amazons! That's what we are, only we ain't got no breasts cut off, at least not yet," yelled Samantha Cartwheel, six months pregnant. She watched a group of scabs hightail it for a barbed wire fence, chased by a passel of screaming vixens.

Three women caught the fleeing men as they tried to slide under the fence. A cluster of others took off in the easterly direction, hounded by flailing sticks and scrambling women.

This wasn't war, yet, but it was getting close, wasn't it?

Danika had caught up with Skubitz. Neda, catching her breath, reached her side.

"Pass the words down the lines," encouraged Skubitz. "Tell em, Danika, we women are tough, strong, and focused. Yeah, focused fer sure."

And the words fit perfectly with the rhythm of marching feet, aching feet, unwashed and dirtied feet, poorly shod.

Tough. Strong. Focused.

The words dove-tailed perfectly with the drum-beat on the lunch pails. Only thing, though, Mary Skubitz did think it a shame, all that food, pitiful as it was, poured upon the ground. Hard boiled egg rolling into ditches. Lard biscuits split, falling, stepped upon. Peanut butter and jelly plastering startled miners' faces.

A waste, fer sure, but, still, our cause is just. Governor Allen's not gonna buffalo us women.

An avalanche of mingling voices rolled before them as a dozen or more flags waved in the southeasterly wind:

"Tough, strong, and focused.*"*

They headed for Gross, a pit mine where the steam shovels growled and bit the earth. They leaped upon trolleys. Climbed back into squashed-springs Tin Lizzies. They tromped by shank's mare on toward Gross.

Reassembling there, where a full shift was working, the steam shovels groaned and hummed like prehistoric creatures, dark, threatening, gulping the coal, rocks, and violated earth.

As at the other mines, the foreman, seeing the over-whelming threats, gave the signal for the monstrous machines to cease, lest someone be crushed.

The women surged down into the excavations. Up over slag heaps and rocks. Finding their second wind they whooped and charged. Those women with narrow skirts knew no shame. They simply yanked their skirts up with one hand, thighs churning, feet thumping, soiled or torn bloomers underneath or not.

Like the workers in the other mines, the scabs caught a glimpse of how they could be pulverized underfoot, and lit out for fence rows, fearless women at their heels.

Mary and Danika stood back in amazement as five Amazons caught the coattail of a miner twice the size of any one of them. Grabbing his arms, legs, coattail, any place where their fingers found purchase, they swung him, "one, two, three," then pitched him into an ice-glazed pond, ice crackling as he fell through.

They'd marched to Central Mines, 45, 48, and 51, disgorging scabs. They'd traveled as far away as Weir, mine No. 21. They'd stopped the gigantic steam shovel north of Frontenac. The Pitt bosses had wilted and complied.

Their flags, now tattered and mud splattered, still waved. Annie Stovich had lost both shoes, her feet raw, blistering. Coats, catching on barbed wire, hung in tatters. They'd drunken ditch water to quench their thirst to keep marching.

Oh, Mary Skubitz reveled in pride of the womens' accomplishment. "We've been to sixty-seven mines, ladies. Sixty-seven mines! Our day will go down in history."

A thin little woman, Fanny Wimler, crept to Danika's side. Pausing for breath, she said: "Wouldn't of missed this even if it was judgment day. We showed em. We learned them something. Our men and boys fit to fight that war in Germany, we showed the Bittners and that Lewis fellow that we are true one hundred percent Americans."

Cheering voices shouted, "Victory." Their soiled countenances wide with grins. Never mind a tooth missing here and there in dirtied faces. "Victory!"

"We've stopped almost all the mines. Scabs still running toward Missouri and Arkansas." Mary Skubitz laughed.

"One more day, sisters. One more day, then we can take time to see what we can do with our poor butchered feet."

But those words were spoken before Mary heard the full news.

CHAPTER THIRTY

Oh, What a Ride

Never had Governor Henry Allen felt so in command, so full of vigor, blood circulating, heart thumping.

Oh, what a ride into Pittsburg!

A former Red Cross administrator in the Great War, now riding high on the back seat of his Cadillac. His august chauffeur, Morris, eyes shielded by his goggles, gloved hands upon the wheel, steered the powerful car down highway 69 southward toward Pittsburg.

Brackets clamped upon each front fender of the car sported American flags, whipping in the wind. Secretary Cliva at his side. Other important staff following afterward.

At the Stilwell, too.

Allen smiled to himself, his soft hands folded at his belly below his watch chain. He couldn't keep his mind from getting mushy over the tantalizing thoughts of the opulent cuisine he anticipated there: Pheasant, roasted in white wine sauce. Frog legs, simmered to perfection in Chardonnay. Kansas City steak, medium rare, melting in his mouth. Glasses of Burgundy with prime rib. His saliva flowed.

Another part of him clutched. His stomach growled. A sour upsurge bittered the back of his tongue.

Just exactly what will I do when I get there?

Was it a trick? Bet Alec Howat is behind this. Getting the miners obeying Bittner's orders to badger me to send in troops now? Could they be laughing behind my back?

Anyway, he never dreamed that he'd be leading the convoy of the Kansas National Guard, three whole units.

Think of it.

Machine gun unit from Lawrence, too. What a spectacle, two thousand armed forces rolling down Broadway into Pittsburg.

Chief of Police, Armstrong, there, setting it up so that the machine gun unit could stack their ammunition in the grand hotel lobby. Citizens frantic about the hordes of women they expected to ravage their city.

Who knew which ones carried the dynamite?

Oh, the rumors. How they soar like blackbirds swooping up from a swamp.

Better be late than sorry. Yep, that's my philosophy.

CHAPTER THIRTY-ONE

You've Got to Get Up

Danika awakened to the dough boys' infantry song running through her mind, so unwelcome, early in the morning.

> *You've got to get up,*
> *You've got to get up,*
> *You've got to get up*
> *In the morning*

She struggled to work her swollen feet into loosely-tied shoes. She noted that the stitching had torn loose on her left shoe and that soon, the sole would flop as she walked. If her shoe string broke today, there wouldn't be a thing she could do except find a piece of wire from a fence, if she needed it.

She grunted. "One more day. One more day. Surely, with one more charge and advance, this will be over."

The few hours she'd slept had been restless, her lower back sore and aching.

"This'll probably be our final day, Ma." Neda had emerged from behind her curtain, her hair frowzy, shoulders dropping, ruined shoes in her hands. She edged herself upon the old bentwood chair, struggling to work her swollen toes into the dirtied shoes.

"I don't believe I could take another day of this, Ma."

They'd each gulped a cup of boiled coffee and poked down a yesterday's busciut, shoving the remaining stale ones into their coat pockets along with a handful of raisins, and a hard-boiled egg for each. Grabbing their coats and their dented pans and wooden spoons, they headed for the door. Danika noticed a big tear in the side of Neda's tweed coat.

Maybe I can find some yarn that'll match and knit it together without too big a seam showing.

The morning sky hung dark and foreboding. They could see only a feeble glow of the electric lights of the Company Store through the fog.

Skubitz'll be there, up ahead waiting.

As they plodded in the darkness, Danika's thoughts picked at her mind.

Has this been the right thing to do? How does one really understand the truth when it comes to battles, the push-and-pull of arguments and the struggle between workers and moneyed investors, speculating on our misery and broken backs? Would operators and millionaire mine owners who never show their faces sneer at us and empty their cold coffee upon us?

Maybe I should have talked to Father Pompeney first. He knows about things like this, doesn't he? Jesus and his words: "Blessed are the poor. Blessed are ye when men revile you, persecute you...."

Yep. Persecute. Right word. Why these last few days we ain't even had time to pee. Mercifully jumping at the chance to hide behind a cedar bush and squat. Never mind the heavier business. Ain't no leaves this season of the year, anyway.

What would Milan think of me?

How did it happen that I threw red pepper into those men's eyes?

She remembered dumping the remains of her pepper in a ditch right after the ordeal, hadn't she? Besides, this was no time for burdensome reflection, get mushy and religious. Duty called.

And those cars? Did we have to do that?

Well, yes, we're tromping for a just cause, that's for sure. Give that Mishmash boy his pay. That what this is, a mishmash?

"Where'd Mary say we were marching today, Edith?" Danika asked the bony woman who'd crossed the path to join her.

"Why, she said we'll be marching on over to another mine between Franklin and Mulberry, didn't she? A hardshell superintendent over there. Some of the women will probably leap off the trolley and others will be loaded in cars."

They watched wobble-wheeled automobiles weave through the fog, chugging in, overburdened as the days before, honking those everlastingly ugly-sounding horns, like ships lost in sea fog. Cars with or without side curtains. In those without, the women huddling together, turning up coat collars, if their coats sported them. Few had gloves.

How can it be, so many of us willing to push ourselves for another day?

Maybe we really have caught the spirit of the Amazons. Weren't they fearless women? Big, muscular, brave women? Did someone say they were especially beautiful?

Well, Lady Liberty lighting that New York Harbor is big and beautiful. Her wraps hang as if she has big breasts and a pregnant belly below. Pillars for legs. Heavy, welcoming, fertile woman. Kind of woman favored by the lustiest men. Maybe Lady Liberty looks like an Amazon woman. Wouldn't that be sumpin?

Has she ever hunched, eyes shut, groaning to give birth? Yep. That poem says she has.

> *...A mighty woman with a torch, whose flame*
> *is the imprisoned lightning, and her name is*
> *Mother of Exiles. From her beacon-hand*
> *Glows world-wide welcome....*

Well, most of us women ain't beautiful. We got warts on our necks and chins. Our hair is straggly and soured from

James D. Yoder

sweat. No time to wash it, and who around here can afford shampoo? Our breasts and bellies sag. Our bodies stink by now. Who had time to take a bath in a tin tub?

Our breath, alone, will drive the scabs back ten yards.

Danika grinned at her revelings.

****

Mary Skubitz led the way as if she never ran out of energy. She looked to the left and saw the women struggling up the rise toward the colliery. Annie Stovich had stumbled; the big flag, tattered and damp, fell.

She caught a fleeting glance of Danika Cratnick's daughter, Neda, run forward and help Annie to her feet. Her words muffled in the din.

"Here, Annie, I'll carry it for awhile."

Yeah, that Cratnick family'll get on in life. Got guts. Women like the ones described in the New York Times. Imagine. New York Times headlines about us coal miners wives. Whoever on this wide, wide, world would ever of thought such a thing? God moves in his mysterious way, doesn't he? And that woman widowed in such a scurrilous way. No justice.

We pitiful put-upon people. Struggling to feed our families and pull our sons and daughters out of the black holes and the cloud of misery hanging over us.

Joey at home baking bread. Sure, he griped, but let him learn. Life ain't easy. Nothing worthwhile is without struggle. Want him to get to one of those American colleges and learn something.

Wouldn't it be a wonder if someday, a miner's son from Arma, Franklin, Ringo, Frogtown, Pittsburg, or Scammon ended up in Washington D. C. helping run the government? Stomping on the toes of men like John L. Lewis. Wonder what Lewis thinks of Amazon Women? Bet he's about to have a stroke. Maybe he already did.

228

Well, one thing, he wouldn't want this horde of women turned loose on him. Let him sit in his big leather chair and breathe fire over the telephone line at our limp-wristed Governor Allen up in Topeka, bowing and cowering at his bullying threats.

Those days will end like a thunderclap announcing the end of a storm. Soon be over. Just wait. Our Alec Howat'll run against the bushy-browed Welshman. Give him a run for his money. Bet Alec's bending the jail bars, trying to squeeze through, hearing about our march.

****

Governor Henry Allen pulled in front of The Stilwell.

Yes, here in the Stilwell Hotel. Three suites for my crew. Hard to keep my mind off dinner tonight but better concentrate upon keeping war from breaking out right outside.

Rumor has it that a mob of crazy women are going to lay siege to Pittsburg. How many? Who knows, six, eight, ten thousand? Fool papers calling them 'Amazon Women.'

Well we got news for that riffraff.

Governor Allen leaned back, a broad smile stretching his mouth. His gold watch chain glittered in a beam of light breaking in from a crack in the opulent velvet curtains.

Chief Ross Armstrong beside himself. Merchants running up and down the streets. Guess the Pittsburg Sun had it right this morning:

"At about 11 o'clock a report released in Pittsburg that the Amazonian host was headed for this city with the object of first entering the Hotel Stilwell and doing bodily harm to Van A. Bittner,...It was also reported that the marchers would raid the offices of the international union, known as the provisional government on West Fifth Street." [2]

---

[2] Source: The Pittsburg Sun, December 15, 1921. (Also Wildcat, Tolly

A streak of jealousy stabbed Allen at the omission of his name alongside that of Van Bittner.

Way correspondents do, leave out important names. I'm in charge. They'll soon understand that.

Warmth flooded his fat-layered body, he could feel his cheeks heat in a glow at the thought of the thousands of machine guns and other artillery stored in the grand entry hall of the Stilwell. Two thousand troops scattered through Ringo, Mulberry, and Franklin. Machine gun unit from Lawrence.

We got em covered.

Sure, nothing coal miners hate more than being invaded by state and federal troops. Showed them back in '19, didn't we? What'd they think? Brought it upon themselves. Defying court orders, my orders. Insulting officials. Don't even mention their wild women and this dreadful Red scare. Why, our ladies here'll have heart attacks from fear.

****

Danika struggled toward the colliery ahead. Before she had noticed it, three rough-looking scabs ran out and gave her a shove, trying to reach Neda and grab the flag.

There it was again.

Something within Danika she couldn't control. Without thought, her arms leaped forward, like the strike of a diamondback, giving two of the men an enormous shove. They stumbled and fell into a side gulch filled with water and sharp rocks. They yelled as the third scab took off running before the big woman with the amazing arms could grab them.

Realizing what she'd done, she mumbled: "Dear Lord, what am I doing? Why..."

Smith in *Journal of the West,* Vol. 43, No. 1, p.60).

Scabs scrambled this way and that, like newspaper pages caught in a whirlwind. The women roared, scattering, chasing, flailing.

Within a few moments the din decreased and Danika could hear Skubitz up ahead, arms up, yelling at them.

Danika turned toward her. She saw Mary squint from the bright sunlight in her eyes. She heard her holler out, "No! It can't be. Soldiers, behind that ridge?"

Those in front heard Skubitz scream:

"TROOPS. UNIFORMEND SOLDIERS. GUNS POINTED."

"Stop the march!" Skubitz yelled. "The march is over!"

Before she had completely mouthed the words they heard the sharp crack of rifle shots in succession. Five shots.

Rifles? Shots? Aiming at us?

A military unit had fired upon them. This time, mercifully, shooting above their heads.

Screams circled like a whirling twister, then began to subside. Mouths flew open. Spoons, sticks, pans, and tubs fell to the ground.

No. It can't be. Governor Allen set troops upon women! Unbelievable!

"Stop the march!" Mary Skubitz called again. "Send the message down the line."

Scattered murmurs spread the words in obedience to Mary's command.

The women waited, listening, wondering.

"We've won. The state and the union have heard us. By sending in troops against women, they've shown their true colors.

"Women! We're not afraid. We're an army. An army of Amazons. But I can't put you faithful women in jeopardy. We've made our case. Just watch. It may take a little waiting but justice will come. It'll come in improved working conditions for our menfolk. It'll come in better housing for us and our children. You'll see. A new day is rising."

By this time the troops, with lowered rifles, had made a circle around them.

The women stood in amazement at Mary, their leader, mouths open.

We won? Did she say we won?

Skubitz continued. "To prevent bloodshed and any more troops firing upon us, we'll head back to Franklin to the Union Hall. Always remember, my sisters, we did it. We women drove the strike breakers right out of Crawford County."

****

The weary Amazonians trickled back to Franklin. Some, desperate for rides, scrambled aboard passing motor cars, the drivers stopping for them. They hung onto running boards, laughing, hooting, screaming, "Victory!"

They waved tattered scarves. Hair pinned up for three days tumbled down and caught in the wind. Heads bobbed, hair flailed.

When Neda looked at the disheveled, gleeful women, she couldn't help but think of Shakespeare's witches around their cauldron, anticipating their own victory over the evil forces.

Instead of the toe of a newt, it'd been the smashed big toe of a reluctant mine overseer. Instead of the hedge pig's whine, it'd been the whine of angry scabs at the onslaughts of the womens' army. Instead of gall of goat...slivered in the moon's eclipse, it'd been their gall infusing their bodies, energizing their surge forward.

A contingent of a women, Danika and Neda included, headed back, still finding the energy to put one foot in front of another.

"Would you look at that?" Danika stared as Neda pointed. Up ahead in one of the strip mines, scabs still worked, in spite of their efforts. Machinery ground, the steam shovel chugged and groaned at an open pit.

When the scabs saw the bevy of women screaming and running toward them, they began to scatter. Clods flew, rocks banged against the iron sides of the groaning steam shovel. It's mighty mouth, half-full of desecrated earth, halted.

Four of the unyielding women ran forward. Danika and Neda leaped to assist. At that very moment an empty lumber truck halted, the driver grinning from ear to ear at the scrambling women and the coal miners trying to flee their wrath.

With Danika's and Neda's aid, the women managed to corral three of the scabs, dragging them back and heaving them upon the truck bed.

"Let's get a goin," they yelled to the driver, who obviously had grasped the significance of the occasion.

"You betcha, ladies. You'all climb on. I heard about you women and whatcha doin. Lordy, never expected to meet you face to face, but I'm mighty pleased. Mighty pleased."

He let out the clutch and they lurched forward, rocking into Franklin.

By the time the truck turned and twisted into town the sidewalks were flooded with citizens who'd heard the news.

The mines now emptied of scabs. Whoever heard of such a thing? And the women had done it, too.

The truck driver, Ace Necessary, taking advantage of the occasion, waved and nodded at his amazing audience, circled through town from street to street, the women proudly exhibiting their catch.

They passed the Company Store as the proprietor stood by a barrel on the porch and scowled. Old men stopped whittling, spat tobacco cuds and hollered, "Well, we'd like to ov had some women like you'uns in our day." They hooted and whistled.

On they rattled. When they came to the Harvey and Ophelia Otis mansion, to Neda's amazement, the Otises scurried to their front porch, feasting their eyes upon the ongoings, listening to the near-hysterical laughter of crazy women, and stare at their smudge-faced captives. They raised their eyebrows at the discourtesy of dirty fingers pointing at them. Snickers and unbecoming words drifted to their startled ears.

"Yeah," Neda thought, almost screaming the words at them, but she held her tongue.

You feeling it? Feeling it now?
Adder's fork and blind-worm's sting.
Fire burn, and cauldron bubble.

Neda had an impulse to thumb her nose at Harvey as they rattled past.

Clowns, buffoons. That's what he'd call us.

She lowered her hand to her side and held it with the other one to prevent herself the humiliation, all the while wondering if baboon's blood still surged in his squiggly veins.

CHAPTER THIRTY TWO

Burley Boy Lifted His Horned Head

The storm was over. Danika's feet were still sore and swollen three days after Ace Necessary proudly offered the exhausted women a ride upon his truck, along with their prisoners for exhibit throughout Franklin.

Neda had come back to the shack to see Toma shepherding Burley Boy, a pout upon his lips as he obviously felt as constrained as the goat.

But mercifully, St. Barbara intervened again.

A mounted army lieutenant, sporting his spick-and-span uniform, polished boots at his saddle sides, toes properly placed within the stirrups, came riding by, leading his unit of mounted soldiers.

Burley Boy, mouth plugged with dried grass and a few green strands that hadn't completely frozen, lifted his horned head.

Toma stood staring, face reflecting a mixture of anxiety and wonder.

The officer cast a sideways glance as if the boy in a half-buttoned jumper and obviously worn and ill-fitting hat was not worthy of recognition.

A miners' boy.

Speedy as a crack of lightning, Burley Boy charged. Head down, horns aimed to hook a saddle, boot, or side of a well-curried horse.

His battering-ram head hit the officer's shiny boot at his ankle. A sharp cry erupted from the officer's lips. Losing poise, he had jerked his horse's reins too forcefully.

Burley Boy backed up. This time he hit the horse on the lower rear flank, baaing, eyes burning with hatred at rivals passing his ditch-site.

Before Toma could grab Burley Boy's dangling stake and attached rope, the officer's horse reared, twisted, neighing wildly.

A melee between horse and officer ensued.

The horse won. A look of wild astonishment glazed Officer Brady's eyes as he sailed out of his saddle, rump thudding upon the dirt road. His fancy-visored officer's cap, floating in Burley Boy's ditch water.

Before the officer could leap to his feet, other horses, upset and nervous at such charging trolls as Burley Boy, proceeded to follow suit. They turned, neighing and rearing in their tracks.

Curses arose. Reins yanked. Tongues clucked. Like a summer whirlwind in a field, the angry horses circled, a few taking the opportunity to release their bowels.

Mounted riders flew, following Officer Brady's example as they watched a good third of the unit's finely-groomed horses gallop riderless with complete disdain down the street toward the Company Store.

Women with shopping baskets threw them and screamed as they scrambled out of the way.

A few men, who'd been leaning at their usual places in front of the store saw the galloping horses and bounded into the intersection, waving their arms to prevent a pile- up between parked Tin Lizzies and wagons at the storefront.

They pushed back their hat brims and raised their eyebrows at the spectacle of a wilted, trotting officer, swearing and sweating as he ran at the side of bolting horses in his attempts to take command.

Two blocks back, Toma Cratnick laughed. He fell upon Burley Boy's road-bank and howled. He hooted until his lungs hurt.

Neda, who'd come out upon the front stoop, hands at her hips, elbows akimbo, caught the whole picture. Her chin went up. She whooped and howled as she trotted over to give her brother a hand.

CHAPTER THIRTY-THREE

Afterward

Alec Howat and Vice-President Dorchy paced in their cells, knowing that their doors would not swing open for months, maybe years. The labor battles between District 14 miners, their women, and the United Mine Workers of America union leaders had erupted in class warfare. Women labeled as aliens, Bolsheviks, Amazons, and communists were spectacular in demonstrating their unity of cause.

The women, pushed to the sidelines, demeaned as foreigners, radicals, and aliens, had disregarded their own differences and marched to make their statement.

Their purpose, clear. It had been a march of protest. Their children were hungry. Husbands were dying and suffering too many injuries, due to the deplorable working conditions, not to mention the ghastly hours and the minuscule pay.

Their bold statement made by the march confirmed that they were, indeed, "loyal Americans."

During the next weeks, sheriff's deputies roamed from mining town to mining town, from Mulberry to Redbud, to Scammon, and on to West Mineral. The prosecuting attorney and deputies were electrified, ready to "bring the lawbreakers in."

All in all, forty-nine of the marchers were arrested. Sheriff deputies, the sheriff himself, plus prosecutors, dragged the women they could snag before the judge, witnesses lined up to testify against them.

****

Danika stood before the Crawford County judge, her dress so faded that the flowers in the print barely showed. She had managed to scrape most of the dried mud from her shoe heels. She locked her fingers before her to steady their trembling.

Her accuser?

Myrtice Hester, wearing one of her favorite outfits, a black voile, which gave her the appearance of one of Shakespeare's witches stirring her cauldron.

"There she is," Myrtice hissed, answering the prosecuting attorney's request to "point out the lawbreaker."

"There, that big woman in that tacky dress. She shoved that poor man, Bud Polsack, into a ditch filled with sharp rocks. His shoulder..."

"Thank you, Mrs. Hester, that'll be enough."

"But I ain't finished, sir. She's the one tricked me to go down into a coal mine. Left me alone down there in the dark. Bats ..."

The attorney, eyes glazed, threw back his head as if he himself was besieged by the vicious creatures.

****

Danika Cratnick settled herself upon the hard bench attached to a cold jail cell wall. She'd sat there, rough hands folded in her lap. Suddenly her face spread into a smile.

I wish you could see me, now, Milan. I think you would be proud of me! I stood up for your principles. Mrs. Skubitz says we won. We women! They called us "Amazons."

Do you know what Amazons are, Milan? I'm sittin here in jail and I feel like a real American Woman. Can't wait to join in with the other women and send Governor Henry Allen scooting, in 1922.

James D. Yoder

Mary Skubitz was snagged and brought in for a variety of charges of molestation and civil disobedience. Her bail was set at seven hundred dollars.

Relenting, in time, the judge showed some mercy. Danika was released when Neda paid the five-dollar bail fee, reduced from the seven hundred, plus court costs of seventeen dollars.

Many miners and their families, hearing of the new demands and laws made by the state officials and the UMWA, gathered their pitiful belongings and scurried out of Kansas, abandoning their shacks behind them.

Deputy sheriffs, energized by Sheriff Milt Gould's puffing and huffing, finally made a raid upon the biggest coal towns, Franklin, Scammon, Mulberry, and a half-dozen others. Over fifteen thousand gallons of illegal moonshine were dumped upon the ground and into ditches. It would have made Carry Nation jealous. Unfortunately, Burley Boy, who slurped generous samples of the brew, got stoned cold.

Considering the ongoing reprisals, on January 13, Alexander Howat ordered all District 14 miners who had obeyed his call to strike, to return to work.

But the grip of the Union and the embittered officers, governor, and attorney general, tightened the ropes corralling them. They made it illegal for any miner who had followed Howat's order to return to the mines without coughing up a ten-dollar fine, money which they did not have.

Further corruption boiled and bubbled. Local union officials and mine operators colluded: "We'll let you back in fer a gallon of wine and five chickens," giving evidence that human nature only changes by degrees and that, by the aid of the Lord.

To make matters worse, they were now forbidden voting privileges in their own union. Insult added to injury.

Governor Henry Allen and District Attorney, Al Williams, not to be outdone, threatened to deport the "worst radical women."

But, in his cell, Alec Howat knew that they had triumphed over arrogance, the bullish threats of Lewis, and the betrayals and malevolence of Governor Allen.

After three years of wrangling, the court finally ordered the Dean and Reliance Coal Company to pay the teenager, Carl Mishmash, the one hundred seventy-eight dollars and sixty-four cents they owed him.

The "Alien Women," strength renewed by their surging efforts, exercised their rights to vote and unseated Governor Henry Allen in 1922, helping elect Johnathan M. Davis, known as "Buckfoot." Governor Davis fought the hated Kansas Industrial Court Law all the way to the United States Supreme Court, where it finally was declared unconstitutional.

Old Lady Bob finally took flight. Took flight off the Company Store roof on an early spring day with a crowd of a hundred spectators, necks stretched, staring at her teetering on a ridge. They pointed and snickered.

Off she sailed in her black dress, arms flapping, disheveled hair stringing behind her. She hit the ground with a loud plop. She lay there as the spectators looked at her, crumpled and still.

Suddenly, she shivered and rose to a sitting position, one arm hanging loosely at a strange angle.

"You ought not to a done that, Lady Bob," one spectator said, thumbs in his galluses.

"Ain't no woman gonna fly," another said.

"You'll have to perfect your technique," this time a woman's voice.

To this, Old Lady Bob replied: "It ain't my technique, you all, it's just that I need more practice."

The local doctor set her floundering arm, which was broken in three places.

CHAPTER THIRTY-FOUR

Resurrection

Three weeks had passed since Danika had been released from jail. The February gloom descended. Their little shack-house sagged in the dreariness enveloping the coal towns.

Gray insipidness weighed at Danika's heart.

She had slept only a few hours at night since she had returned home from her overnight behind the bars.

Neda, no doubt believing that her mother was grieving for her murdered husband, made every attempt to give her loving attention. She fixed fresh grits each morning, raisins thrown in. She bought a new coffee pot that perked nicely and produced tasty coffee.

Still, Danika sagged.

It was the nightly dream.

That dream.

It always started with the joyous calls of a long train of women singing, humming, mouthing the words of *The Star Spangled Banner* in their various tongues. Then they'd switch to *America*, *"My Country 'tis of thee."*

The scene changed abruptly. Automobiles, driven by well-dressed mine operators and dignitaries, rolled down the road toward them. The women screamed and scattered, trying to get to the road edge without falling into the water-filled ditch.

Again, the view changed. Danika, herself, was hollering, "This way, sisters, this way," waving her arm into the air. She realized that she was only trying to encourage a cluster of women to catch up with Mary Skubitz and her contingent, who were already at the entrance of the mine. She glanced up, watching Mary's crew grabbing emerging scabs. They chased the miners who'd returned. She saw metal lunch pails being emptied upon the ground.

"Why, isn't that a waste in hard times?" she said to herself.

But then, Skubitz beckoned to her. She struggled on up-hill toward the giant colliery, its framework and braces rising in the morning gloom like a mammoth insect. A huge pole light blinded her, momentarily. Yet she surged ahead.

She saw, at the ditch-side that women were stopping some kind of grand car, driven by a chauffeur; a derby-hatted operator clutching his briefcase, sat high upon the back seat.

She watched as if in slow motion, her own daughter, Neda, hightail it to the automobile as a clump of angry women blocked the road with their bodies.

When she looked up again, the women were filling the car with boulders, snatching off the side curtains, rocking it, trying to tip it over.

Danika was dumbfounded by such behavior.

Where did the impulse to do such things come from?

Hurrying to get to the cage, where Mary had ordered the manager to bring up the scabs, she saw bewildered-looking men pouring out of the hole.

Black men. Negroes.

She saw herself and other women grab them by their arms and heave them upon the chat and coal-dusted ground. Someone said the words, "red pepper. Throw the pepper."

Before she could control her arm, her fingers dug for the minuscule amount of the burning powder in the bottom of her dented pan.

Someone threw it into those black men's faces.

Fists rose to their eyes. They attempted to open their eyelids, tears flooding down their cheeks. They stared at Danika, startled, confused.

What were they saying?

"Why, ladies, whacha doin that for? We are just working to feed our families like your men. We didn't know we were takin their jobs. Nobody told us."

At this point in her nightmare, Danika, like that woman in the play, *McBeth*, Neda's always talking about, called out some words.

What were the words?

I can't remember the words? What am I saying?

It came to her, as she sat upon the edge of her cornhusk mattress, that when Neda made a mistake and felt guilty about it, she'd grab her hand and say: "Out, damned spot!"

Is that what I'm trying to say? The spot?

****

The next Saturday morning, while Toma and Neda were stirring, she mentioned to them, "I'll be back for breakfast." Danika hurried out of the front door, headed for the little steepled church of St. Phillip Neri.

Father Pompeney hearing confessions this morning.

Like the women in the Gospel who ran swiftly in the morning to what they believed would be a stone-closed tomb, her feet scurried up the sidewalk.

She remembered Mary's words:

"Who will roll away the stone for us?"

Danika recognized that that was the problem.

A stone. A stone in my heart. Nudging me each night.

No, she had not mouthed the words, "out damned spot," but a spot stained her soul.

Those faces. Those tear-stained black faces.

Her feet hit the church steps. The door squeaked as she entered the cold building. where three candles burned at the altar. The curtain on the confessional booth was drawn open.

She clutched her coat collar at her neck and squeezed in and knelt before the screen.

She turned to face the latticed divider where her faithful priest sat, waiting.

"Bless me, Father, for I have sinned."

"What is this sin, my daughter?" His words were spoken with the care of the true shepherd.

She crossed herself before proceeding further, clutching her beads in her fingers.

Danika wept. A poor coal miner's widow, bowed in her own poverty. Muscles weary and sore from the recent tromping. She swallowed a lump in her throat.

"Father, I did something grievous, I..." Her words faltered.

"Go on, my daughter. You need to tell me what burdens you." He waited in patience. She heard the tick of the clock upon the back wall of the church. The smell of the oiled floor rose to her nose.

"Father Pompeney, I performed a disgraceful act. I'm filled with shame." She wiped her eyes with her handkerchief.

"You are fulfilling your soul's need, my sister, by this confession. I'll wait for your words."

Danika choked on a sob, coughed, and cleared her throat. "Father, there were innocent men among the scabs. Men who did not know that they were working illegally. Mine operators misused them. Shoved them into the mines. Ordering them to work. Their own families needed food on their tables, shoes for their children's feet."

"Yes, my daughter. Yes, there are many needy miners. You must remember how Christ loved the poor. He stands by the side of the poor."

"Even me? Father? Even me?"

"Yes, even you. No matter what happened, He is by your side."

"It's hard to believe. I have to tell you. Father, when I saw those men taking our husbands' jobs while we were hungry and out of money, I grabbed...."

"Yes, my daughter, go on."

"I grabbed a handful of red pepper and threw it into those poor negroes' eyes. I did it. I don't know what possessed me. It was like it happened without my will. My arm just flew out on its own."

"Yes, my daughter, sometimes our bodies react before our thoughts fully control them. This is human. This is why we need the forgiving grace of Christ."

"Father, forgive me, for I have sinned. Pray for me."

"It is not I, who forgives you, Danika Cratnick, it is the blessed Jesus and his loving grace that is extended to you. I'm here to remind you of His love. 'Come unto me, all who labor and are heavy-laden.'"

"Yes, father. I could not sleep. I was heavy-laden, indeed. Oh, my heart was sore and heavy. I threw red pepper in those poor men's eyes."

"Do you believe that Christ forgives you, upon your honest confession?"

"How could I doubt the blessed Christ?"

"Then, my sister, you must remember that you are forgiven, and that I confirm Christ's forgiveness to you in the name of The Father, The Son, and The Holy Spirit."

****

The burden lifted. Challenges waited ahead. Danika's feet trod as briskly as those of Mary Magdalene who raced back to tell Peter and John that not only was a stone rolled away, but that there had been a resurrection.

This morning, a morning of resurrection. She could see the peek of the sun shining through the eastern fog. The trees, outlined against the sky, took shape. Today the mines and the growling machinery were silent.

It would come. Mother Earth's resurrection. Already along the sidewalk in the grasses she saw the foretelling. Resurrection.

"O Day of Resurrection!"

Within time the mines would close down. Gaping torn places would be filled. The air would purify itself. The flowers along the roadsides would dance, fresh and bright. The gray and grimy grass would grow green.

Where old shacks stood, there would be fields and pastures. Gardens and orchards. The spring rains would fill the rivers and streams with sparkling water. The trout would leap in *Spring River* again. The bass would rejoice in *The Verdigris*. The falls would be purified in *The Elk River*. The swans would swim and trumpet over in the *Maris des Cygnes*.

Oh, yes, a resurrection was coming.

Danika rejoiced in her own resurrection morning.

A stone rolled away.

Now, she could plan for the future. Now, she could freely give as the widow who gave her mite. Give. Offer forgiveness to confused and blundering Myrtice. Work on forgiving those who murdered Milan.

Oh, God, forgive.

Before she had left the confessional and listened to Father Pompeney's instruction for saying five Novenas, they talked about the other. When she could afford an extra bag of white flour, she would bake two loaves of fresh light bread, find out where those black men lived, and visit their families with her gifts.

Neda and Toma needed her. Oh, yes, there would be resurrection days ahead for them, too. Life called.

She recognized that every day can be a day of resurrection. Only turn the face of one's soul toward the light for the spots to be removed.

ACKNOWLEDGMENTS

I could not have written this story without the aid of the many people who assisted me in research and site visitation. My thanks goes to Hesston Public Library Director, Carie Cusick, and to library staff, Karen White, and Ellen Voth, who retrieved articles and books for me.

Next, I owe a debt of gratitude to Randy E. Roberts, Curator, *Special Collections and Archives* of the Pittsburg State University, Pittsburg, Kansas, who, when researching in the archival library, gave me invaluable assistance. In addition, he invited me to submit research questions to him via email, to which he immediately responded. I considered it serendipitous to have met and received assistance from an authority on this subject.

Though not an exhaustive list, the following sources were of help to me in developing my plot and characters: James P. Cannon's *The Story of Alex Howat*, http.// www.marxists.org/archives/cannon/works/1921/howat.htm, Dee Garrison's (Editor) *Rebel Pen: The Writings of Mary Heaton Vorse*, Monthly Review Press, New York, 1985, *Franklin Centinnial Newspaper - 100 Years From 1907-2007, June, 2007,* Gene DeGrusoen's wonderful poetry book, *Goat's House*, Woodley Memorial Press, Topeka, Kansas, 1973, *GeoKansas- A Place to Learn About Kansas Geology,* http://www.kgs.ku.edu/Extension/home.html.

A special thanks to the stimulating visit with the women and staff at *The Franklin Community Heritage Center*, 701 S. Broadway, Franklin, Kansas, (I encourage all my readers to visit this site).

James D. Yoder

In addition, *Historical Picture of Buildings, Franklin Kansas,* Leonard H. Axe Library Digital Collections, http//axedigital.pittstate.edu.cdm4/item-viewer.php?EISOROOT=itr, Fred N. Howell's *Some Phases of the Industrial History of Pittsburg Kansas,* http//www.kshs.org/publicat/khg/1932 /32_3_howell.htm. Laura Jost's and Dave Lowenstein's *Kansas Murals - A Traveler's Guide,* University Press of KS., 2006, was an outstanding source.

Linda O'Nelio Knoll's (whose grandmother was in the womens' march) website, ttp.www.Franklin/kansas.com/ amazonarmy/amazonarmy%20-knoll, Lecture by Linda O'Nelio Knoll at Lawrence Public Library, *The March of the Amazons,* March7, 2011, attended by my son, Mike Yoder , Chief of Staff, Photography, *Lawrence Journal World.* (Though I was unable to attend the lecture, Mike Yoder's recorded disc made it available to me). The journal, Labor Age -*The Next War In Mingo - Labor's Challenge to the Disarmament Conference,* VX, Nov. 3, 1921, p.p. 8-13, (Includes the Howat Case). Poem, *The New Colossus,* by Emma Lazarus, http:..www.libertystatepark.com/emma/htm, *The Pittsburg Daily Headlight,* Dec. 12, 1921, p. 1, the article, *St. Phillip Neri Catholic Church, Franklin, Kansas,* http//www.franklinkansas.com/st.phillipneri.html, Edward Markham's poem, *The Man With the Hoe,* http://www. ischool.utexas.edu/-wallys/manwhoe.html, Randy Robert's web page about *Alexander Howat,* Miner's Memorial at Immigrant Park, Pittsburg, Kansas) http://www.hmd/b.org/, submitted by William Fischer, Jr. of Frot Scott, KS, 2010, Robert W. Richmond's *A Land of Contrasts,* Forum Press, 1974.

In addition, Dr. Ann Schofield's scholarly article, *The Women's March: Miners, Family, and Communities, Pittsburg, Kansas, 1921-1922, Kansas History,* 7, 2 (1984), Sir Tyrone Guthrie's *Shakespeare: Ten Great Plays,* Macmillan and Co., Ltd. of London and St. Martin's Press, Inc., New York, 1962, Joseph Skubitz's *A History of the*

Development of Deep Mine Production in Crawford County and the Factors That Have Influenced it, Masters Thesis, Kansas State Teacher's College, Pittsburg, Kansas, August, 1934, *The New York Times, Howat Denounces Governor as Skunk,* April 13, 1920, *The New Yourk Times, Howat Sentenced to a Year in Jail,* Feb. 17, 1921, Lewis Untermeyer's poem *Caliban in the Coal Mine,* http://en.wikipedia/wild/Caliban-in-theCoal-. Special thanks for Dr. Tolly Smith Wildcat's comprehensive article, *The Story of Wayne Wildcat's "Solidarity:" Journal of the West,* Winter, 2001, Vol. 43, No. 1.

I encourage all readers to visit The Pittsburg Public Library and see the spellbinding mural in the reading room, *Solidarity, March of the Amazon Army,* painted by Kansas artist, Wayne Wildcat, with apprentices from Pittsburg and Girard High Schools and community volunteers.

Next, I encourage readers to visit *The Miners' Memorial at Immigrant Park,* which is located around the corner from the public library. Here visitors may visit kiosks with both plaques and recorded stories of the mining situation and labor battles during the period.

In addition, visit eight or nine of the mining towns located around Pittsburg, where one may still see the miners' cottages. Eat lunch in an old-time restaurant or visit the bakery in Frontenac. Do not leave out The Franklin Community Heritage Center in Franklin. I also visited the Stilwell Hotel and the restaurateur there took me on a tour of the grand lobby, where the ammunition was stored during the womens' famous march in 1921. If you visit these sites, you will have a vacation experience that you will long remember.

Additionally, I want to express gratitude to my wife, Lonabelle Yoder, who did a lot of proof reading, to Phillip Schoeller, who assisted me with computer operations, and to Mary Rempel for her copy editing.

A special thanks goes to my son, Michael Lynn Yoder (Chief of Staff, *Lawrence Journal World*) for his photograph

James D. Yoder

of the mural, which I'm using for the book cover. Also, if readers are interested in the *Womens' March*, I invite you to read Dr. Tolly Wildcat's article listed in the bibliographic material above.

NOVELS BY
JAMES D. YODER

THE YODER OUTSIDERS*

SARAH OF THE BORDER WARS

BARBARA: SARAH'S LEGACY

SONG IN A NAZI NIGHT*

*(Published in hardback and large print as
Black Spider Over Tiegenhof)*

LUICY OF THE TRAIL OF TEARS*

A BLESSING IN IT SOMEWHERE*

SIMONE; A SAINT FOR OUTSIDERS*

ECHOES ALONG THE SWEETBRIER*

MUDBALL SAM*

THE LONE TREE*

*BOIL AND BUBBLE: THE AMAZON
WOMEN OF KANSAS**

(Books with asterisk may be ordered from Infinity
Publishing at toll-free, 1-877-BUY-BOOK) or
WWW.BUYBOOKSONTHEWEB.COM.

Books may also be ordered directly from the author at
(620) 327-4053 or at web page www.yoderbooks.com.
email: James @yoderbooks.com